ALSO BY SOPHIE LARK

Brutal Birthright

Brutal Prince

Stolen Heir

Savage Lover

Bloody Heart

Broken Vow

Heavy Crown

Sinners Duet

There Are No Saints

There Is No Devil

SAVAGE LOVER

SOPHIE LARK

Bloom *books*

Sourcebooks and the colophon are registered trademarks of
Sourcebooks. Bloom Books is a trademark of Sourcebooks.

Published by Bloom Books, an imprint of Sourcebooks
P.O. Box 4410, Naperville, Illinois 60567-4410
(630) 961-3900
sourcebooks.com

Originally self-published in 2022 by Sophie Lark.

Cataloging-in-Publication Data is on file with the Library of Congress.

Printed and bound in the United States of America.
VP 10 9 8 7 6 5 4 3 2 1

This book is dedicated to anyone who's ever been poor enough to do something desperate 🖤
Xoxo

Sophie Lark

SOUNDTRACK

1. "Sober"—G-Eazy
2. "Hands to Myself"—Selena Gomez
3. "Satisfy"—NERO
4. "Love Lies"—Khalid & Normani
5. "Watermelon Sugar"—Harry Styles
6. "Him & I"—G-Eazy & Halsey
7. "Nobody's Love"—Maroon 5
8. "Bad Reputation"—Joan Jett
9. "Treat Her Right"—Roy Head
10. "Nice for What"—Drake
11. "Whatever You Like"—T.I.

Music is a big part of my writing process. If you start a song when you see a 🎵 while reading, the song matches the scene like a movie score.

Spotify   Apple Music

THE GALLOS

CHAPTER 1
CAMILLE RIVERA

I've been stuck under this Silverado for three hours now. I'm taking out the transmission, one of my absolute least favorite tasks. It's tricky, heavy, messy, and just an all-around bitch of a job, and that's under normal conditions. I'm doing it on the hottest day of the summer so far.

Our shop doesn't have air-conditioning. I'm drenched in sweat, which makes my hands slippery. Plus, BTS just came on the radio for the third time in a row, and I can't do a damn thing about it.

I've finally got all the bolts out and the cross member out of the way. I'm ready to slide out the transmission. I've got to be careful to do it smoothly so I don't damage the clutch or the torque converter.

This transmission weighs 146 pounds now that I've drained the fluids. I've got a jack to help support it, but I still wish my dad were around to help. He crashed right after dinner. He's been exhausted lately, barely able to keep his eyes open to shovel down a plate of spaghetti.

I told him to go to bed, that I'd take care of it.

I ease the transmission down on the jack, then wheel it out from under the truck. Then I gather all the nuts and bolts and put them in labeled baggies so I don't lose anything important.

That was the first thing my dad taught me in car repair—be organized and be meticulous: *These are complicated machines. You've got to be like a machine yourself—there's no room for mistakes.*

Once I get the transmission out, I decide to grab a soda to celebrate. We may not have AC but at least the fridge is always cold.

My father owns a repair shop on Wells Street. We live above it in a little two-bedroom apartment. It's just me, my dad, and my little brother, Vic.

I head upstairs, wiping my hands on a rag. I've got my coveralls stripped down to the waist, and my undershirt is soaked through with sweat. It's also stained with every kind of fluid that comes out of a car, plus just plain dirty. It's dusty in the shop.

My hands are filthy in a way that would require about two hours and a steel brush to get clean. There's oil embedded in every crack and line of my skin, and my fingernails are permanently stained black. Wiping my hands removes most of the mess, but I still leave fingerprints on the fridge when I pull the door open.

I grab a Coke and pop the tab, then press the cool can against my face for a moment before I chug it down.

Vic comes out of his room, spruced up like he's going somewhere. He dresses like he should be in a music video—tight jeans, bright shirts, sneakers he painstakingly cleans with a toothbrush if they get so much as a speck of dirt on them. That's where all his money goes, if he ever gets any money.

I have to resist the urge to tousle his hair, which is long and shaggy and the color of caramel. Vic's only seventeen, eight years younger than me. I feel more like his mom than his sister.

Our real mom dumped him off on the doorstep when he was two and a half. He was this skinny little thing with big dark eyes that took up half his face and the most outrageous eyelashes. (Why do boys always get the best lashes?) No clothes or belongings except for one Spider-Man figure that was missing a leg. He carried that with him everywhere he went, even in the bath, holding it tight while he slept at night.

I don't know where they were living before or who his father is. My dad took him in, and we've all lived here ever since.

"Where are you going?" I ask him.

"Out with friends."

"What friends?"

"Tito. Andrew."

"What are you doing?"

"I dunno." He grabs his own Coke and pops it open. "Seein' a movie, probably."

"Bit late for a movie."

It's 9:40 p.m. Not many movies start after 10:00.

Vic just shrugs.

"Don't be out too late," I tell him.

He rolls his eyes and shuffles past me out of the kitchen.

I notice he's wearing a new pair of sneakers. They look ridiculous to me—white and chunky, with some kinda weird, swoopy gray lines on the sides. They're basketball shoes, but I don't think you'd actually wear them to play basketball unless you were playing on the moon in the year 3000.

They look expensive.

"Where'd you get those?"

Vic doesn't meet my eye. "Traded my Jordans to Andrew."

I know when my brother's lying. He's always been terrible at it. "You didn't shoplift those, did you?"

"No!" he says hotly.

"You better not, Vic. You're almost eighteen. That shit stays on your record—"

"I didn't steal them!" he shouts. "I gotta go. I'm gonna be late."

He slings his backpack over one shoulder and heads out, leaving me alone in the kitchen.

I finish my soda, scowling. I love Vic with every spare inch of space in my heart, but I worry about him. He hangs out with kids who have a lot more money than we do. Kids who live in the mansions on Wieland and Evergreen, whose parents have attorneys on speed-dial to bail their idiot sons out of trouble if they do something stupid.

We don't have that luxury. I tell Vic over and over that he's got to buckle down and study hard in his senior year so he gets into a good college. He has zero interest in working with Dad and me.

Unfortunately, he doesn't have much interest in school either. He thinks he's going to be a DJ. I haven't burst that bubble just yet.

I chuck the soda can in the recycling bin, ready to head back down to the shop again.

I spend another hour tackling the transmission. The owner of the Silverado doesn't want a replacement—he wants us to rebuild it. Since we don't know exactly what's wrong with the damn thing, I'll have to disassemble it entirely, clean all the parts, and check to see what's worn out or broken.

While I'm working, I'm thinking about Vic. I don't believe his story about the shoes, and I don't like that he's hanging out with Andrew. Andrew is the worst of his friends—arrogant, spoiled, and mean-spirited. Vic's a good kid at heart. But he wants to be popular. That leads to him doing a lot of stupid shit to impress his friends.

I wipe my hands again and grab my phone. I want to check Find My Friends to see if Vic actually went to the theater.

I pull up his little blue dot, and sure enough, he's not at any movie theater. Instead, he's at some address on Hudson Ave—it looks like a house. It doesn't belong to Andrew or anybody else I know.

Annoyed, I switch over to Instagram and click on Vic's stories. He hasn't posted anything so I check Andrew's account.

There they are—all three boys at some kind of house party. Vic's drinking out of a red Solo cup, and Tito looks completely sloshed. The caption reads *Gonna set a record tonight.*

"Oh, *hell* no," I hiss.

After jamming my phone in the pocket of my coveralls, I grab the keys to my Trans Am. If Vic thinks he's going to get hammered with those d-bags, he's got another think coming. He's not supposed to be drinking, and he *is* supposed to be working a shift at the Stop & Shop tomorrow morning. If he sleeps in again, they're going to fire him.

I speed over to the location of his little blue dot—or at least I speed as much as I can without overheating my car's ancient engine. This car is older than I am, by a lot, and I'm mostly keeping it alive by sheer force of will these days.

It's only a seven-minute drive to the house. I could have found it with or without the app—the music thuds down the block. Dozens of cars line the street on both sides. Partygoers are literally spilling out of the building, climbing in and out of windows, passing out on the lawn.

I park as close as I can get, then hustle up to the house, where I push my way inside through the crush of people, looking for my little brother.

Most of the partygoers seem to be in their twenties. This is a full-on rager, with beer pong, keg stands, topless girls playing strip poker, couples halfway to fucking on the couches, and so much pot smoke that I can barely see two feet in front of my face.

Trying to spot my brother, I'm not exactly watching where I'm going. I plow right into a group of girls, making one of them shriek with rage as her drink splashes the front of her dress.

"Watch it, bitch!" she howls, spinning around.

Oh, fuck.

I've managed to bump into somebody who already hates my guts: Bella Page.

We went to high school together, once upon a time.

It gets even better. Bella is standing with Beatrice and Brandi. They used to call themselves the *Queen Bees*. Unironically.

"Oh my god," Bella says in her drawling voice, prickling with vocal fry. "I must be drunker than I thought, 'cause I swear I'm looking at the Grease Monkey."

That's what they called me.

It's been at least six years since I heard that nickname. And yet it instantly fills me with self-loathing just like it used to.

"What are you *wearing*?" Beatrice is staring at my coveralls with the kind of horrified expression usually reserved for car accidents or mass genocides.

"I thought something smelled like hot garbage." Brandi wrinkles her perfect little button nose.

God, I was hoping these three had moved away after high school. Or maybe died of dysentery. I'm not picky.

Bella has her sleek blond hair cut into a long bob. Beatrice definitely got a boob job. Brandi has a sparkly rock on her finger. Other than that, not much has changed—all three are still beautiful, well-dressed, and looking at me like I'm shit on the bottom of their shoes.

"Wow," I say blandly. "I've really missed this."

"What are *you* doing here?" Beatrice folds her skinny arms under her new boobs.

"Shouldn't you be back at that shithole garage washing your face with oil?" Brandi sneers.

"I thought she'd be down on Cermak," Bella says, fixing me with her cool-blue eyes. "Sucking dick for ten bucks a pop, just like her mom."

The heat and smoke and sound of the party seem to fade away. All I see is Bella's pretty face twisted with disdain. Even when I'm fucking furious at her, I have to admit she's gorgeous: Thick black lashes around big blue eyes. Pink-lipstick sneer.

That doesn't stop me from wanting to knock her perfect teeth out with my fist. But her father is some bigwig banker, storing cash for all the fancy fuckers in Chicago. I have no doubt he'd sue me into oblivion if I assaulted his little princess.

"At least she gets ten dollars," a low voice says. "You usually do it for free, Bella."

Nero Gallo is leaning against the kitchen cabinets, his hands tucked in his pockets. His dark hair is even longer than it was in high school, hanging in his face. That doesn't cover the bruise under his right eye or the nasty cut on his lip.

And neither of those injuries can mar the outrageous beauty of his face. In fact, they only serve to highlight it.

Nero is proof of the perversity of the universe. Never has such a dangerous object been disguised in such an appealing wrapper. He's like a berry so vivid and juicy that it makes your mouth water just from looking at it. But one taste will poison you.

He's liquid sex in a James Dean frame. Everything about him, from his fog-gray eyes to his pouty lips to his arrogant swagger, is calculated to make your heart freeze in your chest, then jolt back to life if he so much as glances at you.

The girls' moods shift completely when they catch sight of him.

Far from being annoyed at his jab, Bella giggles and bites her lip like he's flirting with her. "I didn't know you were coming."

"Why would you?" Nero says rudely.

I have no interest in talking to Nero and even less in continuing my conversation with the Queen Bees. I have to find my brother.

Before I can slip away, Nero says, "Is that your Trans Am out there?"

"Yes."

"Is it a '77 SE?"

"Yeah."

"Same as Burt Reynolds."

"That's right." I smile despite myself. I don't want to smile at Nero. I would like to stay as far away from him as possible. But he's talking about the one thing I own that I actually love.

Burt Reynolds drove the same car in *Smokey and the Bandit*—except his was black with a gold eagle on the hood, and mine is red with racing stripes. Faded and beat to shit, but still pretty rad in my opinion.

Bella has no idea what we're talking about. She just hates that Nero and I are talking at all. She needs to pull the attention back to herself, immediately.

"I have a Mercedes G-Wagon," she says.

"Daddy must have had a good year." Nero curls that full upper lip, puffier than ever from its bruise.

"He certainly did," Bella coos.

"Thank god there are heroes like him helping all those poor billionaires hide their money," I remark.

Bella whips her head around like a snake, obviously wishing I would leave or die already so she could be alone with Nero.

"Please tell us how you're saving the world," she hisses. "Are you doing oil changes for orphans? Or are you the same loser you were in high school? I really hope that's not the case because if you're still a grimy little degenerate, I really don't know how you're going to pay for my dress you just ruined."

I look at her tight white dress, which has three tiny spots of punch on the front of it. "Why don't you try washing it?"

"You can't throw an eight-hundred-dollar dress in the washing machine," Bella informs me. "But you wouldn't know that because you don't wash your clothes. Or anything else, apparently." She sniffs at my filthy undershirt and my hair tied back with a greasy bandanna.

It makes me burn with shame when she looks at me like that. I don't know why. I don't value Bella's opinion. But I also can't argue with the facts: I'm poor, and I look terrible.

"You're wasting your time," Nero says in a bored tone. "She doesn't have eight hundred dollars."

"God." Beatrice giggles. "Levi really needs to start getting security for these parties. Keep the trash out."

"You sure you'd make the cut?" Nero says softly.

He picks up a bottle of vodka off the counter, slugs down several gulps, then walks away from the girls. He doesn't look at me at all, like he forgot I was even there.

The Queen Bees have forgotten about me, too. They're staring after Nero, wistfully.

"He's such an asshole," Beatrice says.

"A fucking gorgeous asshole," Bella whispers, her voice low and determined. She's staring after Nero like he's a Birkin bag and a Louboutin heel rolled into one.

While Bella's consumed with lust, I take the opportunity to head off in the opposite direction, looking for Vic. Not seeing him on the main level, I climb the stairs and start peeking into rooms where people are either hooking up, snorting lines, or playing *Grand Theft Auto*.

The house is huge but run-down. This obviously isn't the first party it's seen—the woodwork is gouged, the walls full of random holes. From the look of the bedrooms, I'm guessing several people live here—probably all dudes. The guests are a weird mix of slumming socialites like Bella and a much rougher element. I don't like that my brother is mixed up with this crowd.

I finally track him down in the backyard, playing Ping-Pong on an outdoor table. He's so shit-faced that he can barely hold his paddle, not making contact with the ball at all.

I grab him by the back of his T-shirt and start dragging him out.

"Hey, what the hell!" he yells.

"We're leaving," I snarl.

"I don't think he wants to go," Andrew says to me.

I really despise Andrew. He's a cocky little shit who likes to dress and talk like a gangster. Meanwhile, his parents are both surgeons, and I know he got an early acceptance to Northwestern.

His future is secure. He gets to play around at being a bad boy, and when he's tired of that, he'll sail off to college, leaving my brother behind in the gutter.

"Get out of my face before I call your parents," I snap at him.

He smirks at me. "Good luck with that. They're in Aruba right now."

"Fine," I say. "I'll call the cops and report you for underage drinking."

"All right, all right, I'm coming," Vic says blearily. "Lemme get my bag at least."

He grabs his backpack from under the pool table, almost tripping over his own feet in those ridiculous sneakers.

"Come on," I say, impatiently hauling him along.

I drag him through the side gate, not wanting to walk through the house again and risk another meeting with Bella.

Once we're back down on the sidewalk, I relax a little. I'm pissed at Vic for getting drunk, though.

"You're still going to work tomorrow," I tell him. "I'm waking you up at seven, and I don't care if you're hungover."

"Man, I hate that fuckin' place," Vic complains, shuffling along after me.

"Oh, you don't like bagging groceries? Then maybe you should pull your act together and get a proper education so you don't have to do it the rest of your life."

I stuff him into the passenger seat of the Trans Am before slamming the door to shut him in. Then I go around to the driver's side.

"You didn't go to college," Vic says resentfully.

"Yeah, and look at me," I say, gesturing to my filthy clothes. "I'm gonna be working in that shop forever."

I pull away from the curb. Vic leans his head against the window.

"I thought you liked it…" he says.

"I like cars. I don't like changing people's oil and fixing their shit, then hearing them bitch and complain about the price."

I turn onto Goethe, driving slowly because it's getting late and the street isn't very well lit.

Even so, Vic is starting to look a little green.

"Pull over," he says. "I might puke."

"Hold on a second. I can't stop right—"

"Pull over!" he cries, jerking hard on the wheel.

"What the hell!" I shout, yanking the wheel straight again so we don't hit the cars lined up along the curb. Before I can find a good place to stop, red and blue lights flare up in my rearview mirror and I hear the short whoop of a police siren.

"Fuck," I groan, pulling over.

Vic opens his door, leaning out so he can puke in the street.

"Pull it together," I mutter.

The officer knocks on my window, shining his flashlight in my face.

I roll down the glass, blinking and trying to moisten my dry mouth enough to speak.

"Have you been drinking tonight?" the officer demands.

"No, I haven't," I tell him, "Sorry, my brother is sick…"

The cop shines his light on Vic instead, illuminating his blood-shot eyes and puke-spattered shirt.

"Step out of the car," the officer says to Vic.

"Is this really—"

"Out of the car!" he barks again.

Vic opens his door and stumbles out, trying to avoid the vomit. His foot catches on his backpack, pulling it out into the street as well.

The officer makes him stand with his hands on the roof of my car. "Do you have any weapons on you?" he says as he pats Vic down.

"Uh-uh," my brother says, shaking his head.

I've gotten out of the car, too, though I'm staying on my side.

"I'll just take him home, Officer," I say.

The cop pauses, his hand on the outside of Vic's leg.

"What's in your pocket, kid?" he says.

"Nothing," Vic says stupidly.

The cop reaches into Vic's jeans and pulls out a little baggy. My stomach sinks to my toes. There are two pills in the bag.

"What's this?" the cop says.

"I dunno," Vic says. "It's not mine."

"Stay right where you are," the cop orders. He picks up Vic's backpack and starts rooting around in it. A minute later he pulls out a sandwich bag full of at least a hundred identical pills.

"Let me guess," he says. "These aren't yours either."

Before Vic can reply, I blurt, "They're mine!"

Shit, shit, shit. What am I doing?

The officer looks up at me, his eyebrow raised. He's tall and fit, with a square jaw and bright blue eyes.

"Are you sure about that?" he says quietly. "This is a lot of product. A lot more than for personal use. You're looking at posses-sion with intent to distribute."

I'm sweating, and my heart is racing. This is a huge fucking problem. But it's going to be my problem, not Vic's. I can't let him destroy his life like this.

"It's mine," I say firmly. "All of it's mine."

Vic is staring back and forth between me and the cop, so inebri-ated and so scared that he has no idea what to do. I look him in the eye and give him the tiniest shake of my head—telling him to keep his mouth shut.

"Get back in the car, kid," the cop says to Vic.

Vic climbs back in the passenger seat. The officer closes the door, shutting him inside. Then he turns his attention on me.

"What's your name, miss?"

"Camille Rivera." I swallow hard.

"Officer Schultz," he says, pointing at his badge. "Come here, Camille."

I walk around the car so we're both standing in the glare of the headlights.

As I get closer to the cop, I realize he's younger than I thought—probably only about thirty or thirty-five at the most. He's got close-cropped blond hair, buzzed at the sides, and a tanned face. His uniform is stiffly starched.

He's smiling at me, but I've never been so scared of someone in my life. He's literally holding my fate, in the form of a plastic bag of pills.

"Do you know what this is, Camille?"

I look at the pills. They kind of look like Flintstones Vitamins—stamped in the shape of school buses, pale yellow in color. So I'm guessing it's Molly.

"Yeah, I know what they are." My voice comes out in a croak.

"Illinois has strict laws against MDMA." Officer Schultz's voice is low and pleasant. "Possessing just one tablet can result in a felony conviction. Fifteen or more tablets means a mandatory minimum sentence of four years in prison. I'd say you've got about a hundred and fifty tablets here. Plus the ones in your brother's pocket."

"Those are mine, too," I say. "He didn't know what it was. I asked him to hold it for me."

There's a long silence while the officer stares at me. I can't read the expression on his face. He's still smiling a little, but I have no clue what that smile means.

"Where do you live?" he asks me.

"On Wells Street. Above Axel Auto. That's my shop—my father's shop. I work there, too."

"You're a mechanic?" He looks at my clothes.

"Yeah."

"You don't see a lot of girl mechanics."

"I doubt you know a lot of mechanics at all."

It's not the best moment for sarcasm. But I get so sick of the comments. Especially from men. Especially the ones who don't trust me to work on their car, when they wouldn't know a piston from a plug.

Luckily, Schultz chuckles. "Just one," he says. "But I think he's ripping me off."

The silence drags out between us. I'm waiting for him to slap the cuffs on my wrists and throw me in the back of his squad car.

Instead, he says, "Axel Auto on Wells Street?"

"Yeah."

"I'll come see you there tomorrow."

I stare at him blankly, not understanding what he means.

"Get your brother home," the cop says. He drops the pills into the backpack and zips it up. Then he throws the bag in his trunk.

I'm still standing there, frozen and confused. "I can go?" I say stupidly.

"For now. We'll talk more tomorrow."

I get back in my car, my heart thudding painfully against my ribs. My mouth tastes like metal, and my brain is screaming at me that this is very fucking weird.

But I'm not going to argue. I'm drowning in trouble—I'll take any life preserver thrown at me.

I just hope it's not an anchor in disguise.

CHAPTER 2
NERO GALLO

It's Friday night. I'm waiting for Mason Becker outside an abandoned steel mill in South Shore.

This place is a fucking trip. It's right on the water and so huge that it's bigger than the whole of downtown Chicago. And yet it's completely deserted—abandoned since the '90s when the steel industry finally collapsed.

Most of the buildings have been demolished. You can still see the u.s. steel sign all covered with weeds. It looks like the end of the world happened and I'm the only person left to see it.

Actually, this whole area is kinda shitty. They don't call it Terror Town for nothing. But it's where Mason wanted to meet, so here I am.

He's late, as per fucking usual.

When he finally drives up, I hear his car before I see it. His engine is knocking. He drives a crappy old Supra, with a big, long scratch down the panels where his ex-girlfriend dug her keys into the side of his car.

"Hey, why are you so early?" he says, sticking his head out the window and grinning at me. Mason is tall and skinny, with curly hair and lightning bolts shaved into the sides of his fade.

"You've got the wrong spark plugs," I tell him. "That's why your car sounds like a lawn mower."

"Man, what the fuck are you talkin' about? I just got these changed last week."

"Who did it?"

"Frankie."

"Yeah? Let me guess: he gave you a deal."

Mason grins. "He did it for a hundred bucks and a baggie of weed. So what?"

"So he used the wrong plugs. Probably pulled 'em out of somebody else's car. You should've had me do it."

"Will you fix it?"

"Fuck no."

Mason laughs. "That's what I figured you'd say."

"So." I slide off the hood of my car. "What do you have for me?"

Mason climbs out of the Supra, popping the trunk so I can take a look. He's got three FN Five-Seven pistols, a monster .50-caliber rifle, and a half dozen .45s in the back.

They're all different makes and models, the serial numbers crudely filed down. It's not as nice as the stuff we used to get from the Russians, but they're not exactly talking to us right now, seeing as we killed their boss a couple of months ago. So I need a new supplier.

Mason brings his guns up from Mississippi. That state has about the friendliest gun laws in the country. You can buy whatever you like from pawnshops and shows, and you don't have to register it after. So Mason has his cousins pick up whatever we need, and then he brings them up the pipeline of the I-55.

"If you don't like those, I can get others," Mason says.

"How many cousins do you have?"

"I dunno. At least fifty."

"Does your family ever do anything but fuck?"

He snorts. "I sure don't. I like to keep with tradition."

I look the guns over once more. "This is good. I'll take it all."

We haggle over the price for a while: him because he's still trying to get Patricia back, regardless of what she did to the side of his car, and he probably wants to buy her something nice; me because he made me drive way the fuck over here to this ratty-ass neighborhood where the trash is blowing around like tumbleweeds.

Finally, we agree, and I hand him the wad of cash. He transfers the guns to my trunk, into the hidden compartment I built under the spare tire.

If some bitch ever keyed my Mustang, I'd chuck her in the lake. I love this car. Built it up from blocks after I crashed my Bel Air.

"So," Mason says, once business is done. "What are you doing tonight?"

"I dunno. Nothing, I guess."

"Levi's throwing a party at his house."

I consider it. Levi Cargill is a trust fund frat boy who likes to pretend he's Pablo Escobar. I never liked him in high school, and I don't like him now. But he does throw pretty decent parties.

"You going over there now?"

Mason grins. "You gonna come with me?"

"We're taking my car."

"I don't wanna leave mine here—somebody'll fuck with it."

"Nobody's gonna bother with your car unless Patricia finds it again. It's not even worth stripping down for scrap metal."

Mason looks wounded. "You're a snob, you know that?"

"Nah. I like all cars—except yours."

Sulking, Mason gets in the passenger side, and we drive back to Old Town. He tries to fuck with my playlist. I slap his hand away before he can touch it. I do let him roll the windows down 'cause it's hot as balls and the breeze is nice.

We cruise up to Levi's house, where the party is already in full swing.

This was a nice place when Levi inherited it from his grandma. He's abused it ever since, throwing so many ragers that the neighbors probably have the cops on speed dial. They don't say anything to Levi, though. He may be a puffed-up poser, but he has a nasty temper, enough to go off on any octogenarians who dare to give him the side-eye.

I already see a few people I recognize. That's usually the case. I've lived in Chicago my whole life. Went to school at Oakmont, ten minutes from here. Tried a semester at Northwestern, but left six weeks in. I hate sitting in classrooms, and I hate taking tests even more. I don't give a fuck about physics or philosophy. I like things that are practical. Real. Touchable.

I went to one lecture where the professor spent the whole hour yammering on about the nature of reality. If he can't understand reality, then how am I supposed to?

You know what you can understand front and back, up and down? A car engine. You can take it apart down to the last bolt and put it right back together again.

Speaking of which, as we walk up to the house, I see a red Trans Am pulled up to the curb. It needs new tires and a fresh paint job, but it's a classic all the same.

I'm giving it a full once-over until a shapely little redhead draws my eye in another direction. She's walking up to the house in a tight black skirt and ankle boots, her hair pulled up in a high ponytail that swishes as she walks.

I automatically fall into step behind her, walking close enough that she turns around to see who's behind her.

"Oh, hello, Nero," she says, a saucy little smile breaking out on her face. She's got dimples on both sides of her mouth, with little silver piercings through them. She looks familiar and fucking hot in that short skirt and her tight little crop top. Small tits, but that's fine. Like I told Mason, I'm not picky.

"Hey, Red," I say, since I can't remember her name. "What are you doing out here all alone? Aren't you afraid of the Big Bad Wolf?"

"Is that supposed to be you?" She looks me up and down so her lashes swoop down to her cheeks and up again.

"Well, I'm definitely big." I step closer to her.

"I've heard that." She grins up at me.

"Yeah, from who?"

I know girls love to gossip about the guys they fuck, and I know she just said that to be flirty, but I'm irritated all the same. It pisses me off when people talk about me. Even if it's supposed to be a compliment.

Red hears the snarl in my voice. She falters, smile fading.

"Well, you used to date Sienna…"

"I didn't date her," I growl. "I let her suck my cock in the sauna once."

"Yeah." Red giggles. "That's the night she told me about. She said you—"

"Why didn't you text me when you got here?" interrupts a male voice.

A big burly guy in a Bears T-shirt slings his arm around Red's shoulder. He's got one of those faces where everything is almost in the right place, but there's just something off about it. A square jaw, but a long face. Straight nose, but eyes too deep set on either side of it. This guy I do remember, because he's a complete twat. His name is Johnny Verger.

He's got two of his buddies with him, a couple of other washed-up meatheads who probably played football with our boy Johnny once upon a time.

They've all been drinking while waiting on Red. I can smell the beer leeching out of their pores. Johnny most of all—he's bleary-eyed and belligerent.

"I was just walking in," Red says nervously.

"With Nero Gallo?" Johnny sneers.

"Maybe you should put her on a leash," I say. "Then you can make sure she doesn't talk to anybody else."

"Why don't you fuck off?" Johnny snarls at me. "She's not interested."

"I doubt you know what an interested girl looks like."

Red glances over at me from under Johnny's arms, her lashes giving that flirtatious little swoop again.

"See?" I say quietly. "It's that look. Like they want you to grab them and bend them over the nearest table."

Johnny lets go of Red, glowering down at her. Red's cheeks are burning as bright as her hair.

"What the fuck, Carly?" he demands.

"I wasn't doing anything!" she cries. But her eyes are flitting back to me, betraying every dirty little thought in her head.

Johnny shoves Red. She stumbles backward on her high-heeled boots, landing on her ass on the lawn.

"Hey!" she shrieks, tears springing into her eyes.

Nobody helps her up. Johnny and his buddies have their attention entirely fixed on me. I ignore her too 'cause I'm no white knight. She's the one dating this asshole. She can deal with his temper tantrums on her own.

Apparently, Johnny is set on making their little spat into my problem.

"Keep your filthy fuckin' hands off what's mine," he snarls.

"I didn't touch her," I say. "But if I wanted to, I sure as fuck wouldn't ask your permission first."

"Oh, yeah, tough guy?"

Johnny crowds into my space, trying to force me to back up. I'm staying still, watching him, just waiting for him to throw the first punch. He's so big and so drunk that I'll see it coming a mile away.

"Johnny..." one of his buddies says warningly.

"Yeah, I know who his dad is," Johnny snarls. "I know his brothers, too. I'm not scared of a bunch of greasy gangsters. It's not 1920 anymore."

"Is it 1980?" I ask him. "'Cause you look like that douche from *Cobra Kai*."

I don't know if Johnny gets the reference. It pisses him off anyway. He roars and swings a fist the size of a brick at my head.

I duck under it, and then I flex my legs like pistons and drive my head directly upward into Johnny's face. The top of my skull meets his nose with sickening force. In the roshambo of body parts, skull beats nose every time. The sound of the break is oddly hollow, like a baseball bat against a pumpkin. Blood comes flooding out of Johnny's nostrils, soaking the front of his Bears T-shirt in an instant.

"ARGH! FUUUUGH!" Johnny howls inarticulately.

His two buddies rush at me from either side.

I was expecting that. Still, I can only do so much to fend them off. I'm six-two, strong but lean. These dudes probably weigh 240 pounds each. They look like they spend their weekends benching and injecting each other's asses with racehorse roids. I may not have stuck with those physics classes long, but I learned enough to know their combined mass is gonna take me down.

So instead of waiting for them to plow into me, I run at one on the left, skidding into his ankle with both feet outstretched, like I'm sliding into home plate. His ankle bends at a nasty angle, and he topples on top of me.

Unfortunately, that gives his buddy time to kick me right in the face. He gets me in the mouth, splitting my top lip. Kicking is a bitch move, especially three-on-one.

Johnny is still howling and clutching his nose, and Red is screaming, too, though I'm not sure for what reason—because I'm scuffling with these two meatheads, or because I busted her boyfriend's face.

I'm pummeling every inch of the second guy that I can reach. He really pissed me off with that kick to the face. I've got him down on the ground, and I'm hitting him again and again until my knuckles are bloody. His buddy hobbles over and cracks me one in the eye, and I retaliate with an elbow to his face.

At this point, Red's shrieks have drawn a crowd. Five or six dudes yank us apart, pulling me off the face kicker.

While I'm being restrained, Johnny takes the opportunity to slug me in the gut. It slams the air out of me. If I didn't have people holding both my arms, I'd knife the fucker for that one. I have a switchblade in my pocket. I wasn't gonna use it in a friendly fight, but now he's really making me mad.

Before I can get loose, Levi steps between us, shoving us both back.

"All right, all right, you had your fun." Levi's got bleached-blond hair and a bunch of chains around his neck. He's wearing a stars-and-stripes windbreaker and acid-washed jeans. I'd tell him he looks like Vanilla Ice, but he'd take that as a compliment. "If you want to keep fighting, you gotta go somewhere else."

"I'm gonna kill that little shit!" Johnny roars, still cradling his nose.

"Fine," Levi says. "But not here."

He looks over at me. I spit a little blood out on the grass.

"How 'bout you?" Levi says.

"I'm good. I'll come inside."

"Cool." Levi nods at his buddies to let go of me. I straighten, tossing the hair back out of my face.

"You're fuckin' dead, Nero," Johnny hisses as I walk past him.

I just smile, blood in my teeth. If I'm in a bad mood the next time I see him, I'm gonna cut his fucking throat without a word of warning.

I head into Levi's house, which is even hotter than outside and packed with way too many people. The air is so thick with smoke that I could get high just by breathing hard.

The heat makes my lip throb. I head into the kitchen, planning to grab a handful of ice.

Levi's kitchen is a time capsule of the '70s—pine cabinets and avocado-colored fridge. Granny didn't give it a facelift, and Levi sure as hell won't bother. I doubt he's cooked a meal in his life. The counters are covered in half-eaten take-out boxes.

I crack the freezer door. The only thing inside is an empty vodka bottle. No ice at all, not even the trays.

I close it again. Over the thud of EDM music, I hear an irritating drawl that's all too familiar to me. Bella Page, sinking her claws into somebody.

I look over at the girls. It's the three wicked bitches, surrounding some girl with dark curls tied back by a bandanna.

I usually could not give two shits what Bella is doing. In fact, I'd rather avoid her at all costs. There's nothing interesting about her practicing her mean-girl routine—in fact, I'd be a lot more shocked to see her doing anything else.

It's their current victim who catches my eye.

Camille Rivera.

Now that is a blast from the past. I could be looking through an eight-year time-warp tunnel. Bella is sniping at her just like she used to in the good old days. And just like back then, Camille looks like she wants to pop Bella right in the eye.

I was always surprised Bella went to such great lengths to fuck with Camille. It's not like they were in competition or something. Bella had the money, the clothes, the friends, the boyfriends (pretty much anybody worth fucking at school, other than me—though not for lack of trying on her part). Plus, objectively speaking, Bella is way hotter. She's got that supermodel pout, mile-long legs, and the I-had-four-ribs-removed-to-look-this-skinny thing going on.

Camille isn't feminine in the slightest. She dresses like Billy Joel in "Uptown Girl." She's constantly filthy. She's got a low, husky voice that hardly belongs in the same conversation with Bella's bitchy bite. And she's poor as dirt. Her dad does good work, but he never charges enough. His shop is so run-down that it's antimarketing for the business.

Camille was one of the only kids who brought their own lunch to school instead of buying from the cafeteria or snack bar. It was always superdepressing leftovers in old yogurt containers, not even Tupperware. Bella used to rail on her about that, along with a hundred other things.

But the number one thing Bella would give Camille shit about is her mom.

Everyone knows Camille's mother worked as a stripper. She had Camille super young, and she was still stripping when we were all at Oakmont. People used to throw dollar bills at Camille in the hallway. They'd say they were going to visit her mom at Exotica and ask Camille what song they should request.

Maybe that's why Camille tries so hard to be plain. She deflects male attention like it's her job. Trying to prove she's nothing like her mother.

Or maybe she just hates showering. How the fuck would I know?

Bella makes some bitchy comment about Camille's mom.

That's where I insert myself into the conversation. Not because I care about defending Camille but because Bella needs some new material.

All the girls spin around to stare at me, Camille most of all.

Bella smirks at me, one hand on her hip and her chest thrust upward for my approval. "I didn't know you were coming," she purrs.

"Why would you?" I say coldly.

Bella's smile turns into a pout.

She's been thirsty as fuck since the day I met her. It's funny—I've banged a lot of girls I didn't like. But I've always held out against Bella. It's almost a game at this point. The more she wants it, the more I enjoy not giving it to her. She's so damn spoiled, it's probably the one time in her whole life she hasn't gotten her way.

It ain't happening. Not tonight and not ever. I know how hard she'd be to shake afterward—I don't need that kind of drama.

Bella is the one person who might be as vicious as I am. Trust a snake to know a snake. Who knows what kind of crazy shit she might pull if we were alone and naked?

Those shiny pink lips part as she's about to shoot her shot again.

To cut her off, I turn to Camille and say, "Is that your Trans Am out there?"

Camille was trying to sneak away. My question pulls her up short. She turns around again, not quite meeting my eye. "Yeah," she says quietly.

"Is it a '77 SE?"

"Yes."

"Same as Burt Reynolds."

She smiles.

I haven't seen Camille smile very often. I'm surprised how nice her teeth are, how white they look against her tan skin and grease-streaked face.

"I have a Mercedes G-Wagon," Bella says loudly.

Jesus Christ. She would. I bet it's white with rose-gold rims and a bunch of shit hanging from the rearview mirror.

The conversation goes on for a few more moments, but I'm rapidly getting bored of it.

Camille slaps back at Bella about her asshole father, which is fun to see. Even if it has zero effect—you can't force Bella to self-reflect. She's got about as much clarity as a fifty-foot oil well.

My lip starts throbbing again, and I want to be done with all of them. I steal a swig of somebody's liquor off the counter, and then I ditch the girls, thinking I'll challenge Mason to a game of *Madden* if he hasn't gotten too blitzed to play.

Instead, I bump into Red on the stairs. She's looking kind of weepy-eyed, reading something on her phone.

"How's your ass?" I ask her.

"Bruised," she says. "Thanks to you."

"I'm not the one who shoved you. That was lover boy."

"He's such an asshole!" She glares at her phone screen once more, then shoves it in her purse.

I assume Johnny is bitching her out through text, wherever he wandered off to. Probably the hospital if he cares about straightening his nose out.

I lean against the wall, my hands thrust in my pockets. "I know how you could get back at him…"

I'm standing very close to Red—close enough to feel her breath on my arm. Invading women's personal space is a great way to make your intentions clear. You get the scent of your pheromones right in their nose. It makes them go crazy, like dog in heat.

Red looks up at me, her eyes wide and her lips parted. Her little tongue pokes out to moisten her lower lip. "You're trying to get me in trouble again..."

She doesn't say it like she's telling me off. She says it like she's begging me to keep going.

I bend to speak right into her ear. "Well, I don't want to be a bad influence. So here's what I'm going to do. I'm going to touch you. And you tell me when you want me to stop..."

I start at her knee, slowly sliding my hand up to her inner thigh. Her legs are freshly shaved and silky smooth. Her flesh trembles under my fingertips.

Her breath speeds as I slide my hand higher. She isn't stopping me. In fact, she shifts her feet ever so slightly to spread her legs.

My hand goes under the hem of her skirt. Her inner thigh is warm and slightly damp because it's hotter than a Louisiana swamp on this staircase. The pounding music vibrates the walls.

My fingertips reach the edge of her panties. I pause to see if she'll say anything... All I hear are her rapid little gasps against the side of my neck.

I tuck my fingers under the elastic of her panties and find her velvety pussy lips, as smoothly shaven as her legs. I slide my index finger down the crevice of her lips, slick and wet though I've barely even touched her yet. Red lets out a desperate little mew.

She grabs my face and kisses me like she's trying to swallow me whole. She tastes like wine coolers and lipstick. She's darting her tongue into my mouth, splitting my lip open all over again.

I push my fingers inside her, and she groans into my mouth, grinding her body against mine.

"Take me upstairs," she begs.

I grab her hand, leading her up the stairs to the closest bedroom. There's already a couple inside, but they're just making out on the bed, still fully clothed. I grab the guy by the back of his shirt and yank him up before shoving him out the door.

"Hey, what the hell!" he shouts.

The girl blinks up at me, her mascara smeared and her shirt half-unbuttoned so I can see her generous cleavage above her lacy bra.

"Stay or get out," I tell her.

She looks up at me for a second, then smiles. "I'll stay."

"Fine by me."

I throw Red next to her on the bed.

Then I close the door in the other guy's face and lock it.

CHAPTER 3
CAMILLE

WHEN I WAKE UP IN THE MORNING, THE SUN IS STREAMING through the rattan blinds in the little glassed-in porch I call a bedroom. Its brightness fills me with relief, like it's going to wash away the nightmares of the night before.

Then reality crashes down on me. Those were no nightmares. I was absolutely pulled over on Goethe Street by a cop, who now has a backpack full of evidence in his trunk.

It's 7:22 a.m. Vic is supposed to be at work by 8:00.

I stomp into his room and rip the blanket off him.

"Hey..." he groans, too hungover to even protest.

"Get in the shower," I order.

He tries to roll over and put the pillow over his head. I snatch that away, too.

"If you don't get up right now, I'm coming back with a pitcher of ice water to dump on your head," I tell him.

"All right, all right." He rolls out of bed onto the floor, then stumbles out to our one and only bathroom.

I head out to the kitchen to make coffee.

There are only two bedrooms in our cramped little apartment. My dad has one and Vic has the other, the latter of which is tiny, windowless, and closet-less—probably meant to be an office, really. I sleep on the porch. My dad tried to weatherproof it, but it's hotter than Hades in the summertime and freezing in the winter. If it rains, my clothes get damp and my books swell up from the humidity.

Still, I like my room. I like the way the rain and sleet beat against the glass. On clear nights I can open the blinds and see stars mixed with city lights, all the way around.

I hear the shower sputter into life. Vic better actually be washing up and not just letting the water run while he brushes his teeth.

The coffee maker hisses as blessed dark brown wake-up juice dribbles down into the pot.

By the time Vic stumbles into the kitchen, his hair damp and his shoes untied, I've got toast and a poached egg waiting for him.

"Eat up."

"I don't think I can," he says, giving the food a nauseated look.

"Eat the toast at least."

He takes half a piece, crunching it unenthusiastically. He slumps in his chair, running a hand through his messy thick hair.

"Hey, Mill," he says, looking down at my feet. "I'm really sorry about last night."

"Where did you get that shit?" I demand.

He squirms in his chair. "From Levi," he mumbles.

Levi Cargill is the flash-ass drug dealer who owns the house we were at last night. He went to the same high school as me. Like most of the assholes at the party.

"You're dealing for him?" I hiss, keeping my voice down because my dad is still sleeping, and I don't want him to overhear.

"Sometimes," Vic mumbles.

"*For what?* To buy a bunch of bullshit expensive sneakers? To keep up with that idiot Andrew? That's what you're going to throw your future away for?"

Vic can't even look at me. He's staring down at our dingy linoleum, miserable and ashamed.

It's not even his future he threw away. It's mine. That cop is coming for me today. There's no way he's just gonna write me a ticket.

Despite my fury at my brother, I don't regret what I did last night. Vic is smart, even if he's not acting like it right now. He gets top marks in biology, chemistry, math, and physics. If he buckles down and studies this year—and quits missing assignments—he could get into a great school. Get some scholarships, even.

I love my little brother more than anything in the world. I'll go to prison before I watch him incinerate his life.

"Get to work," I tell him. "And no fucking around with Andrew and Tito afterward. I want you to come back here and sign up for those summer AP courses like you said you were going to."

Vic grimaces, but he doesn't argue. He knows he's getting off light with me. He grabs the other half of his toast and heads for the door.

I finish my coffee, then eat the poached egg Vic didn't want. It's overcooked. I was too distracted to pay attention to the timer.

My dad's still sleeping. I wonder if I should put a couple of eggs on for him. He never used to sleep in, but lately he's been crashing for ten or eleven hours at night. He says he's getting old.

I decide to let him sleep a little longer. I grab a fresh pair of coveralls and head down to the shop. I've got to finish up with that transmission, then get to work changing the brake pads on Mr. Bridger's Accord.

It's nearly ten o'clock by the time my dad finally joins me. He looks pale and tired, his hair standing in wispy strands over his half-bald head.

"Morning, *mija*," he says.

"Hey, Dad," I say, fitting fresh seals into the transmission. "You get your coffee?"

"Yes, thank you."

My dad is only forty-six, but he looks a lot older. He's medium height, with a friendly round face and big, thick-fingered hands that look like they could barely hold a wrench and yet can manipulate the tiniest little bits and bolts with ease.

When he was young, he had thick black hair and roared around on a Norton Commando, giving girls rides to school on the back of his bike. That's how he met my mom. He was a senior; she was a sophomore. She got pregnant two months later.

They never married, but they lived together for a couple of years in my grandmother's basement. My dad was crazy about my mom. She really was gorgeous and smart. He told her to keep going to school while he worked days as a mechanic and took care of me at night.

Money was tight. My mom and grandmother didn't get along. My dad started getting chubby because he didn't have time to play soccer anymore, and he was living off the same peanut butter sandwiches and chicken nuggets I was eating.

My mom missed her friends and the fun she used to have. She started staying out later and later, not for school but to go to parties. Eventually, she dropped out. She didn't come home often. In fact, we wouldn't see her for days at a time.

I remember that part, just a little. My mom would drop in once every week or two, and I'd run to see her, this glamorous lady who always smelled like fancy perfume and wore tight dresses in bright colors, just like my Barbie dolls. She didn't like to pick me up or have me sit on her lap. As soon as my dad asked her too many questions or my grandma sniped at her about something, she'd leave again. And I'd stand by the window and cry until my dad picked me up and made me a dish of ice cream or took me out to the garage to show me something on his bike.

Eventually, my dad saved up enough to set up Axel Auto. We moved out of grandma's house into the little apartment above the shop. My mom never visited us there. I didn't think she even knew where it was.

Then, one night when I was ten years old, somebody rang our doorbell. We didn't hear it at first because of the rain. I was watching *ER* with my dad, eating popcorn out of a giant bowl set on the couch between us.

When the bell buzzed again, I jumped up, knocking over the bowl of popcorn. My dad stopped to pick it up, and I ran to the door. I opened it up. There was a lady standing there, not wearing any coat. Her dark hair was soaked, and so was her blouse. It clung to her skin, so I could see how skinny she was.

Neither of us recognized each other for a minute. Then she said, "Camille?"

I stared at her, my mouth open. Maybe she thought I was angry. Maybe she heard my dad walking toward the door, calling out, "Who is it?" Either way, she turned around and hurried back down the stairs. She left Vic behind.

He'd been hiding behind her leg. He was two years old, small for his age, with huge dark eyes and hair that was almost blond then. For a second, I wasn't sure if he was a boy or a girl because of those lashes and because his hair hadn't been cut in a while. He had his thumb in his mouth, and he was clutching that Spider-Man toy.

We brought him in the house. My dad tried to call any friends of my mother he knew, plus her parents and cousins. Nobody knew where she was. He offered to bring the kid over to her parents' house, but they said they'd call the cops if he did. They still hadn't forgiven my mother for getting pregnant with me in the first place.

So Vic stayed with us for a while. That turned into him staying with us forever. Actually, we don't even know what his name was to start with. He didn't talk back then. I picked *Vic* because I was way into *Law and Order*, and I thought the Crown Vic cop cars were cool as shit.

Later, when I was in high school, we heard my mom was working at Exotica. I never went to see her. I think my dad did, to try to figure out what the hell was going on with her. I don't think he got any answers. He just said Vic would be staying with us permanently. By that time Vic was seven years old, firmly ensconced in second grade and T-ball. He didn't remember our mother at all.

So we've all lived here ever since. It's my home and I love it. I love the smell of oil and gasoline and industrial-strength detergent down in the shop. I love the worn-in feeling of my coveralls and the perfect arrangement of my tools, where I can grab the right ratchet without even looking.

My dad zips up his own favorite coveralls, which used to be navy blue but have been washed so many times that they're barely gray anymore. They're hanging off his shoulders. He's lost weight.

"You on a diet or something?" I say, poking him playfully in the side.

"Nah. Just don't have time to eat. I'm lookin' good, huh?" He grins, striking an Atlas pose. He's got no muscle, so his sleeves just hang off his arms.

I smile weakly in return. "Yeah. Lookin' great, Dad."

My dad helps me finish the transmission, so we fit it back into place in the truck. It's much faster with two people. He's so quick and deft with his hands that it puts me at ease again. He certainly hasn't lost his touch.

Still, I notice he's breathing a little heavier than usual and sweating in the heat of the garage.

"You want me to get the fan?" I ask him.

"Nope. It's like a free sauna in here. If it's good for the Swedes, it's good for us."

Still, I grab us both a soda from the upstairs fridge.

While we're drinking them, I hear the bell chime at the front of the shop. New customer.

"I'll get it," I tell my dad.

I hurry up front before setting my soda on the reception desk. We don't have a receptionist—the desk is just there for show and for when my dad tries to sit and muddle through all the bills and receipts we should have organized as soon as we got them.

I see a man in a tight white T-shirt and a Cubbies cap looking through our stack of classic car magazines.

He glances up when he hears me. I see that square jaw and tanned face and friendly smile.

Shit. It's Officer Schultz. I was so distracted with the truck and my dad that I totally forgot about him.

"Camille," he says. "Nice to see you again."

Wish I could say the same. "Officer Schultz."

"Call me 'Logan.'"

I don't really want to, so I just nod stiffly.

"You and your dad own this place?" he says, looking around.

"Uh-huh."

There's nothing fancy about our shop. It's cramped, dingy, and decorated in the saddest way possible with a couple of old posters and a single ficus tree we never remember to water. Still, I don't like his condescending tone or the way he's shown up here like he's marking territory in the only place in the world that belongs to me.

"You live in that apartment up above?"

"Yep."

"And your brother, Victor, too?"

"Uh-huh."

"He goes to Oakmont?"

"Yeah. This'll be his last year."

"I went there," Schultz says, stuffing his hands in the pockets of his jeans. The movement flexes his pecs under the tight white tee. He didn't wear his uniform to come see me. Maybe he's trying to put me at ease. It's not gonna work, and neither is his small talk.

"Yeah, me, too," I say.

"What year did you graduate?"

"In 2013."

"Ah. I was '08. We just missed each other."

"Guess so."

My dad pokes his head out of the garage. "Need any help?"

"No!" I say quickly. "I've got it covered."

"All right. Call me if you need anything." My dad gives a friendly nod to Schultz, not knowing this dude is here to royally fuck with his kids' lives. Schultz gives him a little salute in return.

I wait for my dad to leave, and then I turn my unfriendly attention back onto Schultz. "Let's cut to the chase."

"Sure." Schultz smiles easily. "Let's do that. You were in possession of a hundred and fourteen tablets of MDMA."

Fuck.

"I've logged the traffic stop and the acquisition, but the Chicago PD has some flexibility in making arrests."

"What does that mean?"

He fixes me with those bright blue eyes, smiling pleasantly. "Well, think of your drug charge as a debt. You owe the State of Illinois four years. But you're not going to do anybody any good sitting in prison. In fact, you'll cost the taxpayers a lot of money. So it benefits the good people of this state if you work off your debt another way."

I don't like the way he's standing so close, looking down at me. "How am I supposed to do that?"

"Well…have you ever heard of a CI?"

Yeah. Like I said, I watched a lot of *Law and Order* growing up. I know about confidential informants.

"You want me to rat," I say flatly.

"I prefer to call it 'assisting the police in apprehending dangerous criminals.'"

Dangerous criminals who will slit my throat if they know I'm talking to the police. "You ever heard the phrase 'snitches get stitches'?"

He cocks his head to the side, looking me up and down even though he can't see shit through my coveralls. "You ever heard the phrase 'don't drop the soap'? I don't think you'd like federal prison, Camille. The women there are just as brutal as the men. Worse, sometimes. They love when a pretty young girl gets thrown inside. It's like chum in the water. They don't even want to take turns."

My skin crawls. I hate being threatened. And I'm especially pissed that he's doing it over some baggies of bullshit party drugs.

There are people murdering others every day in this city. He's gonna rake me over the coals because a bunch of rich kids like to get high and dance around to shitty music?

"What do you expect me to do?" I say through gritted teeth. "Wear a wire or something? I don't know any serious criminals. Just a bunch of idiots who like to get high. And we're not even friends."

"Where did the Ex come from?"

"Levi Cargill," I say without hesitation. I've got no problem throwing that guy under the bus after he recruited my underage brother to sell drugs for him. "He lives on—"

"I know where he lives."

"If you already know who he is, what do you expect me to do?"

"Get close to him. Find out where he gets his product. Find the names of all his dealers and suppliers. Report back to me."

"I'm not Inspector Poirot!" I cry. "I don't know how to do any of that!"

"You'll figure it out," Schultz says with zero sympathy. He hands me a business card. On the back he's written his personal cell number. "Memorize that number. Get used to calling it. We're going to be seeing a lot of each other."

I stifle a groan. I would like this to be the most I ever see of Schultz. Or Levi either, for that matter.

"And what if I can't get any more information?"

"Then you go to prison," Schultz says coldly. "And your brother, too. Don't forget, he had product in his pocket. He's old enough to be charged as an adult."

I press my lips together to keep from snapping at Schultz. Vic and I are just tools to him. He doesn't care if he destroys us as long as he gets another tally in his arrest book.

"Memorize that number," Schultz tells me again.

"I'll put it in my phone." *So I can make sure never to pick up when you call.*

"Perfect. You got any more of those sodas?" Schultz nods to the half-empty can on the reception desk.

"No," I lie. "Fresh out."

Schultz chuckles. He knows I'm lying. "Nice to see you, Camille. Let's do this again real soon."

I stand there with my arms folded until he leaves.

When I head back into the garage, my dad says, "What did he want?"

"Nothing. Directions."

My father shakes his head. "Tourists."

"Yeah."

"At least he was a Cubs fan."

"That's the only reason I talked to him."

My dad laughs, which turns into a cough. The cough goes on a while, long enough that when he straightens, his lips look a bit blue.

"You okay, Dad?"

"Of course," he says. "I might go lie down a while, though. If you've got these brakes covered."

"Sure. I'll handle it."

"Thanks, sweetie."

He shuffles up the stairs to our apartment.

I watch him go, my heart full of dread.

CHAPTER 4
NERO

WHEN I COME DOWN TO BREAKFAST, GRETA HAS MADE A BATCH OF fresh biscotti to go with the coffee, plus a red pepper frittata in that ancient iron skillet that's probably older than she is.

She offers me the food. I only want the coffee.

"More for me, then," Dante says, taking a second helping of frittata.

My father is at the end of the table, reading three newspapers at once. We might be the only people who still get the paper delivered—singlehandedly keeping the *Tribune* and the *Herald* in business.

"I can get those on your iPad," I tell Papa.

"I don't like the iPad," he says stubbornly.

"Yes, you do. Remember that game you kept playing, where you have to shoot peas at the zombies?"

"That's different." He grunts. "You're not reading the news if you don't get ink on your hands."

"Suit yourself."

I take a sip of the coffee. It's real coffee—heavily roasted, bittersweet, made in a three-chambered aluminum pot. Greta also makes cappuccino and macchiato on order because she's a fucking angel.

She's not actually Italian, but you'd never guess it by the way she cooks the traditional food my father loves. She's worked for him since before he married my mother. She helped raise us all. Especially after Mama died.

Greta is plump, with a little red left in her hair. She's got a surprising number of stories from her wild youth, once you get some liquor in her. And she's the only person bringing life into the house now that Aida's moved out.

Dante just sits at his end of the table like a ravenous, silent mountain, shoveling up food. Papa's not going to talk unless he finds something shocking in the paper. Sebastian is living on campus and only comes home on weekends.

I never thought I'd miss Aida. She's always been an annoying little puppy yapping at my heels. She loved to follow us around everywhere we went, trying to do everything we were doing but usually getting into trouble instead.

It's funny that she got married first, since she's the baby. Not to mention the last girl you'd expect to put on a puffy white dress.

Hell, she might be the only one of us to get married at all. I'm sure as fuck not doing it. Dante's still hung up on that girl he used to date, though he'd never admit it. And Sebastian…well, I can't guess what he'll do anymore.

He thought he was going to the NBA. Then his knee got all fucked up by Aida's husband, Callum, when our families weren't on good terms. Now Seb's sort of floating. Still doing physical therapy, trying to get back on the court. Sometimes joining Dante and me when we've got work to do. This winter he shot a Polish gangster. I think it fucked with his head. There's being a criminal, and there's being a killer… You cross that line and there's no going back. It changes you.

It certainly changed me. It shows you how a person can leave this world in a split second. Dead in the time it takes to flick off a light switch. And that's it—infinite nothingness, like the infinite nothing that came before. Your whole life is just a brief flare in the void. So what does it matter what we do? Good, evil, kindness, cruelty…it's all a spark that goes out without a trace. The whole existence of humanity will mean nothing once the sun expands and burns the planet to a crisp.

I learned that lesson at a young age.

Because I first killed someone when I was only ten years old.

That's what I think about while I drink my coffee.

Papa finishes his first paper, then switches to the next. He pauses before he starts perusing the front page, looking over at Dante.

"What's our next project now that the Oak Street Tower is done?" he says.

Dante stabs his fork into the last bite of frittata. "The Clark Street Bridge needs renovating. We could bid on that."

Gallo Construction has been taking on bigger and bigger projects lately. It's funny—the Italian Mafia got into contracting so we could control the labor unions. It started in New York. For decades, there wasn't a single construction project in NYC not controlled by the Mob in one way or another. We bribed and strong-armed the union leaders or even got elected ourselves. When you control a union, you control a whole industry. You can force the workers to slow or stop construction if the developers don't make the proper "donations." Plus, you have access to massive union pension funds, almost totally unregulated and ripe for tax-free money laundering or straight-up robbing.

But here's the irony—when you get into a business for nefarious reasons, you sometimes start making a legitimate profit. That's what happened to the Mafia dons who moved to Las Vegas—they opened casinos to launder their illegal money, and all of a sudden, the casinos were raking in more cash than the illegal rackets. Whoops—you're a legitimate businessman.

Bit by bit, that's happening to Gallo Construction. Chicago

is booming, especially our side of the city. The Magnificent Mile, Lake Shore Drive, the South and West Side retail corridors... there's five billion in commercial construction going on this year alone.

And we're getting more of it than we can handle.

We just finished a twelve-hundred-foot-tall high-rise. Papa wants the next project lined up. For once, I've got an idea...

"What about the South Works site?" I say.

"What about it?" Papa peers up at me from under his thick gray eyebrows. His eyes are beetle dark, as sharp as ever.

"It's four hundred and fifteen acres, completely untouched. It's gotta have the biggest untapped potential in this whole damn city."

"You ever see a python try to eat an alligator?" Dante says. "Even if it can strangle the gator, it chokes trying to swallow it."

"We don't have the capital for that," Papa says.

"Or the men," Dante adds.

That may have been the case a year ago. But a lot has changed since then. Aida married Callum Griffin, the heir to the Irish Mafia. Then Callum became alderman of the wealthiest district in the city. As the cherry on the sundae, Callum's little sister hooked up with the head of the Polish *Braterstwo*. So we've got access to more influence and manpower than we ever had before.

"I bet Cal would be interested in my idea," I say.

Dante and my father exchange scowls.

I know what they're thinking. Our whole world has already been thrown into a blender. We were bitter rivals of the Griffins for generations. Now we're suddenly allies. It's been going well so far. But there's no baby to seal the alliance just yet—no shared blood between the two families.

Dante and Papa are fundamentally conservative. They've already had all the change they can stomach.

I'll have to appeal to their competitive natures instead.

"If you don't want to do it, that's all right. The Griffins can probably handle it on their own."

Dante lets out a sigh that's more of a rumble. Like a dragon in a cave, forced to rouse itself in response to an intruder.

"Save the negging for the girls at the bar," he growls. "I get your point."

"Four hundred and fifteen acres," I repeat. "Waterfront property."

"Next to a shit neighborhood," Papa says.

"Doesn't matter. Lincoln Park used to be a shit neighborhood. Now Vince Vaughn lives there."

Papa considers. I don't talk while he's thinking. You don't stir the cement when it's already setting.

At last he nods.

"I'll set up a meeting with the Griffins to discuss," he says.

Flush with success, I grab one of Greta's biscotti, dunk it in the last of my coffee, and head down the stairs to the underground garage.

If I identify with any superhero, it would be Batman. This is my Batcave. I could live in it indefinitely, fucking around with machinery and only coming out at night to get into trouble.

I'm currently working on a 1930 Indian Scout motorcycle, a '65 Shelby CSX, and a '73 Chevy Corvette. Plus the Mustang I've been driving around. It's a 1970 Boss 302, gold with black racing stripes. All original metal, V-8 with a manual transmission, only forty-eight thousand miles on it. I swapped out the vinyl seats for sheep leather.

Then there's my absolute favorite. The car I searched for years to find: the Talbot-Lago Grand Sport. I've spent more hours on that baby than all the others combined. It's my one true love. The one I'll never sell.

The only thing I feel the slightest sentimentality about is my cars. Only machinery gives me that impulse to care and nurture.

It's the only time I can be patient and careful. When I'm driving, I actually feel calm. And even just a little bit happy. The wind blows in my face. Speeding by on an open road, everything looks clean and bright. I don't see the little details—the cracks and grime and ugliness. Not until I stop and I'm walking again.

Anyway, that's why I like summer the best. Because I can cruise around all day long and not worry about my cars getting fucked up with snow and sleet and salt on the road.

I don't even mind being Dante's chauffeur. We've got a bunch of places to go this morning—gotta drop off payroll for our construction crews. They all want to get paid in cash because half of them owe child support and taxes and they still need money for drinking and gambling and rent. Speaking of gambling, we've got to pick up the rake from the underground poker ring we're running out of the King's Arms Hotel.

So much of our day is this kind of tedious busywork. I miss the adrenaline shot of pulling proper jobs.

When I was fifteen and Dante was twenty-one, we used to pull the craziest shit. Armored truck heists, even a couple of bank robberies. Then he enlisted out of fucking nowhere and spent the next six years in Iraq. When he got back, he was completely different. He barely talks. He can't take a joke. And he lost that daredevil spirit.

After we've made the rounds, we grab some lunch at Coco Pazzo. Then Dante has to meet with our foreman. I've got zero interest in that, so I drop him off, planning to head back home and do some work on the Mustang. Ever since I juiced up the engine, it's been overheating like crazy. Doesn't help that it's a hundred degrees out today and Dante's been sitting in my passenger seat like a 250-pound block of granite, putting strain on the engine.

In fact, even though I'm driving slowly on the way home, my gauges keep going higher and higher, and the car's straining to go up the tiniest of hills. Fuck. I might not even make it back.

As I'm driving down Wells Street, I see the weathered sign for Axel Auto. Impulsively, I pull the wheel to the left, turning around the side of the building so I can pull up to the auto bay.

I haven't been here in ages. I used to have Axel Rivera order parts for me before you could buy anything you needed online. And he used to do work for my father before I got to a level where I could fix any of our vehicles myself.

I expect to see Axel working in the bay like no time has passed at all.

Instead, I see a much slimmer figure bent over under the hood of an Accord, wrestling with something in the engine. Camille struggles with a piece, finally wrenching it free. She sets the cap on a nearby bench, wiping her sweaty face with the back of her arm. Then, deciding that's not enough, she strips off her shirt, using it to towel off her face, neck, and chest.

She's only wearing a plain cotton bra underneath, wet with sweat. I'm surprised to see how fit Camille is. Her arms are lean and strong, and there's a line of muscle down either side of her belly button. Plus, she's got more up top than I would have guessed—full soft breasts cupped by the damp, clinging material of the bra. She always dresses like a dude. Turns out she's actually a girl under all that grime.

I clear my throat. Camille jumps like a startled cat. When she sees who it is, she glowers at me and yanks her T-shirt back down over her head.

"This isn't a peep show," she snaps. "Exotica is twelve blocks that way."

"Exotica burned down," I tell her.

Actually, I burned it down myself when I was in a tiff with the owner. It was my first foray into arson. It was pretty fucking satisfying seeing the flames roar up like a living thing, like a demon summoned from hell. I could see how people get addicted to it.

"Really?" Camille says, her eyes wide. She has extremely dark eyes—a deep mocha color, as dark as her hair and lashes. Because she doesn't smile much, her eyes give most of the expression to her face. She seems unnerved by what I said.

Oh, that's right—Exotica is where her mom worked.

"Yeah," I say. "It burned down in the winter. It's just an empty lot now."

She looks suspicious, like she thinks I'm fucking with her. "How did it burn down?"

"Guess somebody spun around a pole too fast." I smirk. "G-string friction. Only takes a spark to start a fire." *Or several cans of gasoline and a Zippo.*

Camille scowls at me. "What do you want?"

"Is that your best customer service? No wonder this place is so busy."

I pretend to look around at a host of invisible customers.

Camille's nostrils flare. "You're not a customer," she hisses.

"I might be. My engine's overheating. I want to look at it before I drive the rest of the way home."

I don't ask for permission to pull it into the bay; I just drive the car into an empty stall. Then I get out and pop the hood.

Camille peeks in, curious despite herself. "Have you been using original parts?" she asks. "You can get almost anything for the '65 to '68 models, but once you move into the '71 to '73…"

"This one's 1970."

"Still—"

"It's all original!" I snap.

"No performance brake kit?"

"Well…yeah."

She makes an irritating little "hmph!" sound, like she proved her point.

I'm starting to remember why nobody liked Camille at school. 'Cause she's a stubborn little know-it-all.

"Did you add a turbo?" she says. "How much horsepower is it at now?"

She's really pissing me off. She's acting like I'm some rich kid down on Wacker Drive, not knowing the first fucking thing about my own car.

"It's not unbalanced."

"Then why is it overheating?"

"You tell me, mechanical genius!"

She straightens, glaring at me. "I don't have to tell you anything. I don't work for you."

"Where's your dad? He knows what he's doing."

I knew that would piss her off, but I underestimated how much. She snatches the closest wrench and brandishes it like she's going to hit me upside the head with it.

"He's sleeping!" she yells. "And even if he weren't, he'd tell you the exact same thing I'm telling you. Which is to *fuck off*!"

She turns around and storms out of the auto bay, heading up the stairs to who knows where. Probably her apartment. I'm pretty sure her whole family lives above the shop. *Whole family* meaning her dad and that little brother who's been selling Molly for Levi. I wonder if she knows about that. I don't think Camille even drank in high school—she's always been the responsible type.

Well, that's her problem, not mine.

My problem right now is getting my car running smoothly again. And if Camille's going to stomp off, then I'm still gonna use her tools. No point letting a perfectly good garage go to waste.

Most of her equipment is older than Moses, but it's well maintained, organized, and clean. I set the radio to a better station so I don't have to listen to Shakira or whatever the fuck that was. Soon I'm elbow-deep in the engine, sorting out the Mustang.

After about an hour, I conclude that there might have been a teeny sliver of truth to what Camille said. With some of the mods I've put on the engine, it's running at double the horsepower it was originally intended to withstand. I may need to rethink some of the additions.

But that's a job for my own garage. For now, I just need to top up the coolant. I sort that out, then toss a few hundred bucks on the workbench in return for the tools and materials.

I may be a criminal, but I'm not cheap.

CHAPTER 5
CAMILLE

I'M SO MAD, I COULD SCREAM!

Who the fuck does Nero think he is, coming into my shop and acting like I just sweep floors around here?

I can hear him down there messing around with my tools. I've got a mind to grab the power washer and blast him out of there like a junkyard dog.

The only reason I don't is because my dad starts coughing again. He's supposed to be taking a nap, but he keeps waking up every ten minutes with another round of hacking and groaning. I feel frozen in place in the kitchen, vacillating between going in to check on him and leaving him alone if he might be falling back asleep again.

I've got a sick feeling of dread, like I'm standing in an abandoned building and the walls are starting to crumble around me. Vic is getting in trouble. That cop is up my ass. And now something's wrong with my dad. It's not just the coughing—he's been sick for a while. But we don't have insurance. We're self-employed. I've looked several times, and the cheapest plan we could get is twelve hundred dollars a month. I'm lucky to have a spare hundred bucks after we pay for utilities, groceries, and the rent on this place, which keeps going up every year.

I keep working harder and harder, just to watch my dreams slip through my fingers like sand. I want my brother to go to a good school and become something great, like a doctor or an engineer. I want him to live in one of those big, fancy houses in Old Town, not an apartment. I want my dad to have a fat savings account so he can retire when the heavy lifting of the job gets to be too much for him. I want him to take a vacation somewhere sunny now and then.

And for me…

I don't know. I don't even know what I want for myself.

I want to not feel like a fucking loser. I want to have time for friends and dating. And I'd love to do the kind of work that really interests me. I love cars, more than anything. But changing brake pads is tedious at best. I'd love to do more creative projects.

There's a huge market for custom mods, and it's growing all the time. If I had the capital, we could be doing matte finishes, wraps, custom lights, body kits—all kinds of stuff.

That's just dreaming, though. We've barely paid off the equipment we've got. And if my dad doesn't get better soon, we're not going to be taking on extra work either.

At least he's quieting down, finally. I think he's actually asleep.

I make myself peanut butter toast and eat it with a glass of milk. When I'm sure he's getting some rest and the noise coming from his room is just snoring, I put my dishes in the sink and head back down to the garage to tell Nero to get lost.

Looks like he's already gone.

The right side of the bay is empty, his Mustang apparently fixed enough to carry him back home.

The radio is playing Drake. He changed my station. Are there no depths to which this man will not sink? I snap it back to Top Hits, swapping over to "Watermelon Sugar" instead. *Thank you, Harry Styles. You're a true gentleman. You would never fuck with a woman's torque wrenches and then force her to listen to Canada's worst export.*

At least Nero cleaned up after himself. Actually…the only thing he left out of place is a wad of bills on the workbench.

I walk over to it slowly, like there might be a scorpion hidden inside.

I pick it up. There's six hundred bucks here. All Benjamins, of course. *Douche.*

I hold the bills, wondering why Nero bothered to leave money. Not because he felt guilty for being an asshole—I've never heard him apologize for anything, not once. Not when he broke Chris Jenkin's arm during gym-class basketball. And certainly not when he got a blow job from the Henderson twins, on the same day, an hour apart, without telling either of the sisters that he was going for a matching set.

And that was just high school shit. He's done a lot worse since then. Serious criminal activity, if the rumors are true. They say he's in the Italian Mafia, along with his brother. I wouldn't doubt it. His father is a don, not just your regular goombah.

I remember the first time I saw Enzo Gallo pull up to the auto bay in a sleek gray Lincoln Town Car that looked a mile long. He got out of the back wearing a three-piece suit, Oxford shoes, and a houndstooth overcoat. I'd never seen a man dressed like that. I thought he must be the president.

He shook hands with my dad, and they talked for a long time. They were laughing at one point. I thought they must be friends. Later I found out Enzo's like that with everybody. He knows everyone in our neighborhood—the Italians and everybody else.

He's a benevolent dictator. My father told me that at one point, every single business in northwest Chicago paid a 5 percent protection fee to the Gallos. The Irish had the northeast. But when the Gallos moved into the construction racket, they dialed back on the old-school extortion.

Now I see their name on high-rise sites in the downtown core. I really can't picture Nero working a backhoe. Now, burying a body under a foundation…that I can definitely see. I bet he'd smile while he did it.

No, if Nero left money, it wasn't to be nice. It's because six hundred bucks is pocket change to him.

Not to me, though. I stuff it in my coveralls. That's two month's groceries or a quarter of the rent. I'll take it, even if it fell out of the devil's pocket.

I finish topping up the fluids on the Accord, and then I head into the tiny front office to pay a couple of bills.

As I'm messing around with our online bill pay, my cell phone starts buzzing. I pick it up without looking, thinking it's Vic wanting a ride home from work.

"Did you miss me yet, Camille?" a deep voice says.

I cringe away from the phone, looking at the name on the display: *Officer Dickhole*.

"I really hadn't had a chance to miss you," I say. "Try staying away longer."

He chuckles. "I knew I picked the right girl. What are you doing tonight?"

"Organizing my socks."

"Think again. You're going to Wacker Drive."

"What's on Wacker Drive?" I ask innocently.

"You know exactly what. I'm surprised I haven't already seen you down there."

"I fix cars. I don't crash them into pylons."

"Well, I'm sure you'll enjoy the show either way," Schultz says. "Cozy up to Levi. Start making best buds with all your high school friends again."

I shiver. Schultz knows my connection to these people. He's learning more about me. Not to be friendly, I'm sure. He's sinking his hooks in deeper and deeper.

I keep all my clothes in the coat closet. My little makeshift room doesn't have a closet or any space for a dresser. I only have a few outfits anyway. Most of them look the same. Jeans. A couple of

T-shirts. Undershirts that come in a pack of five from Hanes. A pair of shorts that used to be an old pair of jeans.

I pull those on, along with some sneakers and a T-shirt. Then I look in the bathroom mirror. I pull off the navy bandanna that holds back my hair. My curls spring up, frizzy in the summer humidity.

I would like to have Beyoncé curls. What I actually have are Howard Stern curls, where they stick up everywhere like I've been electrocuted. Even the ends are a little lighter from the sunshine, like they really did get zapped with ten thousand volts. I usually keep my curls tied down.

There's no way I'm wearing my hair loose. But I can at least put it up properly. I rub a little shea butter in it, then twist it up in a bun on top of my head. Some curls poke out, but I don't care. It's good enough.

I get my Trans Am and cruise down to Lower Wacker Drive. Wacker is like three freeways stacked on top of one another. The top two streets carry traffic, but the lowest road is much less busy. It runs parallel with the river, with heavy support beams bracketing the road on both sides.

I have been here before, once or twice, though apparently not when Schultz was around to see. I couldn't resist watching some of the fastest cars in the city face off in illegal street races.

It's not just drag racing. It's drifting and burnouts, too. Every once in a while, a race gets out of control, and somebody crashes into a parked car or a pole. That somebody was Nero Gallo last fall, or so I heard. He crashed his beloved Bel Air racing Johnny Verger. It was stupid of him to even try—a classic car can't compete with a brand-new BMW, not in speed or in handling, no matter what modifications Nero made to it. But that's his problem. He has his normal level of crazy. And then he has his moments when he seems to crave pure immolation. He's somebody who wants to go out in a blaze of glory. The going out is more important than the blaze of glory.

When I get there, I see half a dozen cars with their headlights on, circling lazily, with a dozen more parked around. I see Supras, Lancers, Mustangs, Imprezas, a couple of M2s, and one chromed-out silver Nissan GT-R.

I park my car and join the loose crowd, looking around for people I know.

I spot Patricia Porter. She's a tall, pretty girl who was a year ahead of me in school. She's got her hair pulled up in a high pony and a little gold hoop through the side of her nose.

"Patricia!" I call.

She looks up, taking a second to fix on me, before she breaks into a grin. "I haven't seen you in forever!"

"I know. I'm boring. I don't go out."

She laughs. "Same. I work a lot of nights, so unless somebody wants to meet for brunch when I get off…"

"Where do you work?"

"Midtown Medical. I'm an X-ray tech."

"I'm surprised you're not glowing, then."

"I mean, I wear a lead apron. But yes, I've developed several superpowers so far…"

I'm happy to see her. It's nice to remember that not everybody I went to school with was an ass. Just most of them, unfortunately.

Speaking of which, there's Bella Page prowling around. Not with her little minions this time, but with some guy I don't know—he's wearing a denim jacket and he's got sort of an Eastern European look, all slicked-back hair and high cheekbones. There's a cross tattooed on the side of his neck.

He's the one who owns the GT-R, apparently. He's got great taste in cars, if not in women. They call it the Godzilla for a reason. You can go around the pilings in one of those like you're doing slaloms down a goddamned mountain.

I was planning to hold really still and hope Bella didn't see me, until Patricia yells, "Hey, Bella—where are your bookends?"

Bella frowns at us, annoyed that we got the first shot off before she even saw us. "They're not here tonight."

"That's weird," Patricia says. "I thought they were surgically attached."

"It's called having friends," Bella says in her sweetest, most condescending tone. "That's why we're the Queen Bees, and you two losers are barely Ds."

I shake my head at her. "You really haven't changed since high school. And that's not a compliment."

"Yeah. You guys gave yourselves your own nickname. That's lame as hell," Patricia says.

I snort.

I don't know who first called them *the Queen Bees*, but I can certainly imagine those three bitches sitting around brainstorming. Probably took them all afternoon.

Bella narrows her eyes at us until they're like two bright blue horizontal slits. "You know what else hasn't changed since high school? You two are still ugly, poor, and completely jealous of me."

"Well, you got one out of three right," I tell her. "I am pretty broke."

"Obviously," Bella says, letting her eyes sweep over the whole of my person. Then she turns and stalks away to rejoin the boyfriend who doesn't seem to have noticed she was missing.

Patricia laughs, totally unconcerned by that little encounter. "God, I thought she'd be living somewhere else by now. Torturing some other innocent citizens."

"Innocent is a stretch…" I say.

A few cars are already lining up—the tight, efficient Japanese models and the roaring American muscle. I see a white Supra with a long scratch down the side waiting alongside a purple Impreza.

Patricia looks keenly interested in this particular race. She's watching closely, biting the edge of her thumbnail.

The cars take off, screeching off the line. The Impreza jolts ahead first, quicker off the line, but the Supra starts to catch up along the straight stretch. There's a curve before the finish line—the Supra is forced to the outside but pulls ahead again when the cars straighten out. They whip across the finish line, the Supra ahead by an inch.

It's only a quarter mile. The race lasted a total of fourteen seconds.

Still, I failed to breathe the entire time. My heart is in my throat, and I'm hit with a vivid bolt of joy.

Patricia seems equally thrilled—she lets out a whoop of happiness, like she was cheering for the Supra the whole time.

"Who was that?" I ask her.

She blushes, looking mildly embarrassed. "This guy, Mason. We're sort of dating."

The two cars pull back around. Patricia hurries over to meet them, running across the beams of their headlights. I follow her, curious to see this Mason guy.

He climbs out of the Supra: tall, skinny, with lightning bolts shaved into the side of his hair, wearing a pair of ripped-up skinny jeans.

He's laughing at the driver of the Impreza. "I told you, you don't have the top-end speed—"

Mason breaks off when he sees Patricia.

"Patricia! Baby! Why don't you pick up your phone?" he cries. "I called you eight hundred times. Listen, I'm telling you, baby, I never cheated on you…"

"I know that," Patricia says calmly.

"You know…" He stares at her. "If you know that…then why… in the fuck…did you key my *car*!?" he shouts.

"BECAUSE YOU LEFT MY GRANDMOTHER AT THE AIRPORT!" Patricia bellows back at him. "You said you were going to pick her up while I was at work! She waited THREE HOURS, MASON! That woman is eighty-seven years old! She saw the

Hindenburg explode. Actually, she heard it—BECAUSE THERE WAS NO FUCKING TV!"

Mason is standing there frozen with a guilty grimace on his face. He definitely forgot all about Patricia's grandma until right this very moment.

"Okay, okay," he says, holding up his hands. "I might have fallen asleep—"

"ASLEEP?"

"But you didn't have to key my car, baby! It's a classic!"

"Nana's a classic, Mason! *Nana!*"

This is so much better than a drag race. A large circle of people formed around us, and I swear to god, somebody is taking bets on whether Patricia is going to smack Mason or go for his car again.

"She had to eat airport Wendy's, Mason! That is so much worse than normal Wendy's!"

At that moment, I see Levi Cargill standing over on the opposite side of the circle. He's wearing a hot-pink tracksuit and a diamond the size of my pinky nail in his right ear. I cannot comprehend why Officer Schultz needs my help tracking Levi when you can probably see him from outer space.

I sidle over toward him, wanting to speak to him alone.

He's talking to a couple of hard-faced guys. When I make eye contact, he peels off from the pack and ambles over.

"You wanna buy something?" he asks me.

"No."

He lets his eyes roam down my body, grinning suggestively. "You want something for free, then? It's big and thick, and I can—"

"Actually, it's about my brother."

"Who?"

"Victor."

"Oh." He stops smiling. "You dragged him out of my party last night."

"Right. He's not coming to those anymore. And he's not selling for you anymore either."

Levi's lips thin out into a long straight line. He sucks in air through his nostrils. "That's not up to you. It's between me and Vic."

"Victor is seventeen," I say quietly. "He's a minor, and he's not selling drugs for you."

Levi grabs my upper arm between fingers that feel like steel pincers. He drags me away from the circle of headlights, behind a cement pillar.

"Here's the problem," he hisses. "Your brother owes me for a hundred and fifty tabs. And he also owes me a new dealer if he's planning to quit."

"It was a hundred and ten."

"He's paying me for one fifty, or that's how many strokes I'm gonna practice with my nine iron on the back of his skull," Levi spits into my face, digging his fingers into my arm.

"What does that cost?" I mutter, trying not to show how much it hurts.

"Ten bucks a tab."

There's no way they cost him that much. But he's obviously determined to extort me.

"Fine," I growl. "I'll get you the money."

"Yeah? What about the dealer?"

I hesitate. I don't want to cave to this guy. I don't want to see him at all after today.

But there's somebody who's not going to let me go home and hide my head under the pillow. Officer Schultz expects me to get information. He's going to expect a lot more than the news that Vic "quit."

"I'll do it," I say.

"You?" Levi sneers.

I yank my arm out of his grip. "Yeah, me. I know a hell of a lot more people than Victor does. They come in and out of my shop all day long. I can probably double Vic's sales."

"I thought you were a good girl." Levi's suspicious. "I heard you don't even suck dick with the lights on."

"I wouldn't touch yours in any fuckin' light."

Levi snorts. "You're not my type either, you Justin Bieber–dressin' bitch."

I want to tell Levi he looks like a cool mom, but I keep it to myself. The only way I'm going to get dirt on this guy is by working for him. And if that's what I have to do to get Schultz off my back, well…I don't have any other choice.

"That's the best I can do," I tell him. "My brother's going to college. He's not sticking around here like the rest of us."

Levi scoffs. "I went to college. There are more drugs on campus than the whole rest of the city."

"Yeah, well, there are also diplomas."

Levi looks me over one last time. "Come by the house tomorrow."

"Perfect. I will."

I turn away from him, trying not to hyperventilate.

Great. I'm a drug dealer now.

I don't exactly feel like celebrating, but at least I'll have something to tell Schultz next time he calls. Unless he gets hit by a bus in the meantime.

CHAPTER 6
NERO

I WASN'T PLANNING ON GOING DOWN TO WACKER DRIVE. RACING IS stupid, I know that. But it draws me back again and again. It's that scent of high-octane fuel and the way the engines snarl like beasts under the hood. A car wants to race just like a horse does.

And I want to be the one behind the wheel.

Time slows down. You can live an entire year in the span of fourteen seconds. I can see everything—every pebble on the pavement, every drop of moisture on the windshield. I can feel the whole operation of the engine through the vibration of the gearshift under my palm.

I crashed my Bel Air here. That was a bad night. I was in a fucking fury. In one of those states where I feel like I want to see the whole city burn down around me. I don't know why I get like that. There's something wrong with me.

If I feel something painful, I want more pain, more rage, more violence.

Maybe it's because you can't get rid of pain. All you can do is try to burn it out.

Anyway, Mason's racing tonight, and I want to see it.

He's got his Supra up against Vinny's Impreza. It's a friendly race—two thousand dollars on the line.

As the cars are lining up, I see a familiar red Trans Am pulling in under the covered road. Camille Rivera slides out of the driver's seat. She's dressed in normal clothes for once—well, normal compared to her usual coveralls. She's talking to Mason's ex-girlfriend.

It's weird. I hadn't seen Camille in years. Now she's come out twice in a week.

Bella Page is here, too, with Grisha Lukin. He's Russian—born here, but his father's an old-school oligarch with *Bratva* ties. My family's on shaky footing with the *Bratva* right now. The Russians haven't picked a new boss yet after the Griffins killed the old one.

Anyway, I've known Grisha a long time. So we should be cool. Or at least cool enough to keep it civil.

He gives me a curt nod when we lock eyes. I do the same. I'm sitting on the hood of my Mustang, drinking a forty of Olde English. It's absolute piss, but it gives a nice buzz. It's all they had at the bodega on Quincy Street.

Mason and Vinny peel off the line, racing down the covered roadway. The Impreza has more kick to start with, but the Supra catches up in the end, and Mason edges him out.

Watching them race makes me want to do it, too. I get that itch, where my head starts to feel muddled and my thoughts are all mashed together, and I know the one thing that will give me clarity is speeding down the road at 160 miles an hour.

"Put me on the lineup," I say to Carlo. He's running the races tonight.

"Who with?"

"I don't care."

I'll race anybody. It's not about the money. It's the challenge.

I notice Camille is talking to Levi Cargill. She looks irritated. No surprise there—Camille is as prickly as a hedgehog, even under the best of circumstances. But I haven't seen it turned on Levi before. Maybe Camille found out he's been using her brother to move Molly.

She'd better watch it. Levi looks like a total poser, but he's got a nasty temper. Sometimes the rich boys are the worst thugs of all. They want to prove they're hard-asses.

I can feel myself tensing. My eyes are fixed on the two of them, on Levi in particular. Just waiting for him to reach in his pocket or raise a hand to her.

I don't know why I should care. Camille and I aren't even friends.

But I guess I do respect her a little. She's not vapid, like Bella's friends, or reeking of desperation, like Bella herself. Camille is…real. She is who she is, and she doesn't apologize. There's honesty in that.

Maybe that's the real reason Bella hates her. Because Bella is trying so hard to be the most beautiful, the most desirable, and the most fascinating person around, which never really works, and she knows it. And then here's this other girl who's not trying to be any of those things. It's like an insult to Bella. Because Camille won't even play the game, so how can Bella win it?

Or maybe I'm drunk.

I don't know what the fuck goes on in Bella's head. All I know is that she's squaring up with Camille again, starting another skirmish in their endless war.

I slide off the hood of the car, ambling over so I can hear it.

"Well, it's too bad all you've got is that rolling trash heap," Bella is saying, "or you could participate, too. But you'd rather just watch anyway, wouldn't you? That's what creepy losers do. They stand on the sidelines watching more interesting people live their lives."

"You might be surprised," Camille says calmly.

"About what?" Bella says.

"How fast that beat-up rust bucket can go. And how few people would consider you interesting."

Bella flushes. She's always doing this to herself, trying to dominate Camille and never getting what she wants out of it. You'd think she would have given up a long time ago.

"I doubt your car could make it over the finish line in the same night as mine," Bella says.

"Only one way to know," Camille replies.

Bella laughs, disbelieving. "What's the bet? Don't tell me your car—I wouldn't take that tin can if you paid me."

"I've got six hundred," Camille says. She pulls the folded bills out of her pocket.

I snort. That's my fucking money; I paid her this afternoon. She's going to blow it on a race with Bella?

It's completely stupid. But I'm sort of enjoying this reckless Camille. Her chin is stubborn, and her dark eyes are fierce.

"Are we doing it or not?" Camille says.

"I want to," Bella sneers. "I'll just feel so bad taking your whole life's savings…"

"Yeah, I bet." Camille stalks over to the Trans Am before climbing into the driver's seat.

Bella's G-Wagon is not at all built for racing. Still, she's got the newest model, a four-liter twin-turbo V-8. It is quick, for a six-thousand-pound tank.

On the opposite side, you've got Camille's Trans Am, which maybe she's juiced up, or maybe is held together with string. I guess we'll find out.

When they pull up to the line, Camille looks ahead down the stretch, cool as a cucumber. Maybe she's nervous, but she won't show it out of pure stubbornness. Bella's trying to look tough, but she doesn't pull it off as well as Camille. She blows a kiss to Grisha. He grins, amused at this whole thing.

Carlo stands between the cars, raising his arms over his head. He counts down. "Three…two…*one!*"

His arms swing down, and the cars peel off the line.

Camille had the quicker reflexes. Still, the G-Wagon pulls away first. Camille has to shift gears manually, which means she has a slower start. But as she expertly moves from second to third to fourth gear, the car leaps forward in bursts, as if it's an old locomotive and she's shoveling in load after load of coal.

It's only a quarter-mile race. Less than fifteen seconds long. Maybe sixteen, with these two cars.

I can see Mason standing at the end of the line, watching to see which vehicle passes first.

Camille edges up. Her car is more than roaring—it's bellowing. A wisp of smoke comes out from under the hood. She keeps pushing anyway.

I can't help admiring her driving. Camille's got balls. And she knows how to get the most out of her car.

Meanwhile, the G-Wagon wobbles unsteadily on its base. It's top-heavy, and Bella probably has the gas pedal floored. Camille deliberately crowds the SUV. Bella jerks the wheel too hard to correct. The wobble turns into a fishtail. Camille flies past, crossing the finish line.

They circle back around, Bella driving recklessly fast as if she can still win, Camille moving cautiously because there's a steady stream of dark gray smoke coming from the corner of her hood.

Before Bella's even gotten out of the car, she's already shrieking that Camille cheated. "That was horseshit! You tried to run me off the road!" she yells.

"I didn't touch you," Camille says.

"'Cause you don't care if you scratch up your piece-of-shit car!" Bella shouts furiously. She turns and boots the side of Camille's Trans Am, putting a dent in the driver's side panel.

This is a big no-no in street racing. You do not fuck with anybody's car.

Camille launches herself at Bella, only held back by Patricia and Carlo, who has thrown himself between the girls.

"Hey, hey, relax!" Carlo stiff-arms them both in opposite directions.

"That is fucking *it*!" Camille shouts.

"Looks the same as it did before," Bella sneers back at her.

"Here." Grisha stuffs a bundle of bills in Camille's hand. "You won. There's some extra for the car."

Bella smirks, pleased to have her boyfriend pay for her mistakes.

Camille takes the money, but she's so pissed off that she's shaking. She's mad that Bella didn't even pay her bet, let alone the damage. It looks like Camille has to silently count to ten before she can turn away from Bella, popping the hood of her car and releasing a cloud of smoke tinged with oil.

"Fucking garbage," Bella hisses, not specifying whether she's talking about Camille or her car.

Camille ignores her, focused solely on her ride.

Mason, Carlo, and I all circle around her, irresistibly drawn by our curiosity to see what went wrong. I stand next to Camille, peering over her shoulder. It's exactly the position we took when she was looking at my car earlier today.

"Here we are again," I say.

She gives me an annoyed look, not seeing the humor in it.

"Yikes," Mason says. "That doesn't look good ..."

"*Cops!*" somebody shouts.

The effect is instant. The word is like a grenade thrown into the center of the group. Everybody scatters.

It's not that I care so much about a ticket. It wouldn't be my first. But I don't fancy spending the rest of the night in an interrogation room if the cops get the bright idea to put the screws to me while they have the chance.

I'm about to take off, until I see Camille standing helplessly next to her car.

"Come on!" Patricia calls to her. "Come with us!"

Patricia is climbing into Mason's Supra. She gestures frantically for Camille to join them.

"I can't leave my car!" Camille shouts back.

Sirens close in on two sides.

I should just leave.

If Camille wants to get arrested, that's her dumb choice.

Camille rests her palm on her car, her expression anguished. Like it would kill her to leave the Trans Am. Like it's her baby.

"Forget the car," I bark to Camille. "You can come back for it tomorrow."

She casts a frightened look in the direction of the cop cars, but she's still glued to the smoking Trans Am. I hear racers speeding off in all directions, while I'm still standing here like a fool.

Propelled by annoyance, I scoop Camille up and throw her over my shoulder.

"Hey!" she shrieks. "Put me down! What are you—"

"Shut up." I jog back to my car before wrenching open the passenger door and throwing her inside.

"I don't need you to—"

I slam the door in her face and run around to the driver's side.

A squad car is heading right for us. We're the only idiots still parked along the main drag. Mason peeled off as soon as he saw me grab Camille.

The cop has his siren blaring and his lights on. Over the speaker, he barks, "Stay right where you are!"

Instead, I set my foot on the gas pedal and press it all the way to the floor.

CHAPTER 7
CAMILLE

"*WHAT ARE YOU DOING?*" I SHRIEK AS NERO SPEEDS AWAY FROM the cops.

Two squad cars chase us, their sirens wailing furiously. The police are driving Chargers, basically the most aggressive cop car ever built. They're new, fast, and built like tanks, with front racks to sweep us off the road if they get so much as a piece of us.

Nero is staring straight ahead. His face is oddly calm. No, strike that—I think he's actually enjoying this. His perpetual scowl is wiped away, and the tiniest hint of a smile tugs at the corner of his lips.

"Hey, psychopath!" I yell at him. "I think they want you to pull over!"

"I'm not gonna do that," Nero says calmly.

Jesus Christ. Just when I think I can't get in any more trouble, now I'm evading arrest.

We're racing down Wacker Drive, nearing the end of the strip that's relatively free of traffic or lights. Soon we'll get jammed up in cross streets.

"Hold on," Nero says.

"What? Why—"

He pulls the e-brake, spinning us around in a tight circle. The tires shriek, and the smell of melted rubber fills the car. The whole world spins like a merry-go-round.

Now we're facing the two cop cars barreling down on us, and Nero has floored the gas again. We're hurtling toward them like it's a game of chicken. I crouch in my seat, not wanting to be seen but also feeling like Nero's about to crash us headlong into the police.

Instead, he shoots the gap between the two cop cars with only an inch to spare on either side. His side mirror hits the mirror of the squad car, ripping it off.

Then we're barreling down the road again, going in the opposite direction. I hear the screech of the squad cars trying to brake and turn around. The Chargers are fast, but they're definitely not as maneuverable. And presumably, the officers driving them actually care about staying alive, so they're not whipping around like a demon in a go-cart.

"Just stop!" I beg Nero. "You're gonna get us killed!"

"Probably not," he says, as if he doesn't much care one way or another.

Nero pulls a hard left down Adams, throwing me against the passenger door. "You should buckle up," he says.

I try to pull my seat belt across my body—not easy to do when Nero is taking each new corner like he's trying to confuse himself, only wrenching the wheel to the side when we're almost past it.

We're weaving through Greek Town. I can hear the sirens still but not actually see the squad cars. I can't tell if they're behind us or one block over.

Nero seems to know exactly where they are, because he keeps doubling back and shifting over.

I have to admit, his driving is masterful. I've never seen somebody handle a car like this, especially an old Mustang that wasn't exactly built for it. He shifts through the gears like they're liquid, tendons standing out on his hand and forearm. His skin is smooth and deeply olive, no hair on his forearms, so I can see every ripple of tension running up the flesh.

His black hair falls into his face as we wrench around the corners.

He tosses it back again with a flick of his head, like a restless horse. His jaw is as tight as his arm. It flexes as he grits his teeth.

As I watch Nero drive, instead of watching the road and all the other cars we're almost hitting, my panic leeches away. I'm mesmerized by the sight of him. I've never seen somebody so focused.

I've also never looked at Nero for so long before.

I never could.

I could only steal glances, knowing that he's so high-strung, so alert, that each time I was risking him turning that blazing stare on me, shrinking me to nothing in the heat of his gaze. I didn't want to draw his attention. I didn't want him to cut me down for daring to look at him.

Now my eyes are fixed on him like I'm seeing him for the first time.

It's too much.

He fills my brain.

Maybe it's the adrenaline of the moment, but I've never seen anything more beautiful.

His jaw is a straight sharp line beneath those ridiculously full lips. His mouth is perfectly shaped—pouting, cruel, mobile, sarcastic. And yet soft and infinitely enticing. He looks the most Italian of any of his brothers, his skin almost as brown as mine. It's smooth and clear. His broad nose is strong enough to balance those lips. And then you have his eyes…

God almighty, why did you give the man with the blackest soul the most heavenly eyes?

They're long, narrow, and light gray in color. Lighter than his skin. The gray almost looks silver, shot through with darker bands that radiate from the pupil like a starburst.

He turns those eyes on me, sparing a glance from the road. It feels like a spike driving into my chest. For just a second, I wish that I were beautiful so he'd want to look at me the way I'm looking at him.

He fixes his eyes on the road again.

The sirens are just a little more distant now. Maybe two streets over.

Nero checks the rearview mirror once more, then jerks the wheel to the right and turns into an underground parking garage. He takes us down to the second level before pulling into a tight spot between a van and a truck. He cuts the lights.

"We'll wait here a minute," he says.

It's only in the sudden silence that I hear my blood rushing in my ears, and I realize how fast my heart has been beating all this time.

I sink back in my seat, gasping for air.

I cover my eyes with my hands, trying to block out the car, the garage, and Nero so I can breathe.

The weight of all the trouble I'm in is pressing down on me like a block of stone. Victor, my dad, Schultz, Levi…I can see them all circling me, all needing something. Now I don't even have my car, and I'm stuck in here with Nero, about to be arrested any second.

My heart is seizing up in my chest. My breath comes faster and more ragged. I feel like I'm dying.

Nero grabs my hand and peels it away from my face. He presses hard on the flesh between my thumb and index finger.

The jolt of pressure cuts through my racing thoughts. It focuses all sensation on that one point in my hand.

Nero keeps squeezing, his strong fingers as relentless as a vise.

Right when the pressure is turning into pain, he starts kneading his thumb into my palm instead. He's holding my hand between both of his, massaging the exhausted muscles of my fingers and palm.

I never realized how tired my hands get, working all day long. The massage is agony and ecstasy. It gives me relief so powerful, I can barely stand it.

My breathing slows. I'm sitting up straighter, focused only on my hand.

Nero drops the left hand and picks up the right. He does the same thing, rubbing all the tension out of my flesh.

He seems to know exactly where to touch, as if he can read my aches with his fingertips.

I never imagined Nero could have a gentle touch. I've seen him get in more fights than I can count. He's like a walking weapon—violent, unpredictable, wreaking destruction on whatever he touches.

I've seen him with girls, too. Even then, he's always been rough and aggressive.

This is different.

Maybe because he doesn't see me as a girl.

He's touching me the way he'd touch a car engine—with a desire to fix it. He diagnosed me, and he's making me run smooth again.

I pull back my hand. "Thanks," I say. "I'm good now."

"Good." Nero nods.

He faces forward once more, scrolling through his phone. He puts on some music, quietly, in case any cops are trolling through the parking garage looking for us.

"Here," he says.

He passes me a bottle of malt liquor with about a third drunk already.

I almost laugh. "This is what you drink?"

"I drink whatever's handy," he says, unsmiling.

I take a swig of it. It tastes spicy and foamy, without the bitterness of beer. It burns on the way down, spreading warmth through my chest, helping to calm me a little more. I take another drink.

"That's actually…not bad."

Nero takes the bottle and drinks several heavy swallows. I see his throat moving with each gulp. He passes it back to me, wiping his mouth on the back of his hand.

I drink again, trying not to think that we're sharing more than liquor, our lips touching the same glass rim.

We're silent. The only noise is the slosh of liquor in the bottle and the music Nero's playing.

The steady rap beat is interspersed with a pretty chorus—melancholy and wistful. I remember how Nero switched my radio station. He must like this kind of stuff. It's not what I usually listen to, but I'm liking it now, with the warmth of the malt liquor spreading through my body and the darkness of the underground parking garage cocooning us.

Nero's car smells good. I mean it really, really smells good. Like expensive leather, spiced liquor, engine oil, and Nero's own masculine scent. I don't usually sit close enough to him to notice it. There's a warm, enticing scent rising from his skin: hawthorn and nutmeg, no hint of sweetness.

It's intoxicating. Or something is. My head feels light, and I get a flush of honesty. Like I should just say what I'm thinking. I never do that, usually. I keep my thoughts locked down tight.

"Why did you do that?" I ask Nero.

"'Cause fuck the cops."

"No. I mean, why did you take me with you?"

He takes another swig, giving himself time to think.

"I don't know," he says at last.

"Why'd you leave the money in my shop?"

"Because I used your tools."

"You left too much."

"Who cares?" he says angrily. "I don't give a fuck about money."

I don't ask him what he does care about. The answer is obvious—nothing.

I'm trying to puzzle through this.

Nero isn't kind. He doesn't do things to be "nice." Especially not to women. He's got a trail of scorned hearts a mile wide behind him. There isn't a pretty girl in this city who hasn't been caught in the flame of his charm, only to burn like a paper flower.

The only reason I can think of is that Nero doesn't view me like one of those women. He's not interested in me, or he'd take me and use me up just like the others.

No. I'm like a starving puppy in the street. He tossed me a scrap because it was easy, and it cost him nothing.

"I don't need your pity," I tell him. I'm glaring at him, anger burning through me. I may not rage out loud like Nero, but I have bitterness inside me, too. I could be dangerous. If I wanted to be.

Nero looks at me with those cool-gray eyes. He's picking me apart, taking in my every flaw and blemish. The frizzy curls escaping from my bun, the dark circles under my eyes from lack of sleep, the grease embedded under my fingernails and in the lines of my knuckles, my chapped lips, and my shit clothes.

"Why are you mad?" he says. "What do you want me to say?"

"I want to know why you're not acting like you usually do."

"Is that what you want?" His voice is low, and his eyes are fixed on my face. His body tenses like he's going to hit me.

My lips part. I don't know what I'm going to say.

I don't get the chance to say anything.

Nero closes the space between us in an instant.

His lips crash against mine. They're soft but also hungry. He kisses me wildly, like this is the last moment of our lives. His tongue thrusts into my mouth, and his taste is as intoxicating as the liquor, rich and warm and head spinning. His hands are locked around my face, his fingers like iron. The music is still playing.

♫ *"Sober"—G-Eazy*

He's sucking the breath right out of my lungs. He might be pulling my soul out, too, if he really is a demon that feeds on the lust of women.

I don't care if he is. My heart is pounding; my whole body is aching with need.

I want him, I want him, I want him.

Then he lets go of me just as abruptly.

He sits back in his seat. "There," he says.

I'm shocked and reeling, my lips still throbbing.

He's still as a statue, like he's feeling nothing at all. That was just a joke to him—giving me a taste of what he can turn on and off at will.

I can't turn it off. My thighs are clenched tight together, my whole body screaming for more.

"We can go," Nero says. "Cops probably gave up by now."

He starts the engine, still not looking at me. Probably because there's desperation all over my face, and it's embarrassing to him.

"Are you sober enough to drive?" I say.

"Yes," he says, putting the car in reverse. "I'd have to drink that whole bottle to feel anything at all."

He's right. Malt liquor isn't that strong.

I wish I could blame this on being drunk. I wish I could black out and forget it all in the morning.

CHAPTER 8
NERO

We're meeting with the Griffins today to talk about the South Shore development.

We meet at the Brass Anchor, which has become our regular spot since that first night where Papa and Fergus Griffin had to negotiate on neutral ground to avoid an all-out war.

We all waited in our cars that night, until Papa and Fergus approached each other in front of the double doors, stiff and formal. Today the mood is completely different. Papa shakes hands with Fergus like he does with all his old friends, gripping Fergus's elbow with his opposite hand, then clapping him hard on the shoulder as he releases him.

"You're looking well, Fergus," Papa says. "Tell me how you never age. Is there formaldehyde in that Irish whiskey?"

"I hope not. Gray hairs are good for business," Fergus says, smiling. "Nobody trusts a young man."

"That's not what I hear," Papa says, turning to shake Callum's hand, too. "I hear you're getting all kinds of things done."

"Yes, we are," Callum says.

The other half of that *we* isn't Fergus—it's Aida, my baby sister. She kisses Papa on both cheeks.

I never thought I'd see the day, but Aida actually looks really fucking professional. She's wearing a man's dress shirt with the sleeves rolled up, the bottom tucked into high-waisted trousers. She's got on heels, and earrings, and even a little swipe of lip gloss. It's not totally conventional, but she looks chic.

"What the hell is this?" I say, letting her kiss me on the cheek as well. "Where are your sneakers?"

"Oh, I've still got 'em," Aida says, tipping me a wink. "If you want to race me."

"I do like racing."

Aida's eyes gleam. "Got any good stories for me?"

She's been down to the street races a few times. I never let her use my car. That would be like handing a speargun to Jason Voorhees—it's just begging for mayhem.

"Bella Page tried to race Camille Rivera," I tell her.

"I don't like Bella." Aida makes a face.

"Who would?"

"I dunno. Maybe those people who like eating weapons-grade hot sauce."

"Masochists," I say.

"Right." She grins. "So what happened?"

"Bella almost rolled her G-Wagon."

"Ugh! Can't believe I missed that. Who's the girl who won?"

"Camille?"

"Yeah."

"Her dad owns that auto shop on Wells."

"Hm. Is she a friend of yours?" Aida's sharp eyes scan my face.

God damn it. Aida is like a heat-seeking missile. If there's some information you're trying to hide from her, she'll home in on it with breathtaking precision, then hound it out of you.

And I'm not even hiding anything. There's nothing to tell.

"I sort of know her."

"In the biblical sense?" Aida teases me, in her most annoying and persistent way.

"No."

"A girl you haven't slept with? What, does she have three eyes? No teeth? What's the problem?"

Jesus Christ. I've already given Aida too much ammunition.

The truth is that Camille isn't my type at all. But I sort of felt like we might be becoming friends—a little bit. I kind of like her. And I don't like anybody. I barely like my own family. In fact, right now, I'm only fifty-fifty on Aida.

So it was a new thing for me, feeling like hanging around with Camille wasn't the worst thing in the world. Then she was so weird in the parking garage. I couldn't tell if she liked me or hated me, if she wanted me to touch her or didn't. So I defaulted to what I always do with women when I want them to shut the fuck up. I kissed her.

And here's the weirdest part of all. The kiss was…good.

With a lot of girls, there's a kind of mechanical routine to sex. They want to go through their list of tricks, like a show pony. And a lot of what they do is so fucking fake. When they ride on top of you, they're posing the whole time, demanding you look at them and acknowledge their hotness. And they're not hot. They're needy and pathetic. I want to get what I want out of them as quickly as possible so I can be alone again.

Before the sex there's the clumsy flirting. And after the sex there's the whining and clinging. I go through the rotation of blonds, brunettes, and redheads. But in the end, they're all the same, and I feel hollow afterward. Spent but not really satisfied.

Kissing Camille was different. She smelled like motor oil, gasoline, and soap—all my favorite scents. Her mouth wasn't all slicked up with lipstick. I could taste her lips and her tongue. They had a mellow sweetness under the spice of the malt liquor—like vanilla. Barely noticeable at first but lingering pleasantly.

The way she kissed was different, too. She seemed like she was exploring me, trying me out. At one point I saw that her eyes were open, looking at my face. Which should have been off-putting, but it wasn't. Her eyes were big and dark and curious. Like we had invented something new, that nobody in the world had tried before, and she didn't want to miss a moment of it.

All those things were odd and confusing to me.

I don't want to share any of it with Aida. But every millisecond I hesitate, she's ferreting out the meaning behind my silence. So I have to say something.

"I'm glad to see that getting married hasn't matured you any," I tell her. "Except for the clothes."

Aida grins. "Kinda seems like you're trying to change the subject with a personal attack…"

"Aida," I snarl, "if you don't get off my ass, I'm gonna—"

We're interrupted by Papa, who's finished the small talk part of this meeting. "Coming inside?"

I'm about to say, *Gladly.* Then I spot a man on the sidewalk, leaning against a lamppost. He's wearing sunglasses, but it's pretty clear he's looking right at us. He's got blond hair buzzed short on the sides, a square jaw, and an athletic build. He's wearing a T-shirt and jeans. Still, there's something in the arrogant posture and the clean-cut grooming that makes me think *cop.*

"Go on ahead," I say to my father. "I'll catch up in a minute."

He glances over to the man, then nods. "See you in a minute."

The others file into the restaurant. I wait until they're inside, and then I stride toward our Peeping Tom. I'm thinking he'll spook and leave. Instead, he stays exactly where he is, his arms folded, a little smirk on his face.

"How can I help you, Officer?" I say as I draw close.

He grins. "Oh, I was just wondering how your car was doing after you put it through its paces last night."

"I don't know what you're talking about. I was home all night."

"You should get a less distinctive vehicle if you want to use that line."

I shrug. "There are a lot of Mustangs in the city. Do you have a plate number for the vehicle in question?"

I've already swapped my plates out. I did it the minute I got home. I've got dozens of spare license plates, none of which can be linked to my name.

"You've caught my attention a couple of times this year," the cop says, his sunglasses like blank bug eyes staring at me.

"Is this an interrogation, or are you trying to hit on me?"

"That's cute." The cop's not smiling anymore. "You Gallos think you can do whatever you want in this city. Your brother gets arrested for murder, breaks out of Cook County Jail, and then somehow gets his charges dropped a few weeks later? I've got news for you: Not every cop has their hand in the cookie jar. Some of us actually care about getting you greedy fucking gangsters locked up where you belong—in a cage, with the other animals."

"Oh, you're a clean cop? Kinda sounds like a friendly mosquito or a gourmet Twinkie. I've sure as shit never seen it."

He smiles again. It looks like a dog baring its teeth. "Just know you're on notice, Nero. I like a fair game, so I'm giving you a warning. I'm watching you. If you step one fucking toe over the line, I'll be there to clap the cuffs on you. And you won't be slipping out of them like your brother did."

"If this is an example of your surveillance skills, I'm not worried."

He doesn't like that. The skin around his mouth goes tense and white. "This is me telling you exactly what's going to happen. And it'll happen anyway. Because that's what you sleazy, arrogant shitheads can't seem to comprehend. You're always going to lose in the end. There are more of us than there are of you. We're smarter, better trained, better funded. I've got the whole city behind me. But you'll keep breaking the fuckin' law anyway. You don't know anything else. You can't *be* anything else."

"Huh, maybe you're right," I say, nodding slowly. "But you sit behind a desk filling out incident reports for sixty-five K a year while I'm sipping champagne at parties with your boss. So I guess I'll take my chances."

I saunter away from him, still feeling his stare boring into my back.

When I join the others in the restaurant, my father says, "Who was that?"

"Some cop."

"What did he want?"

"To inform me that he suspects our family may, at some point, have been involved in illegal activity. Apparently, the police frown on that."

Papa is not amused. He scowls, drawing his thick gray eyebrows together over his broad nose. "Did something happen last night?"

Fuck, he's worse than Aida. Every one of them is like a bloodhound, sniffing out weakness.

"No," I lie.

"Find out who he is and what he actually wants," my father says.

"I will."

With that, we return to the discussion of the Steel Works property. Fergus Griffin admits he's had his eye on it for a while.

"It's going to require an insane amount of capital. Plus every favor we've ever been owed," he says.

"If I were mayor, I could get it done," Callum says.

"Williams is up for reelection in eight months," Papa says.

"Hard to beat the incumbent," Fergus says.

"Not impossible, though," Aida says.

"I've only been alderman for a year." Callum steeples his fingers. "It's a big jump."

"The campaign will be expensive." Fergus frowns. "The Russians cleaned out our cash reserves."

"We're short at the moment, too. We splashed out big on the Oak Street Tower. Won't see the return until it's all leased out," Papa says.

"We might need to bring in another partner," Fergus says.

"The *Braterstwo*?" Callum says.

His father flinches. He hasn't quite accustomed himself to the fact Mikolaj Wilk, the *Braterstwo* boss, kidnapped and married his youngest daughter.

"Perhaps," Fergus says stiffly.

"We'll look at our options," Papa says.

The meeting wraps up quickly.

As I'm driving Papa home, he says, "Catch your brother up on everything we talked about."

Dante handles all the projects we already have in the works, while the rest of us are scheming to add more work to his plate.

I'll summarize for Dante. And then I'll ask him what he thinks about my idea for getting capital.

I've got no interest in trying to bring other investors on board. If we need money, we should get it the old-fashioned way—by stealing it.

As that cop reminded me, we are gangsters after all.

CHAPTER 9
CAMILLE

I WAKE UP EARLY SO I CAN GET AS MUCH WORK DONE AS POSSIBLE before I have to head over to my second job of being a degenerate drug dealer.

I'm so pissed about this, I can barely concentrate. I'm supposed to swap out an oxygen sensor in an old Chevy, and it's taking me twice as long as usual.

My dad is still sleeping. My worry about him is another rock added to the backpack of stress I'm carrying around all the time. If he doesn't perk up in a day or two, I will physically drag him to the drop-in clinic. Even throw him over my shoulder if I have to, like that asshole Nero did to me.

I guess he did save me from a ticket or worse.

But then he had to fuck with me after. There are no favors from Nero. He's always a coin with two sides.

I've known him for years, from a distance. Well enough to know that falling for Nero Gallo is the most stupid, self-destructive thing I could possibly do.

Yes, he's gorgeous. Yes, he smells like pure sex and sin. Yes, he can occasionally be the slightest bit helpful when the whim catches him.

But he's a black hole of selfishness. He eats up female attention with a voracious appetite and never, ever, gives anything in return.

Not to mention that every minute I spend around him is likely to land me in jail, one way or another.

I don't need that. I'm doing a pretty good job of destroying my future all on my own.

Fuck, I've got to get my car back, too. That means a pricey Uber ride or a long-ass journey on public transit.

I finish up the Chevy so I can get going, and then I change out of my coveralls. I'd rather wear my work clothes—that's how I feel most comfortable—but I've got to make Levi take me seriously. I need some kind of dirt on him, or else Schultz is never going to leave me alone.

I take the L and then a bus, and then I walk several blocks over to Lower Wacker Drive. My car is still there, thankfully in one piece and thankfully parked in the shade so it's had a chance to cool off. When I try the engine, it rumbles for a minute, then starts up. It's not exactly running smoothly, but it should get me over to Levi's house.

I roll out cautiously before gathering speed once I'm sure it's not going to blow up in my face. I head back over to Levi's neglected Victorian on Hudson Avenue.

The house looks even worse in the daytime. Trash and empty beer cans are scattered across his lawn. Also an overturned couch and a hammock with somebody sleeping in it. Levi's steps are sloped from the frost and melt of the Chicago seasons. The painted woodwork is so chipped that it looks like peeling skin.

I climb up on the porch, briskly rapping on the door. There's a long wait, and then a big Samoan dude cracks the door.

"'Sup." He grunts.

"I'm here to see Levi."

He stares at me for a minute, then moves his bulk aside just enough for me to slip by.

The inside of the house has that musk of too many people sleeping over and nobody washing the sheets. There are at least five people in various states of consciousness in Levi's living room. They're sprawled over the dusty old furniture his grandmother must have bought in the '70s: Long low couches. Recliners in shades of mustard and puce.

The end tables are studded with beer bottles, ashtrays, and drug paraphernalia. The TV is playing, but nobody's actually looking at it.

Levi himself is wearing a robe, open to show his bare chest. He's got on striped boxer shorts and a pair of puffy slippers that look like bear paws. His slippered feet are propped up on the coffee table, and he's smoking a joint.

"My newest employee," he announces to the room. "Everyone, this is Camille. Camille, this is everyone."

I'm gonna need to get their actual names. I don't think Schultz is going to be impressed with *everyone*.

I nod to the people who actually bother to look in my direction.

Levi takes a long pull off his roll-up. His eyes already look glassy and bloodshot.

"Here." I toss him a wad of cash—my earnings from the race. "That's for the pills my brother lost."

Levi nods to the burly Samoan, who picks up the money and stows it away.

"You get that from Bella?" Levi snickers.

"From her boyfriend."

"He's not her boyfriend. He's just fucking her." Levi laughs.

"Who is he?"

"Grisha Lukin."

"What kinda name is that?"

"Russian," Levi says. His gaze sharpens slightly. "You're kinda nosy, huh?"

"Not really." I shrug. "I just thought I knew most people in Old Town. I've lived here forever."

"Yeah, but you don't ever come out of your little shop." Levi laughs. "I don't think I ever saw you drunk in high school even. Now you'll get your fun, though."

He holds out the joint to me.

"No thanks."

"I'm not asking," he snaps. "Sit down."

I sit on the couch next to him, trying to keep space between us without making it too obvious. He shoves the joint in my hand.

I take a pitiful little puff. Even that makes me cough. The thick, skunky taste fills my mouth, and my head spins. I don't like pot. I don't like losing control.

"There you go." Levi laughs. "Now you can chill the fuck out."

It does make me relax—physically, at least. I sink back in the cushions, feeling mildly dazed and in less of a rush to get out of here.

I recognize the girl on the other side of me. Her name is Ali Brown. She was three years ahead of me in school. Her parents own the flower shop on Sedgewick.

"Hey," I say.

"Hey," she replies.

She's got straw-colored hair and freckles. She's wearing a crop top with no bra and a pair of boxers with Superman logos all over them. She looks half asleep.

After a very long pause, she says, "I know you."

"Yeah," I say. "We both went to Oakmont."

"No," she says. "I saw your picture."

She's way higher than I thought. Still, to humor her, I say, "What picture?"

She pauses again, breathing shallowly. Then she says, "The one where you were eating ice cream on the pier."

I stiffen. My dad had a picture like that. He took it when I was fourteen. "What are you talking about?"

"Yeah," she sighs. "It was in the change room, taped to the mirror. I bet your mom put it there."

Now my face is flaming. She's talking about Exotica. Ali must have worked as a dancer or a hostess.

"Who's your mom?" a guy sprawled on a beanbag chair says.

"She's a whore." One of the other guys snickers.

"Shut your fucking mouth." I try to jump up from the couch, but Levi pulls me back down again.

"Relax," he says. "Pauly, don't be a dick. We call them 'escorts.'"

"My mother wasn't an escort," I hiss. "She just worked as a dancer."

"A *stripper*." Pauly laughs. "She teach you any moves? There's a pole upstairs. Why don't you show us how Mommy shakes it?"

"Why don't I shake your fucking head off your shoulders!" I roar, struggling to get out of the low, sagging couch while weak and enervated from the weed. It's easy for Levi to yank me back down again.

"Nobody cares what your mom did." He slings his arm around my shoulders, which I don't like at all. I can smell his sweat and the heavy reek of weed in his robe. "My parents are a couple of fuckin' yuppies, and that's just as embarrassing. You can't be fighting, though. You gotta be a good girl. Do your work. Make some money. Have some fun."

His fingertips dangle over my right breast. He lets them touch down, with only my T-shirt between us. I force myself not to squirm away.

I see Ali watching us. Not like she's jealous—more like a kid watching the fish in an aquarium.

"Yeah, whatever," I mutter. "I need more Ex, then."

Levi nods to the Samoan. The guy comes back about five minutes later with a paper bag, the top folded over. He hands it to me.

"Where am I supposed to sell this?" I ask Levi.

"Anywhere you want. Parties, raves, campuses…sky's the limit. You're your own boss. Under me, of course." He grins.

"Do you make this?" I ask him. "How do I know it's good? I don't want any of my friends getting sick."

Levi's veneer of friendliness peels back. His bloodshot eyes peer at me from too close, his arm tightening around my shoulder. "You know it's good because you trust me," he hisses.

He's only in his twenties, but his teeth are as yellow as an old man's, and his breath is atrocious.

"Right," I say. "Okay."

He lets go of me at last. I heave myself up off the couch, clutching the paper bag.

"You can sell 'em anywhere from fifteen to twenty-five a pop," Levi says. "You owe me ten each."

I nod.

"Bring me the money in a week."

I nod again.

The Samoan leads me back toward the front door, even though it's only ten feet away.

"See ya," I say to him.

He gives me a disdainful look, closing the door in my face.

Even though it's hot as hell outside, the air tastes fresh after the fug of Levi's house. I do not want to go back there. Especially not in a week.

And where the hell am I supposed to keep coming up with the money for this? I don't want to actually sell Molly.

I drive a couple of blocks away, and then I pull over to call Schultz.

"Hey," I say. "I got another batch of pills from Levi. What do you want me to do with it?"

"Bring it to me. I'll meet you at Boardwalk Burgers."

I silently groan. Is today going to be a tour of all the people I least want to visit?

"Fine," I say. "I'll be there in fifteen."

CHAPTER 10
NERO

THE FIRST THING I DO WHEN I GET HOME IS START RESEARCHING this cop.

It doesn't take long to find him. Officer Logan Schultz, graduated from the academy in 2011, then bounced around the Bureau of Patrol for a while. Two years ago, he transferred to the Organized Crime Division.

That's exactly what I expected. Organized Crime covers Vice, Narcotics, and Gang Investigations. All my favorite things.

But I'm curious to know who this joker actually is.

Am I dealing with a Boy Scout? Or a classic crooked cop who wants to get his beak wet?

Now that's a little trickier to tell. Officer Schultz has several complaints lodged against him, and he's been investigated twice for misconduct. But as far as I can see, he's only gotten in trouble for roughing up suspects, not taking bribes.

He's received a couple of commendations, too. Most recently the Top Gun Arrest Award for recovering illegal firearms.

There's a photo of him getting a medal pinned on his chest by a man with a long crooked nose and thinning gray hair. The caption informs me that this is Chief Brodie. I'm pretty sure I've seen Brodie at those hoity-toity parties I was needling Schultz about. I don't actually enjoy attending those—but it's all part of securing power and influence in Chicago.

Lining up the dates on Schultz's big case, I'm guessing he was involved in that raid on the *Bratva* last year—I heard they lost almost twenty million in high-quality Russian munitions.

So it looks like our boy is a real go-getter. Really making a splash in the Chicago PD.

I try to search his social media, looking for evidence of a wife, kids, girlfriend, or exploitable bad habits. It's all buttoned up tight—no public profiles. Or maybe no profiles at all.

However, I do find an old news article from April 18, 2005:

Off-Duty Chicago Police Officer Slain in South Shore

Officer Matthew Schultz passed away early this morning after being shot at approximately 1:30 a.m. at the corner of East 77th Street and South Bennet Avenue.

Police Superintendent Larson said the officer was driving close to Rosenblum Park when an unknown assailant approached the vehicle at a stoplight. The shooter fired through the officer's car window, hitting Schultz three times in the chest and head.

Larson said officers conducting a traffic stop nearby heard the gunfire and responded to the scene. Nearby security cameras caught partial footage of the event.

Schultz was rushed to Jackson Park Hospital, where he underwent emergency surgery. The doctor's efforts were not successful, and he was pronounced dead at 5:22 a.m.

Schultz is survived by a wife and son. Donations to the family can be made via the Fallen Brothers Fund.

Well, well, well. It doesn't take a bona fide detective to surmise the "surviving son" is the new Officer Schultz. Or that his avenging-angel routine is supposed to make up for Daddy catching a bullet in South Shore.

Interesting that the news article makes no mention of what Dad was doing driving around South Shore in plainclothes in the middle of the night. And I don't see any follow-ups about catching the shooter.

I wonder if Schultz the Younger knows the answer to that little mystery.

Well, that's his problem. I've got my own issue to contend with. Namely, how I'm going to rustle up some capital for the Steel Works development.

I'm going to need a lot of money. Not a few million—serious coin. Which might just mean going back to my roots.

Dante and I used to pull jobs together when I was a teenager. This was back before he joined the military. He was fucking wild then. Absolutely fearless.

And I was in a state of pure mania. Our mother had died. Our father was a wreck. I needed something, anything to grab hold of.

When Dante started planning jobs, I begged him to let me come along. At first, I was just the lookout or the driver. That progressed as Dante saw I had a talent for the work.

We robbed almost a dozen armored trucks while I was in high school, taking anywhere from eighty thousand to seven hundred thousand dollars per hit.

I always stole the getaway cars. I could slip into a parking garage and roll out in a nice, unobtrusive sedan in less than ten minutes. Stealing from the airport long-term parking was best—nobody would even notice the car was gone. So there was little chance of it being reported as stolen while we were in the middle of the job.

For a getaway car, you want something with guts and speed but also a low profile and dull color. Something that blends right into the surroundings. Four doors for easy in and out, plus a big trunk to store the loot.

A Mercedes E-Class was always a good bet, or an older BMW. Even a Camry worked well.

We looked for Brinks drivers who were old and fat. Close to retirement and too tired to keep a look out. No itchy young cowboys wearing combat pants, with visions of glory in their heads.

We liked the Brinks trucks. Regular routes, consistent security routines. We attacked them early in the morning when they'd service the ATMs, before the banks were actually open.

We'd drop the money off at a safe house. Then we'd drive the getaway car out to the boonies, douse the interior in bleach, and set the whole thing ablaze.

Now, that was all good fun and good practice. But I'm going to need a much bigger payout than an armored truck can provide.

I've got to go right to the source.

Right to one of the largest vaults in the whole of Chicago. One that stores gold, diamonds, and undeclared cash for the city's wealthiest citizens.

The vault owned by Raymond Page.

It's right in the heart of the financial district, at the end of the LaSalle Canyon—the long tunnel of skyscrapers that includes the Board of Trade and the Chicago Fed.

Bella's father doesn't own the biggest bank, but Alliance sure as shit is the dirtiest. It's like our own little Deutsche Bank, laundering money for oligarchs and helping the wealthy skirt the pesky regulations of international finance.

From what I hear, his records are more convoluted than a Navajo code and about as factual as *The Lord of the Rings*. Which is all to say, I think I could steal a whole lot of money nobody could track.

Now, the tricky part is that while Raymond Page might be crooked, he isn't stupid. In fact, nobody is as paranoid as a criminal. Alliance Bank probably has one of the tightest security systems in the city.

But no system is perfect. There's always a crack.

And I already know how I'm going to find it. Through Raymond's baby girl, of course.

CHAPTER 11
CAMILLE

I meet up with Schultz at Boardwalk Burgers, down by the pier. He's already eating a double stack and fries at one of the outdoor tables.

"You want anything?" he asks me.

I shake my head.

"You sure? I can expense it."

Everything he says has a teasing tone. It coats all his statements, making it hard to understand his real intent. Is he bragging because he can write off his meals? Is he joking about how silly it is to submit a form for a five-dollar burger? Is he reminding me that I'm an informant now, effectively on his payroll? Or is he trying to flirt with me?

I don't like that last possibility.

But I can't ignore how Schultz is constantly pinning me down with his bright blue eyes. Standing too close to me. Sneaking a suggestive tone into every statement.

Once I've sat across from him at the picnic table, he shoves the half-eaten basket of fries toward me. I shake my head again. I don't want anything in my mouth that he already touched.

"So," he says, taking a slurp of his soda. "What did you find out?"

"I went to the street races last night. Levi was there. I told him my brother's not selling for him anymore. So he made me pay for the product you took, and he said I have to sell for him instead."

"Good." Schultz grins.

"I didn't really see who Levi was hanging around with that night. The cops came and broke it up before anything else happened."

I see a little gleam in Schultz's eye.

"I know—one of the attendees got in a chase with a couple of squad cars. Do you know Nero Gallo?"

Even the sound of his name sends a flush of heat up the back of my neck.

I try to keep my expression neutral. "We went to the same high school."

Shultz points a fry at me. "The officers thought he had a brunette in the car with him. Do you know who that might be? I noticed your Trans Am down there. I stopped them from impounding it, by the way."

"Thank you," I say stiffly.

He finishes the last bite of his burger before dabbing his mouth with his napkin. Staring at me the whole time.

"So was that you? Were you speeding around with Nero?"

I grab one of his french fries to give myself a second to think. It's already lukewarm and soggy. I chew hard and then swallow. "No."

"Camille," Schultz purrs, his blue eyes drilling into me. "This isn't going to work if you lie to me."

"I barely know Nero."

"You do know him, though."

I hesitate. "Yes."

"Have you ever fucked him?"

"No!"

Now the heat has risen all the way up to my cheeks. Schultz is grinning. He loves unnerving me. He thinks it lets him read me.

"Not even once? I hear he's got some kind of golden cock. The ultimate Casanova, right? Girls throwing their panties at him like he's Justin Timberlake?"

Schultz is sneering, but there's an edge of jealousy to his words.

He's handsome, fit. He thinks he deserves that kind of female attention himself.

"Maybe *you* should date him," I mutter.

Schultz glares at me, then gives a fake hearty laugh. "Good one."

"Here's what you need to understand," I tell him. "I was a loser in high school. I know these people because we all grew up in Old Town. We've lived in the same twenty-block radius most of our lives. But we're barely acquaintances. They don't like me or trust me. I can try to get closer to them, but nobody's going to be spilling their secrets to me anytime soon. Least of all Nero Gallo."

"You know what his family does?" Schultz says.

"Yeah. They're old-school Italian Mafia."

"Not just Mafia. His father, Enzo, is the head don in Chicago." I shrug. "So?"

Schultz leans forward, his face alight with excitement. Ambition burns in his eyes. "Can you imagine the promotion I'd get if I took down the Gallos?"

"Yeah," I say, rolling my eyes. "Can't believe nobody's tried before."

Schultz ignores my sarcasm. "The key to Enzo Gallo is his sons. Not Dante—he's too careful. Not Sebastian—he's not even a gangster. It's Nero. That reckless, vengeful little shit. He's the weak point of the family."

Schultz has forgotten about Aida. Or he figures she's too well protected by the Griffins these days.

"I don't know if I'd call Nero a 'weak point.'"

"Why?"

"He's smarter than you think. He got one of the highest scores in the school on the ACTs. His grades were shit because he never handed in any assignments."

"See," Schultz says softly. "You *do* know him."

"I know he's a total psychopath. Asking me to get close to him is like asking me to cozy up with a rattlesnake. He gets one hint that something's up, and he'll stab me in the heart."

"Better not fuck it up, then," Schultz says coldly.

He doesn't give a shit what happens to me. I'm a tool. And not even a very valuable one. Not an air compressor or a fancy impact wrench—I'm just a cheap plastic funnel. Easily replaced.

"Now," Schultz says, sitting back against the fence enclosing the little outdoor dining area. "Tell me more about Levi."

I take a deep breath, almost relieved to be off the subject of Nero. "I went to his place today to get some more product. What do you want me to do with that, by the way?"

"Let's see it," Schultz says.

I hand him the paper bag. He looks inside before pulling out one of the pills. It's small and yellow, shaped like a school bus, just like the ones he took out of Vic's backpack.

Schultz smiles. Apparently, he's pleased Levi's supply is so uniform.

"I'll take these," Schultz says. He counts out a dozen, slips them into a plastic ziplock bag, and hands it back to me. "Keep a few so you can sell them at parties when Levi's watching."

I stare at him. "Isn't that illegal?"

"Obviously."

"So you don't give a shit about people taking Molly. Not really."

Schultz snorts. "I don't give a shit about minnows when I'm hunting for sharks."

I stuff the baggie in my pocket. "I need cash for the others," I tell him. "Levi expects me to bring back ten bucks a pill."

"He's ripping you off." Schultz laughs.

"Yeah, no shit. He's got me over a barrel, thanks to you."

"That sounds fun." Schultz smirks. "Having you over a barrel."

God, he makes me want to puke. "I don't have the money to cover it," I insist.

"Fine." Schultz pulls out a bill clip and counts out the money. "Pay him with this. But make sure you wait long enough that he'll think you really sold the Molly."

I take the folded bills. It's weird that a cop is carrying around that much cash.

Schultz is wearing street clothes again. I've only seen him in uniform that one time, when he pulled me over. I'm guessing this is how he usually dresses and he was just wearing the uniform for effect that night. To intimidate me.

He's obviously been watching Levi for a while. I don't think it was a coincidence that he pulled me over.

"Did you follow me from Levi's house?" I ask him.

Schultz cocks his head to the side, smiling. "What do you mean?"

"Were you waiting for me, after the party?"

"I was waiting for someone," he says. "Someone I could use."

Just my shitty luck that it happened to be me. "You probably know as much as I do about the people in Levi's house," I say.

"Tell me anyway."

I take a breath, trying to remember it all exactly. "There's a big Samoan dude who acts like his bodyguard or something. He's the one who went and got the drugs."

Schultz nods. "Sione," he says.

"Then there were five or six other people in the living room."

"Which was it? Five? Or six?"

I close my eyes, trying to picture the room again. "Five," I say. "A girl named Ali Brown—she went to school with me. I don't think she works for Levi or anything. It looked like she was just there to get high. Or maybe they're dating."

Schultz nods. He might have seen her already.

"Then there was Levi. And three other dudes. One was named Pauly."

That was the asshole who was talking about my mom. My face colors again, remembering it. I used to get so much shit about her when I was in school. Then she disappeared five years ago. It took me a while to notice—seeing as she never called me much anyway.

"What was the other guy's name?" Schultz says.

"I don't know."

"Anything else?"

I try to remember. "Levi must keep the drugs somewhere on the main level. Sione went out of the room to get them, but I didn't hear him climbing the stairs. I don't know who makes the Molly, though. I asked Levi where it comes from, and he didn't tell me anything. Basically said to mind my own business."

"Well, don't be so obvious," Schultz says. "Figure it out another way."

He expects me to do his job for him. Except I have zero training and no desire to do any of this. I feel sleazy just for mentioning Ali's name. I don't want to get her in trouble. She didn't do anything to me.

"I think Ali was just stopping by," I say again. "She didn't do anything wrong."

Schultz shakes his head at me. "These people are criminals and lowlifes. Don't try to protect them."

That pisses me off. What makes him think he's better than them? I bet he's done all kinds of shady shit in the line of duty. It's not moral versus immoral. It's just a bunch of people on two opposing teams.

I've been drafted for Schultz's team. But I don't like being here. I don't want to play the game at all, for either side.

"I better go," I say, getting ready to leave.

"Keep in touch," Schultz reminds me.

As we both stand, he grabs my arm. "Hold on." He brushes his thumb over my cheekbone, under my right eye.

I have to force myself not to flinch.

"You had an eyelash there," he says, smirking.

Right. I just bet there was.

When I get back to the apartment, I see my dad's door still firmly shut. It's almost two o'clock in the afternoon, and it doesn't look like he's left the room. The only mug on the table is the one I used this morning.

I can hear him moving around at least. But he's coughing again. "Dad?" I call out. "I'm home."

No answer.

I grab my mug and set it in the sink, running water to rinse out the coffee dregs.

Dad has another coughing fit that ends in retching. I jump up, sprinting over to his door and knocking. "Dad? You okay?"

I push the door open. He's sitting up on his bed, hunched over, hacking into the crook of his arm.

When he looks up, his face is gray. There's red froth on his lips. "DAD!"

"I'm all right. I just need a rest—"

"We're going to the hospital!"

I pull him up from the bed, holding him steady by the elbow. He's not that hard to hold up. He's lost at least thirty pounds. Why didn't I pay attention sooner? He's been sick for a couple of months. I thought it was just a stubborn cold…

I help him down the stairs, though he keeps telling me he can walk on his own. I doubt it—his color is awful, and he doesn't look steady on his feet. I take him out through the auto bay 'cause my car is parked out back.

"You finish that Chevy?" My dad wheezes.

"Yeah. Don't worry about it, Dad."

We get in my Trans Am, and I take him to Midtown Medical. We have to wait forever because it's Saturday and because "coughing" isn't exactly a high priority in the ER. Plenty of people stumble in with head wounds or dangling arms, plus one dude who shot a nail right through the palm of his hand during a little home improvement gone wrong.

"Now you know how Jesus felt," a blue-haired grannie tells him.

"Jesus didn't have to sit around looking at it," the man says, staring at the nail with a nauseated expression.

Finally, a nurse takes us back, and we have to wait even longer while they run a bunch of tests, including a chest X-ray.

I'm so stressed out that I don't even recognize the technician for a second.

"Hey!" Patricia greets me. "Is this your dad?"

"Oh, yeah." I smile weakly. "Dad, this is my friend Patricia."

"I like your scrubs," my dad says. "I didn't know they made them like that."

Patricia's wearing a set of lavender scrubs with a pretty floral pattern on the top. "Oh, yeah." She grins. "It's a regular fashion show back here."

Patricia sets up the X-ray, then has me stand safely around the corner with her while she takes the images.

"How does it look?" I ask her nervously.

"Uh…well, I'm not really supposed to say anything until the doctor takes a look," she says.

But I see a little stress line appearing between her eyebrows when she looks at the images forming on the screen.

My heart clenches.

I'm thinking he probably has pneumonia. There was blood in his cough, but nobody gets consumption anymore—or whatever that disease was that killed all the Victorians. It's gotta just be pneumonia. They'll give him some antibiotics, and he'll be fine in a couple of weeks.

After the tests are done, Patricia leads me and my dad to a little curtained-off cubicle.

"They'll be with you soon," she says, giving me a sympathetic smile.

Another forty minutes drag by, and then a young, chipper-looking doctor comes in. He looks like Doogie Howser, if Doogie were East Asian and wore Converse sneakers.

"Mr. Rivera," he says. "I have the results back from your X-ray."

He pins the images on an illuminated board, so the white portions of the X-ray glow brilliantly against the black. I can see my father's rib cage, but not the lungs themselves. There are several grayish masses below the ribs that I assume are organs or maybe his diaphragm.

"So we've looked at your lungs, and we're not seeing fluid down here." The doctor points to the lower half of the lungs. "However, you'll see there is a nodule or mass right here."

He circles a slightly pale area with his index finger, to the right of the spine. It's not bright white like the bone. In fact, it's hard to see at all.

"A nodule?" I'm confused. "Like a cyst or something?"

"It's possible," the doctor says. "We need to get a tissue confirmation before we can diagnose. We can do this by a CT-guided biopsy or through bronchoscopy—"

"Wait, diagnose what?" I say. "What do you think the problem is?"

"Well." The doctor shifts uncomfortably. "I can't say for certain until we get a sample back..."

"But what else could it be? If it's not a cyst?"

"Cancer," the doctor says gently.

"What?" I'm staring at him, open-mouthed. "My dad doesn't smoke."

"A lot of things can cause lung cancer," the doctor says. "Exposure to radon, pollutants, diesel exhaust..."

I'm shaking my head. This can't be happening.

"Nothing is certain yet," the doctor says. "We'll take a tissue sample and..."

I can't even hear the words coming out of his mouth. I'm looking at my dad, who's sitting silently on the edge of the gurney, his coveralls swapped for one of those humiliating smocks that don't even close all the way up the back. He looks skinny and pale.

He's forty-six. There's no way he has cancer.

"Don't worry, Dad," I say to him. "It's probably something else." I'm forcing a smile.

Meanwhile I'm sinking down, down, down into deep black water.

CHAPTER 12
NERO

I HEAD BACK TO LEVI CARGILL'S HOUSE BECAUSE HE'S THROWING another party and I assume Bella will be there. He makes a good little racket off these shindigs—charging a cover at the door, asking five dollars for shitty beer, and then selling harder stuff through his little army of minions.

He never touches the product himself. That's what makes him a good kingpin—always delegating.

Also, he loves a good theme. Tonight is some kind of foam party—he's got machines spraying rainbow-hued bubbles all over the front and back yards. The swimming pool is so full of soap that it's more suds than water.

Most of the girls are wearing bikinis, or they were when the party started. Now they're naked and slippery, tossing around beach balls or making out with one another to attract all the more male attention.

Trust me, I'd love to give them that attention. Unfortunately, I've got to find the one girl I'd rather not see.

Sure enough, Bella is reclining on a giant inflatable flamingo in the middle of the pool, along with her best buddy Beatrice. The two girls are wearing matching white bikinis. Bella's is the kind that consists of three little triangles held on with string.

She's tanned and fit. She's managed to keep her makeup in place, despite all the foam. I really should give her credit.

But I'm not going to.

Bella demands I be attracted to her. She expects it.

I hate being told what to do.

Still, I need something from her. So I slouch on one of the poolside lounge chairs, letting Bella float around right in my line of sight. I give her exactly what she wants, which is my eyes on her bare flesh. I watch her giggling and posing with Beatrice, throwing glances my way. Until she finally rolls off the flamingo and paddles over to me.

She climbs up the ladder, water streaming down her body. Her stiff nipples poke through the white bikini top. She tosses back her cap of blond hair, which she carefully kept out of the pool.

"See something you like?" she purrs.

"Yeah. Where can I get one of those floaties?" I say.

"You can have mine."

"That's generous."

"I'm a nice person," Bella says sweetly. "Once you get to know me."

"Maybe you're right, Bella. Maybe we should go for lunch sometime."

She raises an eyebrow, mildly suspicious. "What, like a date?"

"Just two people eating food at the same table. Getting to know each other better."

She's trying not to agree too easily. "I didn't know you were the dating type."

"People change. You're nice now, and I'm a romantic."

Bella bites her lip. She probably thinks it looks seductive, but she's getting lipstick on her teeth.

"When?" she says.

"Tomorrow. You know the Poke bar on LaSalle?"

"Yeah." Of course she does. It's right across the street from Alliance Bank.

"I'll meet you there at eleven."

"Okay."

She's smiling, pleased and excited. I'm trying to hide my smile, too, but for entirely different reasons.

"You want to go grab a drink right now?" she says.

"I can't. I've got to find Levi."

"Oh." She frowns, disappointed.

"I'll see you tomorrow, though."

I leave her by the pool, pretending to head off in search of Levi. In reality, I don't need to talk to anybody else. I've set my plan in motion. Now I can relax and have a couple of drinks without Bella tagging along.

I bump into Mason in the living room. He's slouched on the couch, drowning his sorrows in a half-drunk bottle of rye.

"Hey, dude," I say. "What's your problem?"

He takes another slug of liquor, staring morosely across the room. I follow his gaze to where Patricia is dancing very closely with a handsome muscular man in a polo shirt.

"Who's that guy?"

"Ricky Dean," Mason says bitterly. "He works at Ridgemoor."

"Oh, yeah, he teaches lessons, right?"

"Golf and tennis," Mason says, taking another miserable swig.

"Hm," I say, borrowing Mason's bottle for a quick drink. "Makes sense. Patricia's hot. And that dude's a lot better looking than you."

Mason yanks his liquor back. "Man, shut the fuck up."

"I'm just saying it's not your fault—there's nothing you can do about it. It's just your face. Maybe if you had a better personality..."

He tries to slug me on the arm, and I knock his fist away, laughing.

"She says I have no ambition. I'm going nowhere."

"You do live at your mom's house."

"I need a better job."

I steal his drink again, taking a heavy gulp. "I might have something for you," I tell him.

"Oh, yeah?" He perks up.

"It's not exactly simple. We need a driver, some muscle, a lock picker, and somebody to handle alarms. Plus some custom equipment."

Mason grins. "What kind of equipment?"

"I'll give you a list. Tomorrow."

Mason's handy with fabrication. If I give him the specs, he can put together almost anything.

"Is Dante the muscle?" he says.

"Possibly."

I'm not sure if I can rope my big brother into this one. He's gotten so conservative. It might be best to spring it on him at the last minute, when the wheels are already in motion.

"I assume you're working the locks," Mason says.

"Of course."

"We could use Jonesy for the alarms."

"Yeah, if he's back on his meds."

"What about the driver?"

At that moment, Camille Rivera walks into the living room. She looks like absolute shit—hair a crazy tangle of curls. Huge dark circles under her eyes. Expression like she just watched a car wreck explode in front of her.

"To be determined," I say to Mason.

I intercept Camille over by the kegs. She's just poured herself a cup of Levi's shit beer, and she's gulping it down.

"Where'd you come from?" I ask her.

"None of your business," she snaps. She finishes her beer and pours another, the cup half full of foam.

"You're in a hurry," I say, watching her drink that beer down just as fast.

"I don't need your commentary, Nero." She drains her second cup. "You're about the last person on the planet who should be giving me shit for drinking too much."

Usually, this would be the point in the conversation where I'd tell her to knock herself out—literally. But today I don't. I can see bright tears gleaming in the corner of Camille's eyes. In all the years I've known her, in all the times I've seen her pissed off, agitated, or stressed, I've never seen her cry. Not once.

There's something seriously wrong with that sight. It's like a lion with its mane shaved off. It makes me feel the one thing I don't ever want to feel—pity.

"What's going on? What happened?"

"What do you care?" Camille shouts. "Stop pretending to be nice to me! It just makes it worse."

She's drawing the attention of the people around us, but I don't care.

She tries to stomp away from me, and I seize her arm and jerk her back again. I spin her around, keeping her body pressed against mine. It's hot as hell in the house, and Camille's flesh is even hotter. My blood is rushing hard. I feel myself grimacing, my teeth bared, as I demand, "Tell me what's going on!"

She stares up at me, those big dark eyes wide and furious. "Let go of me, Nero!"

"Not until you tell me what's wrong!"

"She said let go," a masculine voice interjects.

Fucking Johnny Verger. He's shouldering his way over to us, playing the chivalrous hero. He's got that surly look on his face that tells me he's spoiling for a fight again. I'm pleased to see his nose still looks swollen, with two winglike bruises extending under his eyes.

"How's your face, Johnny?" I ask him, without letting go of Camille's arm.

"Better than yours is gonna be," he snarls.

A crowd is gathering around us. I can see Bella and Beatrice on one side, still wearing their bikinis and nothing else. Bella's face is alight with excitement, anticipating the violence to come.

Camille's eyes dart back and forth between Johnny and me. "I don't need your help," she says to Johnny.

"This fuckstick needs to be taught a lesson," Johnny says. "About keeping his hands to himself."

"Maybe you should teach your girlfriend that lesson," I sneer at him. "She seems to put her hands...and her mouth...anywhere she wants..."

Johnny roars and swings both fists at me at once.

I let go of Camille now, shoving her out of the way so she doesn't get hit in the crossfire. In the time it takes me to push her down on the nearest couch, Johnny hits me hard in the left ear with one of those meaty fists. I hear a popping sound, and bright lights explode in front of my eyes.

I fall on my back, and Johnny tries to jump on me, but I kick my heels hard into his gut, flinging him backward. Then I leap up again, without even touching the ground with my hands. I'm running after him while he's still stumbling backward. I hit him twice in the face and once in the body.

The bloodlust is on me. I can barely even feel my fists pummeling his flesh, though I can see each impact. I want to hit him harder and harder. I want to pound him into mush.

Johnny swings back at me. I dodge the first punch. The second hits me across the jaw. The pain is shocking, blinding.

I fucking love it. This is the only thing that feels real. The only thing that feels genuine. I hate this shithead, and he hates me. We want to tear each other apart.

Beating him proves I'm better than him—smarter, faster, stronger.

I've killed men before, when I had to. That's work, and I don't enjoy it.

Fighting is different. It's pure fun. And I'm really fucking good at it. One-on-one I almost never lose.

Johnny is a big dude. A worthy adversary. When he hits me again, square in the chest, I could almost respect him.

I'm still going to take him apart.

I watch for his next haymaker; then I duck under it, and I boot him again in the chest, sending him crashing backward into Levi's grandmother's china cabinet. The glass doors shatter, broken dishes raining down on Johnny's shoulders.

That's when the Samoan hits me with a punch that feels like a redwood log upside the head. I didn't see it coming, and there was no way to brace for it. It knocks my brain halfway out of my head, so I don't even feel myself falling to the ground. One second I'm standing; the next, my face is pressed into the filthy carpet.

I hear a scream—possibly Camille. The Samoan gives me a couple of kicks to the body that rearrange some organs. That would hurt pretty bad if I were still fully conscious.

All I hear is Levi shouting, "I said no fighting in the house!"

Then I fall into blackness.

I wake up in some kind of glassed-in porch. I can see the corner of a neon sign overhead and the edge of a high-rise. The rest is just black summer sky, dense with clouds. The humidity is so thick, it's like gauze.

I'm about to drift away again, until I hear the rumble of thunder. It pulls me back to consciousness.

Somebody is washing my face. They're using a rough washcloth. Their touch isn't rough—it's gentle and careful, cleaning blood off my aching flesh.

My mother used to wash my face like this when I was sick.

She's the only person who ever saw me like this—helpless. Vulnerable.

I try to sit up. Camille pushes me back down, saying, "Relax."

I'm lying on some kind of shitty thin mattress, right on the floor with no bed frame beneath it. The tiny room smells damp. But it also smells like soap and gasoline—like Camille herself. I see a stack of paperbacks in the corner and a couple of potted plants. Those, at least, are thriving.

This is her room. The most pathetic little room I've ever seen.

Camille is kneeling next to the bed. She has a bowl of warm water in front of her, rusty with my blood. She wrings out the cloth, darkening the water even more.

"Did that Samoan hit me?" I say.

"His name's Sione."

"Fucking hell, I've never taken a punch like that."

"I'm surprised you have any teeth left in your head," she says.

"Eh, strike that. I think Dante hits that hard. When he's really mad."

"You seem to bring that out in people," Camille says.

I could be wrong, but I think there's a hint of a smile on her face. She's probably enjoying this. Seeing me get my just desserts for once.

"How'd you get me back here?" I ask her curiously.

"I dragged you. And you're not light, by the way."

"Lighter than a transmission." I grin.

"Not by much."

We're silent for a minute. The quiet is broken by the patter of raindrops on the glass roof. I look up, watching each of the raindrops burst against the glass. Soon there are too many to count. The patter turns into a steady drumming sound that ebbs and flows in a soothing way.

"I love summer rain," Camille says.

"You must like this room."

"I do," she says with a fierce kind of pride.

I look around the room again. It's dingy and tiny. But I can see why she would like it—it's a capsule of complete privacy. A space that belongs only to her. Half outside, half inside. In the rain, and yet sheltered.

"Why do you always do that?" Camille asks me.

"What?"

"Why are you so violent?"

I feel myself flushing. The heat makes my face throb all over again, especially in the places I was hit. My ribs are groaning. Sione might have broken a few.

I want to say something cruel, to punish her. She has no right to judge me. To ask questions.

But for once, I keep my temper. Camille pulled me out of that party. She dragged me all the way back here and tried to clean me up. She did that—not Mason or Bella or anybody else. She didn't have to help me. But she did it anyway.

I look at Camille. Really look at her in the dim, watery light. Her skin glows like it's illuminated from the inside. The humidity has turned her hair into a wild halo of curls, all around her head. Her dark eyes look huge and tragically sad. I see the pain in them.

I know the reasons she should be miserable—she's poor, her mother abandoned her, her father can't keep his shop together, and she's trying to raise her delinquent brother all on her own.

But all that never seemed to bother her before. Why is she finally falling apart?

"What happened today?" I ask her. "Why are you so sad?"

She wrings out the cloth angrily, refusing to look at me. "I'm not."

Even while she's saying the words, two tears run down the sides of her face in perfect parallel.

"Tell me what happened."

It's not an order. It's just a request. Still, she shakes her head, making the tears fall onto her lap.

"No. It's none of your business. And I don't trust you."

"Well," I say. "That's probably smart. I'm not that trustworthy."

Camille gives me a suspicious look, like she thinks I'm messing with her. "I'm not some fragile flower," she says. "I grew up right here in Old Town, the same as you."

"Not exactly the same. You're a good girl."

"No, I'm not." She shakes her head. "You have no idea what I'm capable of doing."

I sit up again, wincing at the pain in my ribs. She doesn't try to stop me this time. I lean closer to her, my hair falling over my eyes.

"I've got some idea," I growl.

I take her face between my hands, and I kiss her. This time I do it slowly, so she could pull away if she wanted to. She stays completely still. She lets me run my tongue over her lips and then thrust it into her mouth, tasting her. She tastes a little bit like beer, a little bit like Coca-Cola, and a little bit just like herself.

Her lips are soft and flexible under mine. The top and bottom are almost equally full.

This time it's me who sneaks a look at her face up close. Her thick dark lashes fan out against her cheeks. Her skin is smooth and clean. Her face is rounder than usual—not a supermodel oval. But that makes her look youthful, especially when her hair is loose. Especially when she isn't frowning for once.

She smells like fresh rain and clean laundry. Her tongue massages mine—gently, softly.

She brings her hands up to my face, too, and I smell the remnants of diesel on her skin. One of my favorite scents in the world—intoxicating and raw. It makes my heartbeat pound against my throbbing ribs.

I pull her down on top of me, trying not to groan from the pain all down my side. We lie together on the narrow, lumpy mattress, still just kissing.

I've never kissed a girl like this, without trying to go further. I'm so wrapped up in how good it feels that I'm not pushing on to the next thing. I simply want to taste and smell and touch her, just like this.

Maybe I'm still floating from that hit to the head, because I barely feel the floor beneath us. I'm wrapped up in the rain and her warm skin. I feel a rush of contentment that I haven't known for years.

I don't know how long it goes on. Maybe an hour or two. The time has no meaning because it's the only time that matters. If you could see my whole life laid out on a string, this would be the one bright bead. The one moment of happiness.

Then my hand brushes her breast, accidentally, and she stiffens.

I don't know if she's pulling away or if she liked it. But the moment is broken.

We're both drawing back, staring at each other. Both confused.

The rain stopped. I didn't notice it when it happened. The room is utterly silent.

"I should go home," I say.

I don't know if I'm saying what I want or what I think she wants. She nods.

"Thanks. For…you know." I gesture awkwardly at the bowl of rusty water.

Camille nods again, her eyes darker than ever.

And that's it. I leave. Wondering what the fuck is happening to me.

CHAPTER 13
CAMILLE

WHEN NERO FALLS TO THE FLOOR, SIONE, JOHNNY VERGER, AND about five other guys start kicking and stomping him from all angles. Nero has more than a few enemies eager to get their licks in while he can't fight back.

Mason tries to intervene, jumping on Johnny from behind, but he's no match for all of them.

I have to physically throw myself on top of Nero to get them to stop.

I do it on impulse because I'm afraid they're going to kill him. In fact, they look like they still want to, whether I'm in the way or not. But Levi backs me up.

"That's enough," he says to Johnny and the others.

He lets me haul Nero out of the party, out to my car. Probably because he doesn't want to get in serious trouble with the Gallos.

"You gonna take him home?" Levi asks me. He looks twitchy, like he thinks Dante Gallo might be back an hour later to set his whole house on fire.

"No," I say. "I'll take him to my place."

I tell Levi that to put his mind at ease. But once I pull away from the curb, it doesn't seem like such a bad idea. After all, I'm not exactly looking forward to facing the Gallos myself—Enzo scares the hell out of me, and Dante isn't much better. Plus, Nero's in no state to defend me.

So I bring him back to my place and haul him up the stairs, which really isn't an easy task. He's heavy as hell, deadweight. Plus, wherever I put my hands, I can't help noticing how hard his body is. Even unconscious, Nero is made of tense, lean muscle just about everywhere.

I lay him down on my bed and try to clean him up a little.

He's an absolute mess. It's almost like he wants to get his face caved in. Like he's trying to destroy its beauty.

It won't work. The cuts and bruises can't hide what's underneath.

With every bit of blood and grime I clean off his skin, I reveal another inch of that perfect face.

It's funny how the most striking faces are atypical. Nero doesn't look like Brad Pitt or Henry Cavill—he looks only like himself.

He's got a long face, high cheekbones, and a sharp jaw. The whites of his eyes and his white teeth gleam against his olive skin whenever he speaks or looks my way. His eyebrows are straight black slashes directly above those light-gray eyes—eyes that sometimes look bright as starlight and sometimes as dark as the underside of a storm cloud. His nose is broad, his lips full and sensitive, beautifully shaped but perpetually twisted in a sneer.

He's got a shock of black hair without a hint of brown that often falls over his eyes until he tosses it back again in an impatient, angry gesture, like he's annoyed at his own hair or anything else that dares touch his face.

He dresses like James Dean, in a battered leather jacket that looks older than he is, torn-up jeans, and boots or filthy Chuck Taylors.

That's the Nero I've known for most of my life.

The one lying on my bed is a little different. For one thing, he's sleeping. Passed out or knocked out, I'm not sure. So that intense look of anger is absent from his face. His features are relaxed. Almost peaceful.

The only other time I've seen him like that was when we were driving together in his car. Granted, we were fleeing from the cops. But it was the only time I've seen him that he almost looked happy.

His T-shirt is torn open from the fight. There's a long gash across his chest. I clean that up, along with his face.

I notice the skin on his chest is as smooth and hairless as the rest of him and as deeply olive. I'm surprised to see he isn't covered in tattoos. Actually, he doesn't have any at all that I can see.

I wash his face clean. He groans as I touch the swollen parts of his face. It's a pitiful sound.

He really is in pain.

I never thought of Nero as someone who could feel pain like a normal person. He always seems to enjoy it.

I look at him lying there, and I think about how young he is, really. Only twenty-five, like me. He always seemed so much older. Especially when we were in school together.

But he was only a kid back then. He's barely an adult now.

He just grew up rough. Rougher than even I did.

The Gallos have money. But how old was he the first time somebody put a gun in his hand?

I look at that hand, curled up on his chest, trying to hold on to something. His knuckles are bloody and battered. His fingers are long, slim, and finely shaped.

I slip my hand into his just for an instant, to give him something to hold. I have long fingers, too. Our hands link together perfectly. Like fingers inside a glove. Like they were made for each other.

Nero's eyes flutter open. I pull my hand away, sitting back on my heels before he notices anything.

He tries to sit up, and I push him back down.

We talk for a while. More calmly than we've ever talked before.

Then he kisses me. Not like he kissed me in the car. That was violent, aggressive, like a punishment. This is the opposite. It's gentle. Almost tender.

We kiss for so long that I forget who he is and who I am. I forget I swore to myself a hundred times that I would never, never, never let

Nero Gallo get a hold of my heart so he could tear it into tiny pieces and stomp on them, like he does to everybody else.

Then his hand brushes over my breast, and I gasp because the feeling of his palm grazing my nipple is like an electric shock shooting through my body. And he pulls away from me, looking surprised and almost horrified.

Then he leaves.

And I'm alone in my bed for hours, wondering why I let him kiss me. And why he wanted to at all.

The next morning, I feel groggy, and my head is thumping. I barely ever drink. Those two beers at Levi's house didn't do me any favors.

I stumble out to the kitchen, where Vic is actually out of bed, with his textbooks sprawled across the table and his nose an inch away from his paper as he scribbles notes.

"What are you doing?" I ask suspiciously.

"I signed up for those AP courses like you said," Vic says.

He looks humble and apologetic, like he's trying to pay penance with me.

He knows I've been shanghaied into selling Molly for Levi Cargill. I haven't told him about Officer Schultz. Working with the cops is one of the most dangerous things you can do in Old Town. If Vic knew the situation, it would only put him in danger.

"What are those notes for?"

"Evolutionary biology," he says. "It's all about natural selection and common descent and speciation."

"Like that stuff with Mendel and the pea plants?"

I vaguely remember filling out a bunch of squares that were supposed to teach us recessive and dominant traits.

"Yeah," Vic says. "Basically."

"What are those charts you do for inheritance?"

"Punnett squares."

"I remember those."

"Well, we covered that in normal biology," Vic says. "This is a bit more advanced. Look…"

He flips the page on his textbook and gestures for me to sit down and read it with him.

"So I'm reading about epigenetics, which is the modification of gene expression, rather than alteration of the genetic code itself."

He's not reading that out of the book. He's just rattling it off from his own brain. Vic is so damn smart. That's why I can't stand the thought of him throwing his life away on some menial job—or worse, no job at all. Rotting in a prison cell because he made the mistake of trusting a guy like Levi.

"But look here." He points. "Here they're talking about inherited mutations. This one's on the FOXC2 gene. It's called 'distichiasis.' It's the same mutation Elizabeth Taylor had. It gives you a double row of eyelashes."

"That's cool." I'm trying to remember exactly what Elizabeth Taylor looked like.

"I have it, too!" Vic says proudly.

"What?" I lean in to examine his face.

He does have very thick eyelashes. It made him look like a girl when he was little—especially when we didn't cut his hair often enough.

"How do you know you have it?" I ask him.

"'Cause look—the lashes aren't just thick. They grow in two lines."

I look closely at his eyes. It's true—the lashes grow on top of each other, not just in a single row. "Is that…bad?"

"It can cause irritation," he says. "Not for me, luckily. Distichiasis is really rare. But it's an autosomal dominant disorder."

I stare at him blankly.

"Passed from parent to child," he adds helpfully.

"Did Mom have it?"

Vic frowns. "How should I know?"

I sometimes forget he doesn't remember her at all. She never came to visit him, after that night she dropped him off at the house.

I think our dad talked to her sometimes. In fact, I'm almost sure of it, after what Ali said. The only way my mom could have gotten that picture of me is if Dad gave it to her.

Ali said my mom kept it on her mirror. That doesn't make me feel good.

Actually, it pisses me off. She had no right to look at a picture of me when she couldn't be bothered to come see her real, actual daughter, who was still living in the same damn neighborhood as her.

"That's really cool," I say to Vic, trying to shake thoughts of our mother out of my head. "Glad to see you studying."

"I should have time to finish the whole course before the summer's up."

"That's great, Vic. I'm proud of you, dude."

I ruffle his caramel-colored hair as I stand from the table.

Vic really is a good-looking kid. He got a lot of our mom's best features, though he's more fair.

I try to remember if my mom had thick eyelashes. She had big dark eyes like me and Vic. But I don't know if the lashes were anything special.

Actually, much as I hate to admit it, I've only ever seen one person with lashes like Vic: Bella Page. And I've known her long enough to know she's had them since we were kids. They're not extensions like so many girls are getting these days. She's always had thick black lashes even when she was a skinny blond kid...

My stomach gives a strange squeeze inside me.

I saw Bella's parents once at our high school graduation ceremony. Her mom was slim and blond, much like Bella. Her father was tall, with a shiny bald head. But he did have one rather striking feature: thick dark eyebrows and lashes. They made his eyes look oddly feminine in an otherwise masculine face.

Just a coincidence, I'm sure.

"Hey, Vic," I say. "How rare is that dis—that mutation?"

"I dunno." He shrugs. "Maybe one in ten thousand?"

Well, shit.

That's a pretty big coincidence.

I'm supposed to be working in the auto bay, but instead I'm downtown, in the financial district.

This is where Bella's father works. He owns Alliance Bank on LaSalle Street. Or at least that's what Google tells me. It's confirmed by the company directory located over by the reception desk.

I'm not stupid enough to talk to the haughty-looking receptionist. I know there's no way on god's green earth that she's going to send me up in the elevator to whatever stunning corner office Raymond Page occupies. Bank managers don't meet with random mechanics who come wandering in off the street.

In fact, the receptionist is already eyeing me suspiciously, based off the fact I've been poking around the lobby for about ten minutes, and I'm dressed in jeans and a hoody, instead of the suit and brief-case apparently required to gain entry to the upper levels.

After setting down the receiver on her most recent phone call, she fixes me with an icy stare and says, "Can I help you?" in the tone of voice usually reserved for telling people that their fly is undone.

"I'm waiting for…my uncle," I say lamely.

She raises an eyebrow in disbelief.

I turn my back on her, looking around for someplace to lurk out of sight while I wait for Raymond to come down.

It's almost lunchtime. Unless he's planning to eat in his office, he probably goes out for a steak and martini in one of the many fancy restaurants within a three-block radius of this place.

The lobby is all black marble and sleek reflective surfaces. There are no good places to hide. Not even a potted plant to crouch behind. I can see the receptionist getting antsy, casting glances in my direction more and more frequently. She looks like she's going to call over one of the uniformed security guards any minute.

At that moment, the elevator pings. The gold doors part, and three suited men step through. The one in the middle is tall, bald, and obviously in charge.

Raymond Page.

I hurry over to intercept him.

The security guard hustles toward us from the opposite side. He knows who Page is better than I do, and he has no intention of letting me talk to him. Unfortunately for the guard, I'm closer. I position myself right in front of Raymond, so he has no choice except to stop or run right into me.

"What?" he snaps, breaking off his conversation with the other two men.

"Mr. Page?"

"Yes?" he says coldly.

He's looking down into my face, his eyes as dark and stern as a hawk's, with those drawn-together brows and his beak of a nose between them. His face is coarse—thick-skinned and heavily lined. But there's no mistaking that incongruous double row of lashes lining his eyes like kohl.

"What is it?" he barks.

"I...I know your daughter, Bella," I stammer.

"Then you should know better than to interrupt me at work."

He pushes past me and sweeps through the doors to the outside, the other two men hurrying after him. The security guard blocks me from following him.

"Time to go," he says, his arms crossed over his chest.

"Already leaving." I head for the opposite door.

I can't believe that. The mention of Raymond's daughter didn't interest him in the slightest. He had no curiosity. No concern that something might have happened to her.

It almost makes me feel bad for Bella.

Until I see her walking across the lobby arm in arm with the last person in the world I'd expect to see here: Nero Gallo.

Nero looks equally surprised. I don't know if I've ever seen him speechless before. His mouth is hanging open in a way that would almost be funny if the sight of him and Bella together weren't such a punch to the guts.

Bella looks back and forth between us, confused and annoyed.

"What are *you* doing here?" she sneers. "Applying for a janitor job?"

I don't look at her. I'm staring at Nero. He's dressed up nicer than I've ever seen before, in a button-up shirt and slacks. His hair is even combed back. If I didn't know him, I'd think he was one of the young professionals in the building. The perfect date for the bank manager's daughter.

"Going for lunch?" I ask them. My lips are dry. It's hard to speak.

"We already ate," Bella says, like I'm a complete idiot. For once, I think she's right. "Nero wanted a tour of Daddy's new building."

"You just missed *Daddy*," I tell them, watching Nero's face.

I think I see a flicker of something there. It's definitely not disappointment.

"How do you know?" Bella demands.

"I just saw him leave."

I'm still looking at Nero, trying to figure out exactly what the fuck is going on here.

He hates Bella. He always has. Did he do this to make me jealous? But he didn't know I was coming down here today. I didn't know myself until an hour ago.

Why would he meet Bella for lunch, dressed like a yuppie? It doesn't make any sense.

Unless he's not here for Bella at all...

I glance swiftly around the lobby to see if any of his friends are lurking around. There's nobody here—except the normal crowd of financiers and wealthy clients.

Nero sees my expression change. His face darkens. He doesn't want me fucking this up for him.

"Let's get going," he says to Bella.

"I don't know if I can show you the vault if Daddy's not here..." Bella says.

The vault...

Nero casts me a look, telling me to keep my mouth shut.

I think I know why he's here.

Still, it makes me burn with jealousy, seeing him freshly scrubbed and shaved, with Bella hanging off his arm. She's wearing a pretty yellow sundress and heels, her sleek blond bob shimmering every time she tosses her head. They make a gorgeous couple.

Meanwhile, I look so scrubby that I almost got booted out of this place before I spoke a word.

"I won't keep you. Enjoy your *date*," I hiss at Nero.

"We will," Bella says with poisonous sweetness.

Nero doesn't say anything at all. But I can feel his eyes burning into my back as I stomp out of the air-conditioned bank, back out into the sweltering heat.

I knew it. I fucking knew it.

Nero doesn't give a shit about Bella, and he doesn't give a shit about me. He'll use either one of us when we suit his purpose.

He's a snake. I was a fool to let him slip his fangs into me for even an instant.

Still, I feel myself pausing on the sidewalk. Like he's going to leave Bella in there and chase after me.

Of course he doesn't.

I'm just standing there all alone, while cars whiz by and pedestrians have to part ways around me.

Whatever Nero has planned in there, it's a hell of a lot more important than me.

CHAPTER 14
NERO

OUT OF ALL THE DEVIOUS AND CRIMINAL ACTS I'VE COMMITTED, taking Bella for lunch is the most repugnant.

I honestly think I would have found kidnapping a school bus full of children less distasteful.

I have to sit across the table from her in the Poke Bar, listening to every stupid thought rattling through her brain, while smiling and pretending to be interested.

I fucking hate pretending.

It doesn't help that I had to dress like Patrick Bateman in *American Psycho*. Button-up shirt, polished shoes…it's not for Bella's benefit. It's so I don't draw the attention of the security guards once we head over to Alliance.

I let Bella think it's her idea. I ask her a couple of questions about where her dad works—questions I already knew the answers to—and she says, "It's right across the street. Do you want to see it?"

I check my watch—12:38. I've already watched Raymond head out to lunch at precisely 12:33, three days in a row. I love a banker who keeps a tight schedule. It makes him conveniently predictable.

I have no interest in actually running into Raymond. Actually, I want him out of the way so I can poke around in all the places I'm not supposed to visit, with clueless Bella as my guide.

But instead of dear old Daddy, we bump into Camille instead.

She looks like I've slapped her.

I know how bad it looks, me and Bella dressed up like a fucking Ken and Barbie doll set. I want to tell her it's not what it looks like. Which is the stupidest excuse in the world. Except for this one time, when it's actually true.

Not that I owe her an excuse at all. Camille and I aren't dating. All we did is kiss.

But that kiss…

Okay, maybe it did mean something. I don't know what, but I can't deny it had an effect on me.

So I'm not enjoying the look on Camille's face, like I've stabbed her in the heart. Even worse is her expression when she starts to figure out there's something hinky about me poking around the bank.

Camille is too damn smart for her own good. Her eyes are darting around the lobby while Bella is blathering on, and I want to put a muzzle on Bella and simultaneously tell Camille not to fuck this up for me because she's looking one part pissed, one part hurt, and a whole lot suspicious. The perfect recipe for disaster if she wants to blow this whole thing up in my face.

Luckily, she takes the hint and leaves.

I really don't feel any better watching her stomp out through the double glass doors. Actually, I kinda want to chase her. I want to explain—or at least assure her that this is a business lunch and nothing more.

I can see her standing out on the sidewalk, looking lost, like she can't decide where to go next. She looks small from a distance. When she's standing right in front of me, her eyes blazing and her arms crossed in front of her chest, she's kind of intimidating. I forget she's actually quite petite.

"What are you looking at?" Bella says impatiently.

"Nothing."

I want to slap myself. I've got to get my head back in the game and soothe Bella's ruffled feathers. She's always had a bug up her ass about Camille.

"What is she even *doing* here?" Bella snipes. "I feel like she's everywhere I look lately! God, it's worse than high school! Why doesn't she just stay in her shitty little shop like she used to?"

I want to tell Bella that when you don't get a five-figure allowance from Daddy every month, you kind of have to go places and do things. But I stuff that thought down deep, plastering a smile on my face.

"So you can't go down to the vault room yourself?" I say to Bella, pretending to check my watch. "I better get going, then. I don't think I have time to wait around for your dad..."

"I really wanted him to meet you." Bella pouts.

Yeah, I bet Raymond Page would love to meet me, too. My father is one of the few movers and shakers in Chicago who doesn't keep his money here. Ironically, it's because he thinks Raymond is too dirty. Papa always says, *Don't break the law while you're breaking the law.* What he means by that is you should only commit one crime at a time. Otherwise you draw attention to yourself. After all, Al Capone never would have gotten caught for bootlegging if the feds couldn't prosecute him for tax evasion.

The fact the Gallos don't do business with Page is exactly why I've got no problem robbing him blind. He's not under our protection.

"Well..." Bella says hesitantly. "I can still take you down! We just can't go inside without Daddy."

"Are you sure?"

"Yeah, of course!" She's trying to sound more confident than she looks.

She takes me over to the private elevator, which is guarded by a scowling gorilla in a suit.

"Hey, Michael. I want to show my friend the vault room."

Michael grunts. "Is he in the appointment book?"

"No." Bella giggles. "I'm never in the appointment book."

"I better call up to Mr. Page." Michael's stubby fingers reach for his walkie-talkie.

"Okay," Bella says carelessly. "He's in a lunch meeting right now." Michael hesitates.

"It's fine," Bella says in a passive-aggressive tone. "He'll be less mad if you interrupt him than if you don't help me."

Michael's fingers drop from the walkie-talkie. "Okay," he says. "You can go down. Don't touch anything, though."

"Of course not." Bella smiles sweetly.

Michael hits the elevator button and lets us inside. The doors close, and we drop to the underground vault.

As we descend, I say to Bella, "I bet your dad knows everybody important in Chicago."

Bella flushes with pleasure. "He knows *everybody*. Every time he takes me to a party, he knows everybody's names, and they all know him. The mayor, all the CEOs, even celebrities…"

While Bella's talking, I'm noting the control panel in the elevator and the location of every camera and sensor.

When we enter the vault room, I walk slowly and deliberately, counting my steps. The stupid cuff links I'm wearing aren't just so I can look like a finance douche. Every time I adjust the one on my right wrist, I'm taking a picture. I can angle the cuff link in any direction to snap shots of the elevator, the vault room, and the vault door itself.

There are no decorations down here. No handy niches or vases I could use as a hiding place. I have a secondary camera I want to stash in situ, but I can only see one good place for it: over by the fire extinguisher. I wander over in that direction, asking Bella, "So what's in the vault? Gold bars or something?"

"All kinds of stuff," Bella says. "Actually…" She sidles over to me, lowering her voice. "I heard my dad talking on the phone. He said he had this big diamond from some Russian guy…but I guess he died? And nobody's come back since then. He thinks the rest of them don't know about it."

My heart skips a beat. It's hard to keep my expression neutral, like this means nothing to me.

The Griffins killed Kolya Kristoff this winter. He was the head of the *Bratva*. And he was a flashy fucker. I could see him stashing some rock in here without telling the rest of his men.

Poor Raymond must be horribly tempted…knowing there's no record of the giant stone in his possession but terrified to sell it, in case the Russians find out…

Maybe I should solve his dilemma by relieving him of the diamond.

While I'm talking to Bella, I reach behind me, out of view of the security cameras, and stick my own little camera under the nozzle of the fire extinguisher.

The only problem with this tiny device is that I have to place the receiver aboveground, within a hundred meters of the vault.

"So your dad built this bank recently?" I ask Bella.

"Three years ago—if that's recent." She giggles.

"Did they build the vault at the same time?"

"I guess so. It was definitely here when I visited. You want to look at anything else?"

"Nah." I grin. "I get the idea."

As we head back up, I say to Bella, "You seemed to know Michael pretty well."

"He's always guarding the elevator. He's a bit of a stick, but he's nice enough."

Meaning he lets her do what she wants in the end.

The doors open, and I hold out my hand to Michael.

"Thanks for letting us take a tour," I say, shaking his meaty paw.

Meanwhile, I stick my receiver right on top of his walkie-talkie. It's black metal, about the size of a screw. Unless he looks closely at his antennae, he won't notice it at all.

It will silently beam the images from the hidden camera right out of this building, all the way to my laptop at home.

"Come back soon," Michael says politely.

I intend to.

CHAPTER 15
CAMILLE

When I get home, I knock on Vic's door.

"Come in!" he calls.

I push the door open. His bedroom is tiny. He only has a minuscule window high up on one wall, like in a prison cell. He doesn't seem to care, though—he's papered the walls with posters of all his favorite musicians, and the space is as cheerfully crowded and messy as any teenage boy's room.

He's got a desk squished in there with his bed. He's currently working at that desk, hunched over the laptop I bought him a couple of years back.

He sits up a little too quickly when I come into the room.

I automatically glance at the screen to check if he's doing his coursework.

Instead, I see some kind of music program. It looks like a bunch of slider bars and squiggly graphs.

"What's that?" I ask him.

"Well..." Vic looks guilty.

"Come on. Out with it."

"It's this thing for making beats," he admits.

"What kind of beats?"

"You know. Backing tracks for songs."

I don't really know, but I'm interested. I come and sit on the edge of his bed.

"Let's hear it."

"Okay…" Vic says nervously.

He places his cursor over the right spot on the screen and presses enter.

The beat plays out of his tinny speakers. I don't know much about this kind of music, but I can hear that it's upbeat and catchy, with a '70s funk sound to it.

"You made that?" I ask Vic.

"Yeah." He grins shyly. "Listen to this one."

He clicks another track. This time the beat is slightly eerie, with an instrumental backing that sounds like it belongs in a kung fu movie.

"Vic, that's really cool!"

"Thanks," he says.

"What do you do with them?"

"Well…I posted a couple online. And I sold them, actually."

"Oh, yeah? What does somebody pay for a beat like that?"

"Well, at first I was charging twenty bucks. But now I'm getting fifty per track."

"Seriously?"

"Yeah."

I'm impressed. My enterprising little brother has found a way to make money that actually sounds legal.

"I wish I had a better mixing board," he says. "If I sell a few more, I could probably buy one. But I know I have to save for college, too," he adds hastily.

"Save for both," I tell him. "Half for college, half for the equipment you need."

"All right." Vic grins. "Fair enough."

I'm really proud of him. I always knew my little brother was brilliant. He just needs to turn his attention in the right direction.

To things that will help him out in life, instead of getting him in trouble.

I look at his handsome thin face, dominated by his dark eyes and girlish lashes. The truth is, he doesn't look entirely like my mother. She was 100 percent Puerto Rican. Vic is fairer. It's possible his dad was a white dude.

I search his features, trying to find evidence of Raymond Page in his face. Could my mom have known a man like that? Dated him or slept with him?

All kinds of men visited Exotica. As far as strip clubs went, it was one of the fancier ones in the city. People said my mother worked as an escort, too. I didn't want to believe it. But it's possible she met Raymond and accidentally fell pregnant.

That's not information Page would want anybody else to know. He would have been married to Bella's mother at the time. And even if she's okay with him philandering, I doubt that extends to unprotected sex with strippers.

God, it makes me feel sick just thinking about it.

"What?" Vic says. "What are you looking at?"

"That eyelash thing," I tell him.

He laughs. "It's kinda cool."

"Vic," I say hesitatingly. "Did Mom ever tell you anything about your father?"

"No." He frowns. "I told you she didn't."

"Do you remember any guys coming around her apartment? Anybody she was dating when you were little?"

"I don't remember anything about her at all." Vic scowls.

"What about a tall bald man?"

"Why are you asking me all this stuff?" Vic says angrily. "I don't care who my real dad is. Axel's my dad."

"I know that, of course he is." I try to soothe Vic. "It's just... maybe your real dad has money. He might owe you child support."

"I'm not a child anymore," Vic says. "It's too late now."

I don't think that's true, strictly speaking. Vic's still seventeen. Raymond Page is a wealthy man. I might be able to get something for Victor, to help pay for college.

Because I'm not going to be able to chip in on that anymore. My dad got his test results back from the hospital. He's got stage three adenocarcinoma. His doctor says it doesn't seem to have spread yet, and Dad's got a decent chance of recovery if he gets in right away for surgery.

But we have no insurance. I told the hospital we're broke. They're trying to get financial aid for us, setting us up with a payment plan in the meantime. That's going to sap every dime I've got, without anything left for Vic.

Which makes me think it might be worth hitting Raymond up for money. I don't love the idea—he's wealthy and powerful. And if his daughter is any indication, he's probably a complete asshole. But what other choice have I got? If he really is Vic's dad, he owes him something.

Jesus. I just realized that means Bella is Vic's sister. Or half sister, I guess. The same as me.

That pisses me off. I don't like Bella having any connection to my baby brother. It makes me jealous and territorial. I'm the one who raised Vic. I'm the one who always protected him and took care of him.

Well, it doesn't matter. It's not Bella I need to talk to. It's Raymond. And I need a better plan than just ambushing him at work. He won't want to hear what I have to say. I need proof.

"Don't forget about your schoolwork," I say to Vic, ruffling his hair on my way out.

I head back down to the auto bay. It's just me down here today—my dad's at Midtown Medical going over his treatment plan with Doctor Yang. I wanted to go with him, but he reminded me that we had two cars that were supposed to be finished by the end of the day. And there's nobody else to do the work but me.

Even though the tasks are menial, I'm fully immersed. After cranking the radio so loud that I'm sure it's echoing down the street,

I get elbow-deep in grease, losing myself in the intricate engine of a 2018 Camry. It's a relief focusing on this and nothing else.

I can't think about my dad, or Vic, or Nero. I'm just working hard and fast, getting it all done as quickly as possible.

I get so lost in the work that I'm actually starting to feel good. That old Joan Jett song comes on the radio, and I start singing along, forgetting the auto-bay doors are open, and anybody could hear me.

♫ *"Bad Reputation"—Joan Jett*

"Is this your theme song?" a masculine voice growls in my ear.

I shriek, straightening so fast that I slam my head on the open hood of the Camry. Bright stars burst in front of my eyes like flashbulbs. I put my filthy hand up to my temple and feel warm blood trickling down.

I spin around before coming face-to-face with Officer Schultz, who's standing way too close to me.

"What are you doing here?" I gasp.

"You weren't answering my text messages. Or my phone calls."

"I'm working," I snarl. "I don't exactly have my phone attached to my hip."

He hasn't backed up, so only a few inches of space separate us. He has me pinned between him and the Camry. My head is throbbing, and my heart is still pounding from the shock of the surprise.

"Can you move?" I say. "My head is bleeding."

"Let me look at it."

"I don't need your help."

Schultz pushes me down on the nearest bench, not listening. He grabs a handful of paper towels and presses them against my temple. He's sitting right next to me, his tanned face only inches away from mine. I can smell the spearmint gum on his breath.

"Sorry I surprised you," he says. He's smiling. He doesn't look sorry at all.

"You shouldn't be here," I mutter. "If anybody sees you—"

"I'm not wearing my uniform."

"So what? You don't live here. People will notice you. And not to burst your bubble, but you reek of cop."

"Come on," he says. "In these clothes?"

Today he's wearing some kind of Tommy Bahama shirt and cargo shorts. It's slightly less obvious than his sports gear, but it still doesn't strike quite the right note if he's trying to look like a tourist. It's that military haircut, the stiff set of his shoulders, and the watchful way he looks around the room. Tourists are a lot more clueless.

"So what do you have for me?" he says.

I rattle off what little information I gathered at Levi's last party—mostly the names of people I saw buying drugs.

Schultz doesn't seem very interested in any of that. "What about his supplier?"

"How am I supposed to figure that out? Levi doesn't even like me, let alone trust me."

There is one piece of information that might interest him.

"Sione beat the shit out of Nero Gallo," I say. "You could arrest him for that."

"Arrest him?" Schultz scoffs. "Give him a medal, more like."

I sigh in irritation. "You don't give a shit about any of the crimes I've actually witnessed. So I don't know what to tell you."

"You could tell me what you were doing at Alliance Bank," Schultz says coolly.

My throat tightens.

How does he know about that?

This motherfucker is following me.

I want to tell him off, but I try to play dumb instead.

"I was opening an account," I say.

"Nice try," Schultz sneers. "You don't have the bank balance to interest Raymond Page."

"You'd be surprised. Once I dug through the couch cushions, I had almost thirty-eight dollars."

Schultz is not amused. He presses the wad of paper towels hard against the cut on my head, making me wince.

"Is everything a joke to you, Camille?"

"I don't find stalking very funny." I glare right back at him.

"I wasn't following you," Schultz says. "I was tailing your buddy Nero."

"I didn't even see him there," I lie.

"Did you see his new girlfriend?" Schultz asks, his voice a soft hiss.

Now my throat is clenched up so tight, I can barely breathe. I feel that same rush of bitter jealousy, remembering how beautiful Nero and Bella looked, standing side by side. She is the type of girl he should date, if he actually wanted to date someone. Rich. Gorgeous. Well-connected.

I'm a fucking nobody. An embarrassment. Can you imagine Nero introducing me to his family? He'd never do it. My dad vacuumed Enzo Gallo's car for god's sake. You might as well date your maid's daughter.

"Are you talking about Bella?" I rasp.

"Of course. Who else?"

"I didn't know they were dating. Good for them."

My lie is incredibly pathetic. Schultz shakes his head in wonder at how stupid I sound.

"I hear they've had some kind of on-off thing since high school," Schultz says, staring right into my eyes. "I bet she's a hellcat in the sack. Girls with daddy issues always are..."

"I told you," I whisper. "I'm not friends with any of these people..."

"Right." Schultz nods slowly. "You're just a loner. A loser. Is that right, Camille?"

God, I fucking hate him. He's still pressing that wad of paper towel against my skull, digging his thumb into the cut. Deliberately trying to hurt me.

"Yeah," I say. "I'm guessing you're in the same boat. Seeing as we went to the same school, and I never even heard your name before."

I see a muscle jump in his jaw. Oh, he didn't like that. Schultz can dish it out, but he can't take it.

"You look like the sporty type," I say. "Let me guess—you made the freshman team, but not varsity…never got that letterman's jacket…"

"No," Schultz says quietly. "I never did. But I've gotten plenty of awards since then. Locking up the scum of Chicago. The fucking rats that feed on the filth of this city."

I push his hand away, standing from the bench.

"You know," I tell him. "Not everybody chooses to be a rat. Some of us just happened to be born in the gutter."

Schultz stands, too. He can't bear me being taller than him. He has to look down on me. "Spare me your sob story, Camille. You make choices every day, same as everybody else."

"Do you actually see a hero when you look in the mirror?" I ask him.

"I like what I see just fine. I know you're close to Nero. It's no coincidence you two are always in the same place at the same time. You stick to him, and you report back to me. No more fucking around, Camille. This is your last warning."

He puts his hands in his pockets, lifting the edge of his stupid tropical shirt. I see the gleam of a gun tucked in his waistband. A silent threat, aimed right at me.

"Don't come here again," I tell him.

"Don't make me come back," he spits. "This place fucking stinks."

He turns around and stalks away.

I sink back down on the bench, my legs giving way beneath me. Schultz is an idiot.

There's nothing wrong with the smell of gasoline and oil.

What stinks is his breath, under the cover of that spearmint gum.

CHAPTER 16
NERO

I'M PLANNING THE ROBBERY OF THE ALLIANCE VAULT.

If I were to make a to-do list, it would have about eight thousand items on it.

A robbery succeeds or fails in the planning stage. Dante used to do all the planning for the armored truck heists. My big brother is smart. But I'm smarter.

Yeah, that's right. I'm not just a pretty face. I'm a fucking Moriarty underneath. So this robbery is going to be planned down to the tiniest detail, with contingencies and contingencies for contingencies. In the end, I'll walk out of that bank with eight figures of loot and zero evidence left behind. And I hope to do it all without firing a single shot.

I'm not opposed to violence. Actually, I rather enjoy it. But there's no elegance in a smash-and-grab. Not to mention way too much chance of catching a bullet yourself.

I want to rob Raymond so cleanly that he has no idea who took the money or where it went.

This kind of strategizing requires a clear mind. I've laid off the drinking and smoking. I'm even sleeping eight hours a night.

And yet…I'm not experiencing that mental clarity I need.

For one reason alone: Camille.

I've known this girl most of my life. I never thought about her at all unless she was standing right in front of me. So why in the fuck is she popping into my head twenty times a day?

Every time I'm sitting still, poring over stolen blueprints from the bank or trying to make a list of supplies, there's her face, swimming in front of my eyes.

Every time I pick up my phone to call one of my soon-to-be-accomplices, I get the itch to call her instead.

I keep thinking about her hands touching my face so gently as I came back to consciousness. I think about those huge dark eyes that seem to speak directly to me even when she's not saying a word.

I never thought she was pretty before.

Now I wonder how I could have been so blind.

Everything about her is lovely when you look close enough. The shell-pink beds of her fingernails. Her small round ears peeking out from all those wild curls. The little line between her eyebrows when she frowns. The natural glow of her skin, without makeup or glitter dusted all over it. The slight pink flush under her brown cheeks. Those expressive eyes, so dark and yet so brilliant. Sometimes looking at me with fury or disdain. Sometimes amused, even though she doesn't want to be. And sometimes, sometimes letting slip something more... Sadness. Fear. Worry. Or longing...

You have to look closely to see any of those things.

But once you do, it makes other girls seem flashy and overblown by comparison. Even at the bank yesterday, Bella was dolled up to the nines, in an outfit that probably cost five figures. And all I could think was that she looked cheap and fake next to Camille. The lacquered nails, the pushed-up cleavage, the bleached hair, the shiny new purse the size of an atlas...it was all too much. I just wanted to look at the single curl falling over Camille's forehead and the way she brushed it back with one slim little hand.

Jesus, I sound like a lunatic.

I don't know what's happening to me.

Camille doesn't even like me. Why should she? I've been a total ass to her. Nothing personal—I was just being myself. But I'm not a good guy. Not boyfriend material. I've always known that. I'm selfish. Impulsive. Easily offended. Chasing whatever I want and then hating it as soon as I get it.

I don't think people can change. And I don't know how to be any other way.

And yet...

For once in my life, I wish I were different.

When I lay next to Camille and kissed her, I actually felt happy for a second. I felt connected to her. I felt like she opened her shell just the tiniest bit, and so did I, without worrying that the other person was going to stab us in our most vulnerable place.

Then it ended, and I don't know how to get back there because I don't know how it happened in the first place.

I pick up my phone once more before finding her number. I got it from Mason, who got it from Patricia.

I could call her. I could ask her out on a date.

But the idea of sitting across the table from a girl just reminds me of my stupid lunch with Bella. I hated that. It was so fucking fake.

I set the phone down again, scowling.

Dante comes into the room. I've got my papers spread all over the ancient oak table in the dining room. We never eat in here anymore. We used to have family dinners when Aida and Seb were still here. Now we mostly eat at the little table in the kitchen, where Greta doesn't have to walk so far to bring us the food. Half the time our meals don't even overlap—Greta just keeps the food warm on the stove.

I kinda miss those family dinners. I think the last one we had was the night of Nessa Griffin's party. We all ate up on the roof, under the grapevines. We could see fireworks breaking over the bay.

That night changed so many things. Aida wanted to crash the Griffins' party. I agreed. We had no idea what would follow from that silly little impulse: Seb's star ripped away from him. Aida married against her will. An alliance with the Griffins. A war with the *Braterstwo.*

It's not that I want things to go back. But I wish you could know when a moment will change your life forever. I wish I would have enjoyed that dinner a little longer and not been in such a hurry to get up from the table.

"What's all that?" Dante grunts.

He's dripping with sweat, having just come in from a run.

My brother was already a beast by the time he was sixteen, and he's only gotten bigger since then. I think he spent most of his time in Iraq working out on base. He came home the size of a half-grown bull. Now he's a fucking Kodiak bear.

I often hear him in our basement gym grunting and straining. We've got an ancient set of barbells speckled with rust. Dante slings a couple of giant chains around his neck, and then he does push-ups and pull-ups and dips until his muscles are bulging in places that people shouldn't even have muscle.

"You look wrung out. Have you tried getting a girlfriend instead?" I ask him.

Dante says, "At least I had one, once."

Oh, yes. But we don't talk about her. Unless you want Dante to rip your arm off and feed it to you.

"I've had a lot of girlfriends," I say. "For an hour or two."

Dante snorts. "Mama wouldn't like you talking that way."

Now it's my turn to stiffen. That's the one woman *I* don't want to discuss. "We don't know what she would have liked. Because she's not here."

Dante looks at me quietly, trying to decide if he should say anything else. He returns to the scattered papers instead.

"Is that a vault?" He points to the topmost diagram.

"Clearly."

"Why do you have the schematics for a vault?"

"Is it Obvious Question Day?"

Dante gives a long sigh. Since his lungs are like bellows, it blows several papers off the table.

"Does Papa know about this?"

"Doctor Bernelli says stress is bad for his heart. I was planning to tell him afterward."

My father is currently out on the back nine with Angelo Marino, the head of the second-largest Italian family in Chicago. Papa hates golfing, but he's supposed to be getting more exercise. Marino has lured him out with promises of clubhouse BLTs and pretty waitresses. In return, Marino gets to talk Papa's ear off about how his four worthless sons can advance inside the organization.

Papa won't be home for hours, which means I can work uninterrupted. Other than Dante, of course.

Dante is silently looking over the blueprints, his dark eyes darting from page to page.

"This is Page's bank."

"Guessed it first try."

"You're planning to rob him?"

"Not him, exactly. Just whoever keeps their money at his bank."

"You know he deals with some serious people. You're not stealing from a bunch of doctors and lawyers."

"That's why I'm going to keep this one anonymous. I won't leave a business card like I usually would."

Dante doesn't crack a smile. "Raymond's no bureaucrat. He gets his hands dirty."

"Dante." I scowl. "Are we the baddest motherfuckers in the city or not? I'm not scared of Raymond Page. Or anybody else who keeps an account there."

Dante thinks silently. "What's the take?" he says at last.

"Substantial. Eight figures. And that's not including the Winter Diamond. I think Kristoff stashed it in the vault. Nobody knows except me."

The St. Petersburg *Bratva* liberated that particular gem from the imperial collection at the Hermitage Museum, eight years ago. I don't know if Kristoff bought it or stole it from his brothers. But I guarantee if the other *Bratva* knew where it was, they wouldn't leave it in Raymond's hands for long.

The diamond alone is probably worth fifty million to the right buyer.

"One score. And we can fund our entire project on the South Shore."

Dante shakes his head slowly. "That's risky."

"Large-scale construction is one of the best ways to wash dirty money. The Russians do it all the time."

"You could make a lot of enemies."

"Only if I get caught." I grin. "Besides, we're hardly swimming in friends right now. How much worse can it get? We'll still have the Griffins on our side. As long as we leave their lockbox alone."

"You're not going to bring them in on it?"

I shake my head. "I don't think they're into breaking the law in person anymore. They've got an image to maintain."

"Not you, though." Dante smiles.

"No. My reputation is about as bad as it can get."

Dante looks over my papers again. I don't interrupt him—there's no point trying to rush my brother. He likes to think things over.

But his thoroughness extends further than my patience. Eventually, I say, "So, are you in?"

"No."

"Why the fuck not?"

Dante crosses his arms over his massive chest. "Because you're going behind Papa's back."

"I told you, I don't want to raise his blood pressure."

"Bullshit. You know he wouldn't like it. He'd say it's too risky."

"Neither one of you cared about that when we knocked over all those armored trucks."

"That was different." Dante frowns. "We needed the money back then."

"We need money now!"

"No we don't. We can get it another way. Take on partners—"

"I don't want more partners!"

"You're reckless."

"And you've lost your nerve!" I shout. "What happened to you? You used to love a challenge."

Dante looks truly angry now. It takes a lot to light his fuse. But once you do, there's a whole lot of dynamite behind it. He clenches his jaw, biting back what he actually wants to say.

"I used to make a lot of stupid decisions," he growls. "Then I grew up."

I don't have the same self-control as Dante. I've fully lost my temper.

"You just don't like that all this is *my* idea," I spit. "You want to be the boss forever."

"I don't give a fuck about being boss." Dante growls, turning away from me. "I wish you were mature enough to take over."

With that, he stalks out of the dining room, heading to his bedroom in the back of the house.

"Yeah, go take a shower!" I shout after him. "You fucking stink!"

It's not very satisfying being left all alone with my scattered papers.

But I don't give a damn what Dante says. I'm going to do this job, and I'm going to pull it off brilliantly. I'll sink every penny into the South Shore and triple our empire over the next five years. I'll take us from Mafia kingpins to one of the wealthiest families in the whole damn country.

The Griffins aren't the only ones with ambition.

I may have a temper, but I've got intelligence and vision, too.

I'm going to make this happen.

And nothing will stand in my way.

CHAPTER 17
CAMILLE

I HAVE TO SEE LEVI AGAIN BECAUSE I'VE GOT TO GIVE HIM THE cash for that bag of Molly I was supposed to sell. Also, much as I'd like to avoid it, I need to see Bella Page.

I figured out how I can confirm if Raymond is actually Vic's father. At first, I thought I'd need to steal his empty coffee cup or chewed-up gum. I can't pull a hair out of his head because the guy is bald as an egg, and I doubt his security guards are going to let me get within ten feet of him again.

But then I realized I don't have to test Raymond's DNA. I've got the next best thing—his daughter.

Of course, I doubt Bella's gonna want to spit in a tube for me. But if I can get her at a vulnerable moment…I'm sure I can come up with something.

Then there's the other person I'm both hoping and dreading to see…Nero.

Just thinking about him makes my heart race.

I want to see him again. I just do. It's stupid, and I hate admitting it, but I can't help the way I feel.

I call Patricia to see if Levi's throwing any more parties in the near future.

"Not that I know of," she says. "But everybody's going to some bonfire on the beach tonight."

"Are you going?"

"Yes. But *not* with Mason. I had a perfectly good job interview lined up for him at my cousin's restaurant, and he tells me he 'has something else in the works.' And I'm like, are you kidding me, dude? It better not be anything illegal because you told me you were done with all that shit, and now you're suddenly too busy for a serving job that makes a hundred and fifty in tips a night? That doesn't make sense…"

I'm listening to Patricia, but my ears perk up at the first part of her rant. Mason has something in the works? So does Nero, as far as I can tell. Something at Alliance Bank. It doesn't take a genius to guess what that might be.

"He wanted your number, by the way," Patricia says.

"Mason?" I say in confusion.

"No. Nero. Mason asked me for it, and I know it was to give it to him."

Nero asked for my phone number?

He didn't call it. Didn't send a text either.

But maybe he wanted to…

"Did something happen after the race?" Patricia asks.

"No!" I say, a little too quickly.

"Are you sure?" I can hear the disbelief in her voice, and the teasing tone that means she's smirking on the other end of the line. "The way he dragged you out of there like a caveman…kinda hot, wasn't it?"

"He was just keeping me from getting arrested." I'm glad Patricia can't see me blushing.

"But why, though? He's not exactly the chivalrous type…"

"I dunno. I guess we're friends. In a way."

"Friends that have each other's babies…?"

"No!"

Patricia is laughing, enjoying having something to tease me about. Usually, she's the only one with a dramatic romantic life. This might be her only chance to stick it to me.

"My god, girl," she says, "if you end up fucking him, you have to tell me what it's like."

A little shiver runs down my spine. "I'm not doing that," I say quietly.

"Why not? It's like climbing Everest or skydiving. My friend Jess did it, and she said—"

"I don't want to hear about it!" I say sharply. I can't stand hearing about Jessica or any other girl that Nero's been with. I'm burning with jealousy, and he doesn't even belong to me. Not even a little bit.

This is why I could never date him, even if I wanted to. It would eat me alive.

"Sorry," Patricia says, chastened.

"No, I'm sorry. You didn't do anything wrong. I'm just wound up. You know my dad—"

"Yeah," Patricia says gently. "I saw his file. I'm really sorry about that. You want me to bring over some dinner or something? I make this amazing soup with rotisserie chicken and carrots…"

"I think he went to bed already. Thank you, though. That's really kind."

"Oh. Well…come over here, and we can get ready for the bonfire together," Patricia says. "Have a glass of wine before we go and relax a little."

"Sure. That sounds really nice."

"Ten o'clock, then."

"All right. Thanks, Patricia."

"Of course. See you soon."

———

I drive over to Patricia's apartment on the corner of Willow Street at 9:45 p.m. I'm early because I wasn't exactly sure how long it would take me to get here.

She lives on the twelfth floor of a pretty white brick building. I take the elevator up, then tap on her door. She opens it immediately, wearing a pink robe and fluffy slippers.

"Hey!" she says. "I'm not dressed yet."

"That's okay! I'm early."

I follow her inside. I haven't seen her place before—it's clean and bright and decorated in that way that some people seem to instinctively understand, where everything doesn't match exactly, but it all coordinates to make the place look classy and comfortable and like an actual home. She has a large bookshelf in the living room, with all the books arranged by the color of their covers, so they run down the shelves like a rainbow, from red to violet.

"Have a seat!" Patricia says cheerfully.

She gestures toward a spotless white couch with blue Aztec pillows. I don't know if I'm supposed to move the pillows or sit on them. Also, I'm scared of smudging the couch or spilling the glass of wine Patricia hands me.

"Your apartment's so nice," I tell her. "How long have you been here?"

"About a year."

"Jesus. I've lived in my place almost my whole life, and I think we have like, maybe one picture up."

Patricia laughs. "I always told myself I'd have my own place, no roommates. With a fireplace, a nice shoe collection, and a view."

She pulls back the gauzy curtains so I can see out the window.

"Check that out," she says proudly.

Sure enough, between the various buildings, she has a corridor view down to Lincoln Park.

"Absolutely perfect," I say.

Patricia takes a sip of her wine, looking out at the green treetops with satisfaction.

"That's why I always liked you," she says to me. "You were a hard worker. So was I. We knew what we had to do. I don't think Mason's ever gonna grow up and be somebody I can count on."

"He cares about you, though."

"I know," Patricia sighs. "But I keep trying to change him. And you know that never works in the end."

"You'd know better than me." I take a gulp of my wine. "I think my longest relationship lasted a month."

"Why is that?" Patricia sets her glass down on the coffee table. "You know you're beautiful, Camille. Much as you try to hide it."

"I dunno." I shake my head, too embarrassed to meet her eyes. "Just busy with work and family stuff."

"It's okay to be selfish, sometimes," Patricia says. "My whole family's a fucking mess. That didn't stop me from going after what I want. I'm going to keep working. Keep saving money. Make something of myself. If they want to stay in the same cycle forever, that's their problem."

"That makes sense..." I twist the slender stem of my wineglass between my fingers. "It's complicated for me... Vic and my dad need my help. And they deserve it. My dad always worked super hard. He's just unlucky."

Patricia nods sympathetically.

"Well!" she says. "You can have some fun tonight, anyway. Did you bring clothes to change into?"

I look down at my jeans and T-shirt. "I was gonna wear this."

"To the beach?" She shakes her head at me, then grabs me by the hand and pulls me toward her bedroom. "Come on, you dummy. You can borrow something of mine."

Patricia's closet is as nicely organized as the rest of her apartment. She flips through the hangers, pulling out a few items to hold them up in front of me, then putting them back again. Eventually, she takes out a printed romper that reminds me of the pillows on her couch.

"Put that on," she orders.

"Uh-uh." I shake my head. "No offense, but those onesie things remind me of something a toddler would wear. Also, how do you pee once it's on?"

"You just pull it down." Patricia laughs.

"Like, all the way?"

"Yes."

"So I'm totally naked?"

"Basically."

"How am I going to do that down on the beach?"

"Sometimes you have to suffer to look sexy," Patricia informs me.

"That doesn't sound like a great trade-off."

"Not even for Nero?" She gives me a mischievous look.

Man, she is really not going to let that die. "Especially not for him."

"Bullshit!" Patricia cries. "I know there's something going on with you two. You're coming to parties all of a sudden. He's saving you from cops…"

I press my lips together, like that's going to suddenly help me become a better liar.

"Out with it!" Patricia says.

This is not a friendly glass of wine. She's a goddamn CIA interrogator.

"Fine!" I crack like I'm being waterboarded. "We did kiss."

"I knew it!" she whispers, her eyes alight with glee.

"But that's it!" I hastily add. "And it's probably never happening again."

"Probably…" Patricia says.

"Most likely. Almost definitely."

"Right." She grins. "And?"

"And what?"

"Does he taste like cherry pie?"

"No." I laugh. "He smells amazing, though…"

"God, I know…" Patricia groans. "I tried his jacket on once in high school. I wanted to live inside it forever…"

"His sweat is catnip. I feel like I'm high."

It feels good to admit this to someone.

Patricia's loving it—discovering that I do have feelings after all. Every once in a while.

"That's it," she says. "We're going all the way tonight. You're going to look fucking gorgeous."

I let her pull me into the bathroom. She spends almost an hour on my hair and face.

The hair is the trickiest bit.

"Do you use a pre-shampoo treatment?" Patricia asks me.

"Like...brushing it?"

"Sweet baby Jesus, please tell me you don't brush your hair."

"I mean...I kinda have to."

"Oh my god. A wide-tooth comb, woman, never a brush. What about your deep conditioner? And do you use a satin wrap at night?"

"I use Suave shampoo..."

Patricia gasps like I've shot her. "You're *killing* me."

With a lot of leave-in conditioner, and an infinite amount of patience, Patricia manages to tame my mane and turn it into something that actually looks intentional—or at least less electrocuted.

She spends a long time on my face, too, moisturizing my skin and shaping my brows before she even starts applying makeup.

As she rubs the moisturizer under my eyes and across my cheeks with smooth, steady strokes of her thumb, I could almost cry. I've never been taken care of like this. It's so gentle and so loving.

"What's wrong?" Patricia says.

"Sorry." I sniff. "I just...uh...my mom never showed me how to do my hair and all this stuff."

Patricia puts down the bottle of moisturizer and hugs me.

"Sorry," I say again. "I know this is stupid. I'm an adult. I could have learned it myself..."

"It's seriously no problem," Patricia says. "Just please, show me how to change the oil in my car because I haven't done it since I bought it."

"Deal." I hug her back a little too hard.

"All right," Patricia finally says when she's finished working on my face. "Take a look."

She turns me around to face the mirror.

It's funny because I don't look so different—it's still me. Just a version of me that glows like a fucking angel. A hint of shine on the lips and cheeks, a little swipe of eyeliner, and a mane of soft, spiraling curls, dark at the roots, fading to a sun-kissed caramel at the ends.

Even the romper looks pretty damn cute, with patterned bands of green, blue, and cream that look pretty and summery without being too bright. The sleeves hang off my shoulders, leaving them bare.

Patricia lends me sandals and little beaded hoop earrings, until suddenly I've got an actual outfit.

Then Patricia gets herself ready, which takes a quarter of the time, with no less stunning results. She puts on a loose summery white top with shorts that make her legs look about a mile long and pulls her hair into her signature high ponytail.

"Okay, damn," I say. "Why are you so good at making people look hot?"

Patricia grins. "I missed my calling as a celebrity stylist."

We drive Patricia's car over to Osterman Beach. It only takes a few minutes, since it's right on the opposite side of Lincoln Park. It's almost midnight by now, and I'm confused because usually the public beaches are closed by this time. Not to mention the fact that bonfires and alcohol are banned at all times.

"Aren't we going to get kicked out?" I say to Patricia.

"Nope." She shakes her head. "Miles Kelly is throwing the party. His dad is the super of the Parks Department. As long as we don't murder anybody, we'll be fine. And even then…depends who does the murdering."

Sure enough, even though the long stretch of cool sand is deserted, nobody stops us walking from down to the water. I can see the bonfire already blazing out of its cubby of sand—at first, a distant torch, and then as we draw closer, a beacon that shows the silhouetted figures clustered around.

I look back toward Lincoln Park. From the water, you see three distinct layered vistas—the beach, then the leafy green park behind, and beyond that, the jutting fingers of the skyscrapers in the downtown core. It looks odd, like the three different views don't belong together.

It's equally strange to see the beach so empty. I can hear the waves crashing gently on the sand. I can see faint stars in the black half dome of the sky.

It's difficult to recognize anybody around the fire. Everybody looks orange and glowing, only parts of their faces illuminated. Levi and Sione stand out because Levi's blond hair is impossible to miss, as is Sione's bulk. I'm guessing the figure next to them is that idiot Pauly. When I spot Ali Brown, I wave to her.

She ambles over to Patricia and me.

"Drink?" She offers us each a Heineken.

"Thanks." Patricia pops the caps off with her keys.

"You look different," Ali says, gazing at me with her dreamy eyes.

I say, "Patricia dressed me up…"

"Not the clothes," Ali says. "It's your face. You look excited."

I'd just been scanning the rest of the partygoers, searching for Nero. I blush, embarrassed that I was being that obvious.

I don't see him anywhere. Though I do see that Russian guy Bella was dating—Grisha Lukin. He's crouched on the sand, playing some dice game with a couple of other guys. It might be a drinking game, or else he's taking shots to cheer himself up when he loses.

"Nobody's Love" is playing on a Bluetooth speaker. People are sitting on sand-dusted logs, others on spread-out Mexican-style blankets. A couple of girls dance in a mellow sort of way, just swaying to the music.

The vibe is peaceful. Maybe because Nero isn't here, nor is Bella. Only Beatrice, who seems a lot less aggressive stripped of the rest of her squad. She actually sends a little wave in Patricia's and my direction.

One of the girls brought a pack of marshmallows. Beatrice tries to roast one in the bonfire, but the flames are too high, and it instantly incinerates. She shrieks and swings the stick out of the flames, flinging the charred gooey mess in the direction of Levi and Sione. It barely misses Levi's shoe, landing in the sand right next to his foot.

"Watch it," he growls at Beatrice. "Or I'll throw you in the fuckin' lake."

"Sorry." She cringes.

Levi looks like he's in a sour mood. I don't know about what. He's sprawled on a blanket, not talking, just glowering at everybody else. Sione tries to make some comment to him, and Levi doesn't even bother to reply.

Ali sits on the lid of a cooler. She has one of those little plastic bottles of bubble solution, and she's blowing bubbles away from the bonfire, out over the dark smooth sand.

I sit next to her.

"Wanna try?" She hands me the bubble wand.

I haven't used one of these since I was a little kid. It's harder than I expect to create a steady stream of perfect bubbles like Ali is making.

"You're blowing too hard." She laughs. "Look."

She takes the wand back before pursing her lips and blowing a slow, steady, and gentle breath of air into a dozen glossy round bubbles that go spinning away over the sand.

"How's your week been going?" I ask her.

"Good. It was my birthday on Tuesday."

"What did you do?"

"Nothing," she says serenely. "I went for a walk by myself in Lincoln Park. It was perfect."

"Levi didn't take you out?"

She laughs. "No. He said we'd go for dinner, but then his brother called, and they got in a big fight. And he didn't want to go anymore."

"What were they fighting about?" I ask casually.

"Oh...his brother is coming back from Ibiza."

"So?"

"So he wants his house back."

"I thought Levi owned that house?"

"No," Ali says patiently. "The other one."

I frown, confused. Ali is such a conundrum because she's strangely innocent and seems to say whatever comes into her head. But she also seems to assume I already know what she's talking about, when in fact I have no fucking idea.

I want to keep talking to her, but I can see Levi watching us with a malevolent expression on his face. Catching my eye, he motions me over with a jerk of his head.

I get up reluctantly, then join him on his blanket.

"What's up?" I say.

"Why are you talking to Ali?" he demands.

"Uh...because she's cool?"

"You know she used to dance at Exotica."

"Yeah, she mentioned that."

"That's where I met her."

"Good for you," I say, trying to sound sincere. The idea of Levi hitting on Ali by shoving dollar bills in her thong is not at all romantic to me.

"I saw your mom there, too," Levi says. "Before she quit."

My skin prickles with anger and disgust.

I don't give a shit that my mom used to strip or whatever else she got into. That's her choice. What I fucking despise is how everyone tries to use it as a weapon against me—to shame me and degrade me.

"She was really hot," Levi says, an ugly smile on his face. "Hotter than you."

"I know that."

Everybody always said how beautiful my mom was. She wanted to be an actress when she was young. She wanted to go down in history as one of those timeless faces, like Sophia Loren or Ava Gardner.

Instead, she got pregnant with me.

I'm not angry at her for abandoning me. She was sixteen years old when she had me—way younger than I am now. Younger than Vic, even. Just a kid.

I'm mad because she never came back. I have to hear about her from shitheads like Levi. I have to know she's still here in Chicago. I have to wonder if she's okay. And I have to wonder why she doesn't ever call me anymore. Is she ashamed? Is it painful for her? Or does she just not care?

Levi is still smiling at me in that cruel way.

Why do men enjoy hurting women? Why does he feel good making me feel low?

"I have your money." I hand him the wad of bills Schultz gave me.

"Good." Levi passes the money to Sione. "I'm glad to see we're not gonna have a problem."

Not right this second anyway.

"You have any Ex left?" Levi asks.

"A little."

"Let me see it."

I take the baggy out of my pocket—the one Schultz told me to keep in case I needed it. There are about twelve pills inside.

"Good." Levi nods again. "Take it."

I stare at him.

"Take it where?" I say stupidly.

Levi sits up a little straighter, the smile falling off his face. His eyes are boring into mine. His pupils are tiny dark pinpricks in the expanse of his pale blue irises.

"Take one. Right now."

I try to swallow, my mouth dry. "Why?"

"Because I don't fucking trust you."

My heart is beating fast, but my breathing is slow. I've never taken a single drug in my life besides a few puffs of weed. Mostly because I was trying to be responsible. But also because this stuff really freaks me out. I don't like not being in control of myself. Not to mention, I have no idea where Levi gets it. There could be rat poison in here for all I know.

"I'm not into Molly," I say weakly.

"I don't give a *fuck* what you like," Levi hisses. "Take one right now, or you'll fucking regret it."

I cast a swift glance around at the group. Nobody's looking at me. Nobody's coming to my rescue. Patricia is in conversation with Ali. Beatrice is dancing with the other girls. The only person paying any attention to me at all is Sione, who stands a few feet away, silently keeping watch in case Levi needs him. He's not going to be any help to me—he'd probably shove this whole baggy down my throat if Levi gave the order.

"Okay..." I say hesitantly.

I take out one yellow pill. It's hard and chalky, like an aspirin.

I put it on my tongue before washing it down with the dregs of my Heineken.

"Open your mouth," Levi whispers.

I open my mouth and stick out my tongue, showing that I swallowed it.

Levi laughs, breaking the tension. "All right," he says. "Go have some fun."

I try to laugh, too, but I can't even smile properly. I get up from the blanket, then stumble away from him.

Oh shit, oh shit.

I have no idea what's about to happen to me. I really don't know anything about Molly, which is ironic since I'm supposed to be one of Levi's army of dealers. How long does it take to kick in? Can I go hide somewhere and puke it up before anything happens?

I'm already feeling anxious and sweaty, but I don't know if that's from the drug or just nerves.

Jesus, why do people do this for fun?

I'm freaking the fuck out.

Patricia grabs my arm. "Hey! What's wrong?"

"Nothing. I just…uh, can I talk to you for a second?"

"Sure. What do you—"

I was going to ask Patricia what the hell I should do. But at that moment I'm distracted by the sight of Bella Page joining Grisha and his friends on the opposite side of the fire. Grisha slings his arm around Bella's shoulder as soon as he sees her, apparently not aware she was out on a date with Nero the other day.

I'm not interested in ratting her out. Actually, there's just one thing I want from Bella.

"Never mind," I say to Patricia. "Let's go talk to Bella."

Patricia stares at me like I've lost my mind. "What? Why would we want to do that?"

"Just humor me, okay?"

Sighing, Patricia trudges across the sand with me, toward the little knot of people.

"Hey! It's Mario Andretti!" Grisha says as we approach. He laughs and holds out his fist to me for a bump, apparently not holding any grudge about my race against Bella.

Bella is less pleased. She frowns at me, probably thinking she can't go one damn place in this city without seeing me.

Well, she's right. I'm going to be all up in her face until I get what I want.

"Hey, Bella!" I say, with false friendliness. "How was your lunch the other day?"

Her eyes get big, and her cheeks flush, as she realizes I could blow up her relationship with Grisha if I wanted to.

"It was great," she says, forced to be civil.

"What lunch?" Grisha asks.

"Bella and I bumped into each other outside her dad's office," I say cheerfully. "I was eating at River Roast."

"Love that place," Grisha says. Turning to Bella, he says, "You should have invited me!"

"I didn't think you'd want to meet my dad just yet," Bella says awkwardly.

"Parents love me." Grisha grins. "I'm very charming."

"My father doesn't like anybody," Bella says seriously. Her face looks sad, like that includes herself.

Not allowing myself to feel pity for her, I reach behind her and twine my fingers in a couple of strands of her hair. With a quick tug, I pull them out, making Bella yelp and spin around like a bee stung her.

"Ouch!" she yelps. "What the hell?"

"Sorry," I say vaguely. "I thought there was a hair on your shirt. Guess it was still attached."

Bella narrows her eyes at me, silently fuming. She knows I'm fucking with her, but she can't say anything in case I wreck her stupid lunch story.

I tuck the hairs into my pocket, hoping I got enough of them to serve my purpose and that they won't be ruined by sitting in the pocket of a romper for a few hours. I really don't know how all this forensic stuff works. I could ask Schultz if he weren't such a dick.

At that moment, the strangest thing happens to me.

I'm hit with a wave of warmth and relaxation.

The night suddenly seems ten times prettier than it was before. The movement of the water lapping against the shore looks peaceful and rhythmic. I hear every crackle of the fire behind me. The reflected light looks beautiful on the faces of the people around me. Their eyes are sparkling, and their teeth shine brightly every time they smile.

I feel a rush of love for all these people, even the ones I

barely know. I look at Patricia, and I think about how much I admire her—she's strong and intelligent and hardworking. It was incredibly kind of her to dress me up so nicely tonight, to let me borrow her clothes. I wish I would have known her better in high school.

Then I look at Bella, and I think she really is beautiful. I didn't want to admit it before, but there are some similarities between her face and my brother's. Her big blue eyes can be sad and vulnerable just like Vic's. Those gorgeous, thick lashes are just the same. They remind me of when Vic was little and achingly sweet. They make me feel nostalgic and wistful.

Bella's always been awful to me, but in this moment, I finally see her behavior as a reflection of her own pain, directed at me but not actually having anything to do with me—not really. Once I can separate those two things, it doesn't hurt me anymore. It just makes me realize how badly she must be hurting inside, to lash out like that all the time.

I feel a compulsion to share that thought with her. To be totally honest.

"Bella," I say. "I wish you and I could be friends. I don't think we're actually that different. You're smart and determined. And I think you've been through some rough shit, the same as me. I bet we have a lot in common."

"What the hell are you talking about?" Bella says with a horrified expression.

Her disgust at the idea of us being anything like each other makes me giggle. I'm drifting in a cloud of peacefulness. She can't upset me at all.

"I was jealous of you…" I say to her. "You have money and friends. But your dad sucks. And I've got a great dad…but he's really sick. I guess I just realized everybody has something tormenting them…"

Bella is speechless. I can tell she's trying to figure out if this is some new strategy on my part, some new way to get at her. Every interaction we've ever had is combative, so she doesn't know how to process this at all.

Patricia grabs my arm and pulls me away from Bella. "Dude, what is up with you?"

I laugh. It's funny because even though Patricia's pulling on my arm kind of hard, it actually feels good…

I try squeezing her arm, and that feels good, too, the way my fingers kind of sink into her skin.

"What are you doing?" Patricia says.

I laugh even harder at the baffled expression on her face.

I'm having so much fun. I don't think I've ever actually had fun at a party before. It's always been shades of awkwardness. Now I couldn't feel awkward if I tried. I don't care whatsoever about what happens. I'm just peaceful and interested in everything.

Everything looks lovely. Ali is still blowing bubbles from atop the cooler, like a stream of translucent gems floating away on the wind.

I follow the bubbles along until my eye is drawn to the parking lot, where Nero's Mustang is just pulling in.

"Look!" I say to Patricia happily. "Nero's here!"

I start marching off toward his car.

"Uh, I don't think you should go talk to Nero right now…"

"I'm fine!" I tell her blithely.

I'm hurrying across the sand toward Nero's car. It's hard to hurry because my whole body feels limp and relaxed, in a dreamlike state.

Nero is just stepping out of the vehicle. His silhouette stands out starkly against the streetlights behind him. I see his tall frame. Broad shoulders, strong legs in his tight jeans. He turns to the side, and I see his thighs flexing and notice the curve of his ass, which is as lean and powerful as the rest of him.

A surge of lust almost knocks me off my feet.

I'm aware on some level that the pill Levi made me take has kicked in. But here's the thing—the Molly is not manufacturing emotions where none existed before. Instead, it's like a key, turning the locks on every door inside my brain. It's flinging those doors wide open, letting everything I shut away come pouring out all at once.

When I walk up to Nero, it's with the intention of throwing myself on him. I need him. Desperately. If I don't get him, I'll die.

He catches sight of me, and he turns to face me fully. He runs his hand through his hair to push it back from his face. This gesture seems to take an endless amount of time. I see the ink-black strands of hair sweeping through his fingers, some escaping to fall over his eyes again. I see his straight dark brows drawing together. Those steel-gray eyes focus on me. He bites his full bottom lip and releases it, a movement both uneasy and infinitely sexual.

"I was hoping you'd be here," I say.

I would usually never say anything so vulnerable. But with whatever the fuck this is coursing through my veins, I've lost the ability to hide. I'm compelled to be honest.

"Yeah?" Nero says, surprised.

"Yes. That's why I came."

"I thought you were mad at me. Because I was with Bella."

"It hurt my feelings for a minute," I admit. "But I know why you were at the bank."

He's staring at me, trying to figure out what the hell is going on. "Are you...going to tell anyone?"

"No," I say simply.

"Why not?"

"Because I don't give a shit what you do. I only care...how you feel about me."

Nero frowns. "What's going on with you?"

"Levi made me take Molly."

He lets out a surprised snort, like he thinks I might be joking. "Are you serious?"

"Yeah."

"Are you okay?" he says. "Let me look at you." He puts his hand on the side of my face and tilts up my chin so he can look in my eyes.

The moment his fingers touch my face, I feel an intense swoop of pleasure, like his fingertips are stroking down raw nerve. It's a rush of warmth and sensuality that seems to leave visible sparks in its path.

"Oh, yeah," he says, looking into my dilated pupils. "You're high as fuck."

He leans into his car before pulling out a bottle of water. "You better drink this."

He twists off the cap. I drink down half the bottle. It tastes delicious and refreshing, even though it's not cold.

"You want me to take you home?"

"No," I say dreamily. "It makes me sad being at home. I want to spend time with my dad, but also I want to cry every time I see him. I can't stand it."

"What's wrong with your dad?" Nero asks sharply.

"Lung cancer."

"Oh." There's an uneasy mix of anger and sympathy in his voice. "I didn't know that."

He seems to be searching for what to say or what to do. I can tell he feels uncomfortable and helpless, and that makes him even angrier.

Usually, that would make me feel awkward, too, and one of us would say something stupid that would offend the other person. But right now, nothing can offend me. I feel like I'm seeing things in a completely different way. I understand Nero, and I understand myself.

"Do you want to go for a walk or something?" Nero says desperately.

"Yeah. I would."

We walk along the lakeshore, away from the bonfire. We're walking right along the waterline on the wet sand. I've taken off my sandals, and Nero left his shoes behind, so the cold water laps against our bare feet. For me, this feels utterly incredible. Nero doesn't seem to mind it either.

For once in my life, I'm talking openly and freely without holding anything back. I'm telling Nero absolutely everything. About my dad and my brother. About the fact I'm flat fucking broke and have no idea how I'm going to pay for Vic's school or my dad's treatment.

I even tell him about my mom. How I miss her so badly. And then I hate myself for missing her because I know I shouldn't care when she obviously doesn't give a fuck about me. And how I feel guilty for having that hole in my heart when my dad has always tried to make our family complete, with or without her.

We've walked far enough from the fire and the city lights that it's almost completely dark. I can't really see Nero's face anymore. That removes the last shred of reserve. I feel safe telling him anything.

We sit on the sand, and I rest my back against his body to keep warm.

"If I lose my dad, I won't have anything," I tell Nero. "He's the only person who ever tried to take care of me. I'll have to help Vic all on my own. And I'm not that great of a sister. I don't even have my own life figured out, so how the fuck can I tell Vic what he should do?"

Nero is quiet for a long time. Long enough that I think I've said too much.

Then, finally, he says, "My mom got sick when I was little. My father thought it was a flu. She was up in their bedroom. He told us all to leave her alone and let her rest. I didn't listen, though. I wanted to show her a pocketknife my uncle gave me. So I snuck in there."

I can feel his heart beating hard against my back. I'm silent, picturing Nero as a boy, already too handsome in a way that would be unusual and almost frightening in a child.

"I went up to her room. She was lying in bed. Very pale, not breathing normally. I felt…afraid. I thought I should leave. But she saw me and motioned for me to come over to her. She had…very pretty hands. She was a concert pianist."

He swallows hard, his throat making a clicking sound.

"I lay down on the pillow by hers. She tried to brush my hair with her fingers. Which she did all the time. But this time, she couldn't seem to move her hand right, and her fingers got tangled. I pushed her hand away because I was scared. Her hand was clammy, and her breath smelled like metal."

His arms are tightening around me, squeezing me too hard. I don't say anything to interrupt him.

"I kept thinking I should go get my father. But I knew I'd be in trouble for waking her up when she was supposed to be sleeping. Then, all of a sudden, she started choking. Not out loud, though. Silently. I was right there, so I could see her face. Her mouth was open, without any sound coming out. Her body was jerking. I kept thinking I had to yell for my father, had to get up and run down and grab him. But I was frozen in place. I couldn't move. I couldn't even shut my eyes. I was just staring into her face while the blood vessels burst in her eyes. I didn't understand what was happening, that she was suffocating. She looked possessed, with the whites of her eyes all bloody. And then her eyes went flat and glassy, and I still didn't move. I couldn't speak or make the tiniest sound. I just watched and let it happen. I let my mother die."

I turn around to face Nero, to see his face the best I can.

In the darkness, I can only see the gray gleam of his eyes and the wetness on his cheeks.

I have to feel my way to kiss him. I kiss him softly, tasting the salt on his lips.

"That wasn't your fault." I kiss him again. And then I repeat, "That wasn't your fault, Nero."

I'm hoping that after all the things I told him tonight, with total honesty, he'll know I'm telling the truth right now.

For a moment he seems frozen, unable to respond to me.

Then he kisses me back, deeply and intensely.

All my senses are heightened to a fever pitch. I can feel his lashes tickling my cheek, his tongue tangled with mine, his fingers thrust in my hair.

I'm cold because the heat of the day is finally leeching away. I pull Nero's shirt over his head so I can run my hands over his warm flesh. I kiss his neck. I run my tongue down his throat, all the way down his chest.

I can taste the salt on his skin. It seems to burst against my tongue with visible sparks. The smoothness of his skin is incredible—it would almost be like a girl's, except there's nothing feminine about Nero. His energy is wild, angry, vengeful, animalistic...but never feminine.

Nero comes alive in response. He pulls down the top of my romper and presses his bare chest against mine, holding me tight. Then he runs his hands over my breasts, feeling their shape without really being able to see them, as if he were blind.

"Fucking hell, Camille," he groans. "Your body is unreal."

I laugh. I can't help it. "You thought I was a boy under the coveralls?"

"No. I saw you that day in the garage. I knew you were hiding the most gorgeous fucking breasts imaginable."

He takes them in his mouth, flicking the nipples with his tongue until they harden to aching points of flesh. He sucks on them in turn, going back and forth between them as the sensation builds and builds in waves.

Now I realize why MDMA is called *Ecstasy*. The heightening of physical pleasure is acute and extreme. Even the smallest things become insanely pleasurable—Nero's hand sliding down the outside of my arm or his fingers twining in mine. Things that would already be sexual become near orgasmic. I want him to suck on my breasts forever. It is so achingly good that all I can do is moan and writhe against him, grabbing the back of his head and pressing his face harder into my breasts.

Nero pulls the romper all the way down so I'm completely naked. Then he grabs me by the hips and buries his face in my pussy.

I'm not a virgin. I've hooked up with a couple of guys before. But what I'm learning is that Nero possesses skills on an entirely different level. I thought girls threw themselves at him for aesthetic reasons. What I didn't know is that he's a master of sex. It's no wonder women turn into desperate Ophelias when he moves on—after five minutes of this, I think I'm completely addicted. I don't know how I'll live without it.

He's using his fingers, lips, and tongue in ways I never imagined. He's gentle yet intent. Seeking out all my most sensitive areas, then teasing and tormenting them until I could almost sob with pleasure. He's licking my clit, the folds of my pussy, and even my ass.

When he ventures down there, I try to squirm away, but he holds me pinned with those big strong hands, forcing me to let him put his tongue absolutely everywhere he wants to go. And that part of my body I never even imagined as sexual suddenly seems to be made of a thousand pleasure receptors, just waiting for the right kind of touch. It's kinky and naughty and outrageously intimate.

He moves his tongue back up to my clit, using his fingers to apply just the slightest amount of pressure to my ass. He's not penetrating me with his finger, just rubbing his thumb over that tight little bud, which has become as slick and wet as the rest of me. It intensifies all the other sensations, creating pleasure in an entirely new way.

He slides two fingers into my pussy, increasing the pressure of his tongue against my clit. I'm rolling my hips against his fingers and tongue, so wildly stimulated that I barely even have the breath to moan anymore.

I look up into the dark sky and see much more than stars—I see streaks of light like a meteor shower. It's like rain made of lightning. I don't know if it's real or imagined, and I can't ask Nero because he's more than busy. All I know is that the light seems to rush across the sky as an orgasm finally explodes inside me. It's an arc of bright white brilliance, so dazzling and intense that I could cry.

My legs are shaking; my whole body is shaking so hard that my teeth chatter.

"Oh my god," I whisper. "What the fuck did you do to me...?"

Nero is pulling my clothes back on my body, trying to find my sandals in the dark.

He gets me entirely dressed again before I think to say, "Don't you want to keep going?"

"Of course I do," he growls. "My cock's gonna rip through my pants. But I'm not doing anything else until you're sober."

"I'm totally lucid!"

"That's not the same thing as sober."

I try to kiss him again, but he stops me.

"Camille," he says. "I want you. But not...not like I usually do. Not to just fuck and get off."

Before, I would have thought that was an excuse. But I felt the way he kissed me, the way he touched my body. I know Nero wants me as badly as I want him.

He's exercising self-control. Something I couldn't do to save my life right now.

"I'm going to take you home. Tomorrow...if you want to call me..."

"I do," I say.

"We'll see how you feel in the morning."

I'm too limp to argue.

He half walks, half carries me back to his car.

I let him take me home, my body and brain still flushed with pleasure.

CHAPTER 18
NERO

Dropping Camille off back at her house is the hardest thing I've ever had to do.

I've almost never turned down sex. And definitely not from somebody I actually liked. But I never really liked anyone before.

It scares me.

I know how sex can twist emotions. How it causes pain and conflict.

For the first time, I actually feel a connection to a woman. I'm terrified that I'm going to fuck it up by acting like I always do. Terrified that I'll destroy this fragile thing between us, like I destroy everything else.

God, Camille looks stunning. She's dressed up in this cute little outfit that I know she must have put on for me. The fact she did something so outside the norm, when she's usually so practical and stubborn...it pricks at me.

And on top of that, it really suits her. The blue looks beautiful against her skin. She's got this wild mane of curls, her cheeks are flushed, her lips are swollen, and her eyes look bigger and darker than ever with her pupils dilated like a cat's.

She's lolling back against my car door, exposing her smooth brown throat and the tops of those luscious breasts. Fucking hell, I wish I could have seen them in the light.

But it's no good thinking about that now. My cock is still raging inside my jeans, painfully bent down my pant leg against my thigh, throbbing continually.

God, the taste of her pussy…I can still smell her on my fingers and face. It's intoxicating. I want more.

No. Fucking no.

I'm taking her home, and I'm not taking advantage of her while she's rolling.

Camille rests her hand on mine, where I'm holding the gearshift.

She looks at me with those liquid dark eyes. "I meant everything I said."

My chest feels tight. "Me, too."

I can't believe I told her about my mother. I've never told anybody that. No one knows it. Not my brothers or sister. Not even my father.

After my mother died, I lay there staring at her for almost an hour. Then, finally, I touched her hand. It wasn't sweaty anymore. It was cool and dry.

That seemed to break the spell. I rolled off the bed and ran out of the room. I ran up to the attic and hid there until Dante finally found me. He said Papa had to take our mother to the hospital. But I could see from the expression on his face that Dante already knew she was dead. They just didn't know I'd seen it. That I watched it happen. And had done nothing to help.

I never told anyone because I was so ashamed. I know I was a kid. But I was still a fucking coward.

I hated myself for that. Then hating me turned into hating everything and everyone.

But I don't hate Camille.

I respected her when she was tough and wouldn't give in to anyone.

And now I feel confused and almost humbled that after all this time, when she finally opened up to somebody…it was me.

I don't deserve it. I'm not kind. I'm not understanding.

But…I want to deserve it. I want to be a haven for her. Even if I don't exactly know how to do that.

"I have to tell you something else," Camille says.

"What is it?"

"There's a cop who's been hassling me. He's making me sell Molly for Levi."

"What?"

"Yeah. He caught my brother doing it, and to keep Vic out of trouble, I said I'd work for him as a CI."

"Is his name Schultz?"

"Yeah," she says. "Logan Schultz."

I can feel that anger rising inside me again. I have to hold my body stiff so my hands don't shake.

Camille can feel it anyway, with her hand resting over mine. She looks at me with a frightened expression. "I'm sorry," she says.

I am angry, but not for the reason she thinks.

I'm furious that one more person is piling onto Camille, bending her and bending her far past the point where anyone else would break.

I don't give a fuck that some ambitious cop wants to take a shot at me. But he has no business messing with Camille. The thought of him waiting outside her shop like he waited outside the Brass Anchor, with that stupid smirk on his face…

It makes me want to track him down and put a knife in his heart.

"Did you tell him anything?" I ask Camille.

"A few things about Levi."

That's not good. If Levi finds out what Camille is doing, he's violent and reckless enough to try to hurt her.

I'll fucking kill him, too, if he even thinks about it.

"I didn't tell him anything about you!" Camille hastens to assure me.

"I don't care about that. I'm not scared of Schultz. I'll put him in the ground if he threatens you."

Camille blanches. "I don't want you to kill anyone for me. I'm serious, Nero. I don't want anyone to get hurt because of me."

I look her in the eyes. "Then how can we be together? I can change some things about myself. But not that."

A shiver runs through her. I don't know if it's the idea of us being together as a couple or if she's disturbed by what she knows about me. That I'll use violence when I have to, without hesitation.

We've reached Axel Auto. I pull up to the curb before turning off the engine.

"Do you want me to take you up to the door?" I ask her.

She shakes her head. "I can make it. I'm back to normal now, I think."

"I'll call you tomorrow," I tell her.

She leans forward and kisses me softly on the lips before getting out of the car.

I watch Camille go inside her shop, but I don't go home myself.

If Schultz is leaning on Camille, he's a bigger problem than I thought. I need to look into him again but from a different angle this time. I want to know about Matthew Schultz.

I spend the rest of the night driving around, visiting old friends. People forty and older, who lived in the South Shore neighborhood in 2005, when Schultz Senior was an officer.

I want to know who shot him that night.

Nobody rolls up on an off-duty cop and puts a bullet in his head by accident. That was no carjacking gone awry.

Not to mention very few family men with a wife and kid at home are driving around at 1:30 a.m. Not by Rosenblum Park. I'm expecting to discover a mistress, a gambling habit, a corruption scheme. Schultz Senior had an enemy—I want to know who it was.

I talk to Jeremy Porter, an old-timer who owns a bodega on the corner of Seventy-Sixth and Chappel, right by the park. He says he remembers the night the shooting happened because he was running his shop, and he heard the gunshots and the sirens after. But he says he didn't see anything.

"The news article said there was security footage," I tell him. "Did that come from your shop?"

He shakes his head. "Nah. You couldn't see a thing from here. I didn't have cameras back then anyway."

"Where do you think the footage came from?"

He shrugs. "Mighta been from the funeral home on Jeffrey. But that's gone now."

I check with the Chinese Kitchen sitting next to where the funeral home used to be. The owner doesn't know anything about it, and he doesn't want to talk to me.

"I don't want trouble," he tells me. "I'm closing up for the night. Don't come back here."

In the end, it's August Bruce who gives me my lead. He owns a pub in South Shore, not close to the park but still in the neighborhood.

He's about sixty years old, with a bulldog jaw and Popeye arms. He offers me a drink on the house, even though I know he's about the cheapest motherfucker alive. He likes Papa, so he's trying to be hospitable.

I take the beer, ignoring the dusty bottle and the filthy rag Bruce is using to wipe down the bar.

"Yeah, I knew Schultz," he says. He lights a hand-rolled cigarette, ignoring the fact he's not supposed to be smoking inside his own pub. It smells like he does that a lot in here.

"How'd you know him?"

"His sister married my nephew. Plus, he grew up on the South Side. Baseball star. Won all-state competitions as a pitcher. Got drafted by South Bend but never got called up. So everybody knew him in the neighborhood."

"Then he became a cop."

"That's right." Bruce chuckles. "People only know two kinds of careers here. Crime, or catching criminals. You choose a team, just like sandlot."

"But he was a dirty cop."

Bruce frowns, taking a puff off his cigarette, then picking a piece of tobacco off his tongue. "Who told you that?"

"Somebody capped him. That doesn't happen by accident. Plus, law of averages…"

Bruce shakes his head. "Schultz was as clean as they come. Actual hero type."

"You sure?"

"As much as you can know anybody."

"Who shot him, then? Somebody he locked up? Somebody he was investigating?"

"Could be." Bruce shrugs. "Or…"

I wait, letting him enjoy the suspense.

"You know who hates a hero cop?" Bruce says, squinting at me. "A dirty cop."

"Is that based off fact or just a guess?"

Bruce shrugs his heavy shoulders. "Couple of cops got there pretty quick. Funny they were running a traffic stop at one thirty a.m. in South Shore. Never seen that in all the time I lived here."

I think that over.

Then I stand and clap Bruce on the shoulder. "Thanks. You raise some interesting questions."

"Yeah, well be careful who else you raise those questions to," Bruce says. "Nobody likes digging up old garbage."

No, they don't.

But I never really gave a fuck what people like.

CHAPTER 19
CAMILLE

WHEN I WAKE UP IN THE MORNING, THE SUN SEEMS HORRENDOUSLY bright and my head is pounding. I stumble into the kitchen, still wearing Patricia's romper, and pour myself a giant tumbler of water from the kitchen sink. I gulp it down, feeling like a raisin dried out in the sun.

I drink and drink until my belly is sloshing. Then I set the cup down, wincing at the loud clink it makes on the counter.

I remember that line from the Jay-Z song—*MDMA got you feelin' like a champion...*

Well, the morning after, it has me feeling like a boxer who took a hundred hits to the face and fell right out of the ring.

And that's before I remember how I verbally vomited every single thought in my head to Nero Gallo.

I'm blushing redder than a Ferrari just thinking about it. I told him everything. Every last secret I had. Including the fact I'm completely infatuated with him.

But...it's not a total disaster.

Because Nero told me something, too. I haven't forgotten about it—he told me what happened to his mother. I get the feeling that's not something he shares with a lot of people.

And then...oh, I definitely remember what happened after that.

Only the most brain-bending, earth-shattering, back-breaking orgasm of my life. An orgasm that probably should be illegal because there's no way something that feels that good can be handed out willy-nilly. It's too much for a human being to handle.

Oh, yes, I remember every second of that encounter. It's seared into my brain forever.

And yet we didn't have sex after. Nero drove me home instead.

I almost think he was trying to be a gentleman. Though I must still be high to believe that. Because Nero is about the furthest thing from a gentleman I've ever encountered. Or at least he was…until last night.

This is too much of a conundrum for my throbbing brain to ponder. I've got something entirely different to worry about. Five blond hairs tucked in the pocket of my romper. They're still there—a little sandy but relatively unharmed.

I tuck them into an envelope before googling the closest place to get a paternity test. I find a place called Fastest Labs, which sounds like exactly what I'm looking for. *Immediate and Comprehensive Testing Services—Walk-Ins Welcome!* Perfect.

I drive over there with my envelope of stolen DNA clutched in my sweaty little fist.

I haven't showered or changed my clothes or washed the makeup off my face from the night before, so I'm looking significantly less cute than I did when Patricia finished working her magic on me. But I don't give a damn. I fit right in with the rest of the people waiting for their mandatory drug and alcohol testing.

I give the envelope to a female technician. She dons a pair of plastic gloves, then uses a pair of tweezers to grab the hairs out of the envelope before holding them up under the bright fluorescent light and squinting.

"We usually want seven to ten hairs," she says. "But you've got some decent follicles attached. This might work."

"I've got a toothbrush from the other subject."

I pass her Vic's toothbrush in a plastic baggie. I could have gotten a swab from inside his mouth, but I didn't really want to tell him what I was doing any more than I told Bella. Vic is insistent that he doesn't care about his biological father. And maybe he really doesn't want to know. But he needs money for school. We're too poor to be prideful.

"I want to know the familial relationship," I tell the technician. "If there is one."

"No problem," she says. "It'll take a couple of hours. Assuming we can gather enough DNA to run through the system."

"That's fine. I'll wait."

I snag a chair in the waiting room, one positioned in the corner so I can lean my head against the wall and try to take a nap. Several times I nod off, only to be jerked awake again when the receptionist calls someone's name at about ten times the volume necessary for the tiny space.

At least they have a water cooler. I drink about eight more cups of water, then visit the bathroom several times.

"You part fish?" an old man teases me, after my fifth or sixth drink.

"I wish," I groan. "Then I wouldn't be able to hear Nurse Ratched over there."

"NAGORSKI!" the receptionist bellows at the top of her lungs, making the windows rattle.

"That's the benefit of going deaf," the old man says serenely. "I just turn down my hearing aid."

It takes another hour for the receptionist to shout, "RIVERA!"

As soon as she does, I jump up to pay my $149 fee and receive my results.

I'm out of cash, so I have to put the charge on a credit card. It takes a couple of tries to find one that's not already maxed out.

"You should really pay those off," the receptionist tells me, as my Mastercard finally allows the charge. "Carrying a balance is bad for your credit score."

"It's this fun game between me and the bank. I like to keep them guessing."

She narrows her eyes at me. "Financial accountability is nothing to joke about, young lady."

"You're right." I snatch the envelope of results out of her hand. "I'll pay off those cards the moment I win the lottery."

I take the envelope outside to open it.

My hand is shaking a little, and I feel a sense of dread.

I went to all this trouble to prove my theory, but the truth is, I'd rather be wrong. For the past fifteen years, Vic has belonged to me and my dad, nobody else. He was the center of our world. We loved him like crazy. My dad built him a Transformers Halloween costume that really could transform from a robot to a fire truck. I made his lunch every day for school and drew little cartoons on the bag to make him laugh. We planned his birthday parties, his Christmas presents. We all went to Cubs games together—sitting in the shittiest seats, but it didn't matter because we were the perfect little family unit. Happy with our nosebleed seats and our hot dogs.

I don't know why I ever thought it was a good idea to fuck that up.

Except my dad and I are sinking. I can't bear to drag Vic down with us. If we can't give him the future he deserves, then somebody else has to do it.

So I rip open the envelope and pull out the results.

It takes me a minute to understand what I'm looking at.

Subject 1: Victor Rivera.
Subject 2: Unknown Female.
21.6% shared, 29 segments.
Possible Relationships: Uncle/Niece, Aunt/Nephew, Grandfather/
   Granddaughter, Grandmother/Grandson, Half Siblings.

Right. The test can't tell the age of the subjects, so it's just guessing how they might be related. But I know Victor and Bella. Bella's not his aunt or his grandmother. Which means...she's definitely his half sister.

I let out a long sigh. I don't know whether to be relieved or deeply unhappy.

I think I'm leaning toward the latter.

You could tear it up right now. Throw it in the trash. Never tell anybody.

I could do that. But I'd be doing it for me. Not for Vic.

I give myself five minutes to feel a sense of loss. Then I stuff the paper back into the envelope and square my shoulders.

I'm going home to take a shower. Then I'm going to track down Raymond Page. I'm going to make him listen to me this time—even if I have to stuff that envelope right down his throat.

I get back to Alliance Bank just in time for Raymond's lunch break.

This time I'm a little smarter. I cleaned myself up, putting on the one nice dress I own—it's black, and I wore it to my grandma's funeral, but it helps me fit in a little better in this neighborhood. I wait outside the bank, then follow Raymond to his restaurant of choice, staying back a good half block so he won't catch sight of me.

He leaves the building at almost exactly the same time as before, with a different employee by his side this time—a pudgy guy with glasses who keeps trying to read information to Raymond out of a folder while simultaneously trying to match Raymond's long stride, which forces him to jog alongside his boss.

Raymond takes no account of the pedestrians in his path. He plows straight ahead, trusting the self-preservation of everybody else who has to jump out of his way.

He enters a fancy-looking seafood place, La Mer. I watch through the window while the hostesses practically fall all over themselves to greet and seat him.

When I enter, they give me a much less friendly "can I help you?"

"I'm here with Uncle Ray," I say, pointing in the direction that Page disappeared.

"Oh," one of the girls says. "I'll take you to the table."

"That's okay." I push past her. "I want to surprise him."

As I sneak up to Raymond's table, I see the pudgy guy take a quick sip of his water, then hurry over to the bathroom.

Perfect.

I slip into the booth opposite Page. He barely glances up at first, thinking it's just his buddy back already. Then he sees me sitting across from him, and his expression changes from mild surprise to pure fury.

"You'd better have an *extremely* good reason for bothering me again," he hisses.

"You didn't bother to ask what I wanted the first time."

"I don't give a damn what you want." His dark eyes are the only striking feature on an otherwise craggy face. The lashes that are so pretty on Vic are utterly disturbing on Raymond. They make him look like a creepy doll—the kind that would sit on a shelf in a horror movie, then come alive at night to stab you.

I can't let him intimidate me. I'm here for Vic.

"Maybe your wife would be interested in what I have to say," I remark. "Unless she's okay with you cheating on her."

Raymond doesn't like that at all.

His hand whips across the table, seizing me by the wrist.

"You think you can threaten me? Do you have any *fucking* clue who I am?"

I refuse to wince, no matter how hard he tries to twist my arm. "I know exactly who you are. That's why I'm here."

With my free hand, I pull the envelope out of my pocket and slide it across the table toward him. I've already scanned the test results in case he tries to tear it up or something.

"What the fuck is this?" Raymond says.

Without waiting for my answer, he pulls out the paper and reads it in a glance.

I covered over Vic's name with a black Sharpie, but the rest of the information is there.

"Explain," Raymond says curtly.

"You have a son," I tell him. "I compared his DNA with Bella's."

I see his eyes flick up quickly from the page, then back down again. It's hard to read his expression. He's angry, obviously. But he lets go of my wrist, reading more closely.

I wonder if he's actually pleased at the idea?

Bella is his only child as far as I know. He doesn't seem to give much of a shit about her. Maybe he always wanted a boy?

"Who is this *supposed* son?" he says.

I hesitate. I was going to tell him. But now I'm realizing I could be creating a dangerous situation for Vic. I don't know Page at all. Except that he's connected to a whole bunch of criminals, and he himself isn't afraid to break the law.

"I'm not going to tell you that right now."

"Why not?"

"Because I want to know your intentions first."

Raymond lets out a barking laugh. "My *intentions?*"

"That's right."

Raymond's colleague has returned to the table. He's a short tubby guy with a carefully trimmed beard and an expensive suit that still doesn't fit him very well. His tinted glasses look like the kind Tony Stark wears but a lot less cool.

He stops short when he sees me occupying his seat. "Oh, hello…" he says awkwardly.

Without looking at him, Raymond says, "Go wash your hands again, Porter."

"Right." Porter turns on his heel and marches back to the bathrooms without a second glance.

"You've got your employees well trained," I say.

"You can't imagine what I could tell him to do." Raymond's tone is ice. "If I asked him to drag you out of this restaurant and throw you directly into oncoming traffic, I wouldn't even have to say 'please.'"

My skin is clammy. I desperately want to blink but won't let myself drop his stare for a second. Men like this feed off fear.

"Look," I say. "It's pretty clear that you don't like being inconvenienced. I won't waste your time. You got an escort pregnant, and now you've got a son. He has no interest in creating some big public scandal. Neither do I. I don't know what you'd owe in child support—probably some insane number. We're not greedy—I'm just asking for a one-time payment to make this disappear, permanently. Fifty thousand for your son's education. And you never have to hear from either of us ever again."

It's not much money. Page is wearing a watch that probably costs that much. Hell, his suit might, too.

Raymond seems to be thinking the same thing. He slowly folds the test results into a perfect rectangle, then slides it back into the envelope. He passes it across the table to me.

"What assurance do I have that you won't come back for more?"

"My word," I tell him.

He looks at my stern, steady expression.

Then he reaches into his breast pocket and pulls out a checkbook. He slips the cap off his pen—fancy, gold-tipped, engraved.

He writes out a check, rips it out of the book, and pushes it across the table to me. "That's what I'm willing to pay."

I pick it up. The check says *$0.00.*

"Not. One. Fucking. Cent." Raymond seethes. "If I ever see your face again, or this so-called spawn of mine, I'll introduce the pair of you to a colleague of mine who isn't nearly as friendly as Porter. I like to call him 'the Dentist.' He'll pull out every one of your teeth with pliers, down to the last molar. And I'm afraid he doesn't use anesthetic. We'll see how well you negotiate then, with a mouthful of gums. You have my *word* on that."

I set the check down on the table with trembling hands.

"No," Raymond spits. "Take it with you. As a reminder. If I hear one fucking whisper in this city about a bastard son…I don't think it will be hard to find you. And stay the fuck away from my daughter."

I stand from the table. I'm terrified that Raymond is going to get up, too, but he remains seated. He doesn't do anything to stop me as I stumble out of the restaurant.

CHAPTER 20
NERO

I was up till the early hours of the morning, tracking down info about Matthew Schultz, so I end up sleeping in much longer than usual. It's past noon when I'm finally woken by a knock on my door.

"What?" I groan, not bothering to lift my head from the pillow.

"There's someone at the door for you," Greta says.

"Who?"

"Come see for yourself," she says impatiently.

I roll out of bed—literally roll out of it, onto the floor. I'm only wearing boxer shorts, and I can feel my hair sticking up in all directions, but I don't particularly care. If it were somebody important, Greta would have given me a heads-up. It's probably just Aida—though god knows she wouldn't wait on the doorstep. She'd march right into my room if she felt like it.

Maybe it's Cal.

Greta has already stomped off without waiting for me. She hates when we sleep in. It's the Puritan in her. She likes to bang the pots and pans around in the kitchen when she thinks we're being lazy. Luckily, I was exhausted enough to sleep through it this morning.

I stumble down the rickety staircase, so narrow that Dante has to turn sideways every time he comes up. That's probably why he has his room on the main level. I can't stand having people creaking around over my head. I like to be as high up as possible, someplace with a view. Sort of like Camille's room.

Well...speak of the devil.

Camille Rivera is standing on my doorstep.

She looks somber and pale, wearing a black dress that doesn't really fit the last days of August. She flushes when she sees me, dropping her eyes to her shoes. I remember that I'm practically naked. I lean against the doorframe, standing close to her, because she's cute when she's nervous.

"You're up early," I say.

"It's two o'clock in the afternoon," Camille says, goaded into looking at me by her need to correct me. As her eyes run over my bare chest, she blushes harder than ever.

"Still," I growl, my voice husky with sleep. "I thought you'd be tired after the night you had."

Camille darts another look at me, then covers her face with her hands to hide the color. "Could you put a shirt on, please?"

"Why would I want to do that?"

"So I can talk to you without—"

"Without what?" I say, leaning even closer.

"I'm not looking till you're dressed," she says, her hand over her eyes.

Her lips look very tempting beneath the blindfold of her hand. I could lean over and kiss her right now, without warning.

But I don't want to tease Camille too much. I know she came here for a reason.

"All right, come on in," I tell her.

"In there?" she squeaks. "In your house?"

"Why not?"

"Who's home?" she asks nervously.

"Just Greta. You already met her."

Hesitantly, Camille follows me inside. I see her looking around at the ancient dark woodwork, the handblown lamps, the leaded windows with their panes of colored glass.

It's still a grand mansion, though it is extremely old. Most of the main features are just the same as when it was built: A complicated, asymmetrical shape. Steeply gabled roofs with gingerbread trim. Odd textures on the interior walls.

Some things we've added, like the huge underground garage, the gym, and the sauna.

The Gallos belong to this house, in a way you rarely see in America anymore. We were raised in it. Shaped by it. Old Town is our home and always will be. While other Mafia families moved to the trendy Gold Coast or farther north, we stayed right here, in the heart of our own people.

Camille can see that. She sees the photographs of the generations that came before. The furniture older than I am.

"How long have you lived here?" she asks, her eyes wide.

"Well, my great-grandfather built it in 1901, so...a pretty long fucking time."

Camille shakes her head in amazement. She's forgotten about making me get dressed. She seems shocked by this house that's got to be ten times the size of her little apartment. Maybe even bigger if you count the basement levels.

"I forgot how rich you are," she says dully.

"I thought girls like that," I say, trying to lighten the mood.

Camille shoots me a pained look, and I immediately regret my stupid comment. Why can I never think of the right thing to say to her? I always knew how to get what I wanted from women before. It was easy to manipulate them.

But I don't want to manipulate Camille.

I want us to be in that space we sometimes stumble into by accident, where we understand each other. Where everything is clear between us.

I can never seem to get there intentionally. The harder I try, the more I fuck it up.

"You look really nice," I say desperately. "But you know, I like the other way, too…"

"The coveralls?" Camille says, the ghost of a smile on her face.

"Yeah. I like those. Actually…you want to see something?"

"I guess…" Camille looks scared that I might be about to show her my gun collection or a room full of dead bodies.

"Come on." I grab her hand.

Her fingers link with mine. Her hands are small but strong. I like the little bits of grease in her knuckles. I have the same thing on my hands. If I were to lift her hand to my face and inhale, I know exactly how her skin would smell. Like diesel, soap, and vanilla.

I lead her through the kitchen, past Greta, who seems startled to see Camille actually inside the house.

"Hello again," Greta says.

"This is Camille," I tell her.

"I know. We met at the door."

"Greta's the one who raised me," I say to Camille.

"Don't you dare try to put that on me." Greta scowls at me. "You've never listened to one thing I said."

"I'm still your favorite." I grin.

As I lead Camille down to the garage, she asks me, "Is that true?"

"What?"

"Are you Greta's favorite?"

"No." I snort. "Not even close. It's Sebastian for sure."

"Who's your father's favorite?"

"Aida. Or Dante."

We've come to the bottom of the stairs. Camille looks up at me, her dark eyes searching my face.

"Does that bother you?"

I don't let myself actually think about the question before answering, "No. Why would it?" I pull her onward, flicking on the overhead lights.

Camille gasps. It's a sprawling space, low-ceilinged, supported by pillars. The cement floor is freshly painted, and each of the cars has its own berth. There are eight cars and two bikes. Two of the cars belong to Papa and one to Dante. The rest are all mine.

Camille runs around touching each of them in turn—the Scout, the 'Vette, the Jag, the Shelby. But she lingers longest by my absolute favorite: the Talbot-Lago Grand Sport. Still a work in progress, totally unable to drive. It's going to be fucking beautiful, though. My magnum opus.

"Where did you get it?" she whispers.

"I bought it at an auction in Germany. It only ever had one driver. This old man who bought it in '54. It sat in his barn for years. I had to get it shipped here by freight."

"Have you done all the work on it yourself?"

"Every last bit of it."

"God…" Camille moans. "Look at that body…"

The Grand Sport is all sleek, smooth lines—long like an American classic car, but with a posh European vibe. It's a bit like a Rolls-Royce and a Porsche mixed.

"I know," I say. "It's the only one like it—they sold the basic chassis, and then the bespoke bodywork was done by a custom coach builder."

"What color are you painting it?"

"It was black, originally."

"That's good…" she says. "But imagine it in oxblood red…"

"They never made it in that color." I laugh.

"I know. But they should have."

I never bring anybody down here. Even Dante barely ever comes in. Camille is the one person I know who loves old cars the way I do—like they're living things. I can tell she's dying to look under the hood, to get her hands on every bit of the engine. Usually, that would make me antsy and territorial, but I can't help enjoying it, watching her run around as eager as a kid.

"Ohhh!" Camille groans, looking at all my tools. "You

have everything in here. You did it, Nero. You finally made me jealous."

Her eyes are bright as jet, and her cheeks are full of color. Her lips and cheeks look very red next to the black dress.

"I thought I made you jealous once before," I say in a low voice. "When you saw me with Bella."

"I know you don't like her." Camille goes very still.

"But you were jealous anyway."

I take a step toward her, and she takes one back, so she's backed up against the hood of the Grand Sport. Her eyes flit down to my bare chest once more, remembering that I never did put on any clothes.

I run my hand through my hair, pushing it back from my face. I watch her eyes follow my hand, then run down my arm, down my bare torso, all the way to my boxer shorts. I know she can see the bulge of my cock through the thin material. Especially now that I'm starting to get aroused.

Camille licks her lips nervously.

I'm close enough that I can almost feel the warmth of her breath. The scent of gasoline is heavy in the air. It spikes my heart rate, though not as much as the scent of Camille herself.

In one motion, I wrap my hands around her waist and lift her so she's sitting on the hood of the car. I'm standing between her thighs, her face exactly level with mine. We're eye to eye, nose to nose.

"I don't ever want you to be jealous," I tell her. "There's nobody else, Camille. Nobody who ever made me feel like this."

She looks into my eyes, her lips trembling.

I don't know if she believes me.

I'm a lot of things but never a liar…

"We started something last night," I say. "Are you ready to finish it?"

In answer, Camille grabs my face between her hands and kisses me.

It's like she injected straight nitrous in my engine. My arousal cranks up 1000 percent in an instant. I shove her down on the hood, attacking her with my lips and hands. I'm licking her, kissing her, sucking her, all over her mouth and down her throat. I yank up the skirt of her dress and thrust my hand down the front of her panties, finding that hot, soaking-wet pussy. I sink my fingers inside her, making her moan into my mouth.

I hate that she has clothes on. I'm sick to death of getting bits and pieces of Camille, never all of her at once. The feel of her breasts in the dark, the taste of her pussy…it's not even close to enough.

I grab her panties, and I tear them apart, the fabric ripping like cotton candy under my fevered fingers.

My cock has already escaped from my boxer shorts. It's raging hard, demanding to be put inside her. All I have to do is grip the base of it and point it in the right direction.

I know I should get a condom. I've always used one before. I don't want kids or any other nasty surprises.

But I want to be with Camille fully and intimately. I don't want to fuck her with a barrier between us.

I want my first time to be with her. So I thrust inside her, into that warmth and wetness that grips every millimeter of my bare cock. The sensation is ten times stronger than I expect. My knees almost give way beneath me, just from that single thrust.

I'm eight inches deep into this woman who has invaded every fiber of my body, who is driving me absolutely fucking insane. I almost blow right then and there. It takes every shred of control to hold back.

Once I regain control, I start fucking her hard and fast, desperately and wildly. I can't seem to slow down. It's like street racing— I've got pure adrenaline pounding through my veins. All I want is more, more, more.

I've never experienced anything like this. I'm used to giving in to wild emotion. Lust, violence, rage…this tops them all, and it's not even close. The feeling of Camille's burning-hot pussy clamped around my cock, her fingernails clawing at my back, her teeth nipping at my lips, her tongue thrusting deep in my mouth...

We're trying to tear each other apart. But not out of hatred. Out of a desire to find that raw, vulnerable center again. Camille's got more walls around her than a medieval castle. And I'm equally determined to keep people out—with a barrier of anger, carelessness, and cruelty.

Yet we scaled each other's walls. Because we recognized in each other what we know about ourselves. That we're both hurting. Both alone. Both wanting someone who could understand.

I want Camille like I've never wanted anything in my life.

I want her to love me.

She's the only one who knows me, so she's the only one who can. And I want to love her.

I'm fucking awful at it—I've never had any practice.

But I want to take all that passion and jealousy and obsession inside me, and I want to give it all to her. I want to give her the best of me, whatever that might be.

I only hope it's enough.

Camille is clinging to me with her whole body. She's got her arms wrapped tightly around me, and she's whispering in my ear, "Nero...oh my god, Nero..."

Her thighs clamp around me. Her pussy squeezes me tight, clenching over and over as she starts to come. I kiss her swollen lips, tasting the difference in her breath as her body dumps all the pleasure chemicals of a climax: serotonin, oxytocin, dopamine.

Camille's mouth tastes better than any food I've ever eaten. It satisfies me and makes me ravenous all at once.

I feel a rush of wetness around my cock from her climax. Her pussy relaxes just a little, so I can fuck her even deeper than before. I don't want to stop. I want this to go on forever.

It's impossible, though. I can't believe I even lasted this long.

Camille is looking at me with those huge dark eyes. Looking right into my eyes like she did the first time we kissed.

It's her expression as much as her body that makes me come. The way she looks at me and the way she makes me feel. I explode. Absolutely fucking explode. The orgasm wrenches through me. It makes me cry out with a sound like a sob.

I collapse on top of her, pinning her to the hood of the car, both my hands holding on to hers, our fingers interlocked on either side of her head. I bury my face in her neck, my body still shaking and twitching with the last of the orgasm.

Her legs are locked around my waist. I haven't pulled out of her.

I can feel her heart beating on one side of her chest and mine on the other. They're just a couple of inches apart, separated by flesh and nothing else.

When I finally stand, my cock is still so hard that it pulls out of her with a popping sound. Hot cum runs down the inside of her thigh.

"Is that okay? I should have asked," I say.

"It's fine." Camille blushes. "We can be more careful next time."

"I've never done that before," I tell her. "Bare like that."

"Me neither."

I help her stand and pull down the skirt of the dress. The underwear's ruined.

Camille looks as dazed as I do. It's not an unpleasant feeling. Actually, it's peaceful. It's completely silent in the garage, without any noise from the house above or the city streets beyond.

There's no awkwardness between us. We've separated physically, but I still feel connected to Camille.

She looks up at me, tucking one wild dark curl back behind her ear. "I have to ask you something, Nero."

"Anything."

"Are you going to rob the vault at Alliance Bank?"

"Yes," I say without hesitation.

"When?"

"In two weeks."

She takes a deep breath. "I want in on it."

"You want...what?"

"I want to help you rob the bank. I need the money. And also, *fuck* Raymond Page."

My heart rate, finally starting to slow down, picks up again.

This isn't a good idea. First of all, Camille has zero experience in criminal activity. Second, we're both being tracked by a very nosy cop at the moment. And third, this is no Sunday picnic. This is grand larceny on the highest scale, stealing from a ruthless and well-connected grade A asshole.

"What?" Camille's eyes search my face. "You don't think I can do it?"

I sigh. "I think you can do pretty much anything, Camille. But nobody can rob a bank without some chance of getting caught. Or shot. Or worse."

"I could be a lookout?" Camille says. "I don't need a full share. Just enough to help my brother and my dad."

"I could give you money."

"No!" she cries. "I'm not looking for a handout. I just want a job."

God, I can't even look at her. Those big dark eyes can make me do anything.

I'm dragging this out because I don't want to say yes.

Yet I already know I can't refuse her.

"All right," I sigh. "But you have to do what I say for once."

CHAPTER 21
CAMILLE

THE WEEKS THAT FOLLOW ARE THE MOST BIZARRE OF MY LIFE.
Nero and I are planning an actual honest-to-god bank robbery.
And every minute outside that, whenever we're alone together, we
can't keep our hands off each other.

What started in his garage has progressed to hooking up in his
car, my car, his house, my house, the beach, an elevator, the bathroom
at an Irish pub, and anywhere else we happen to find ourselves.

I never imagined I could feel something like this. This kind of
obsession with someone.

When I'm not with Nero, I'm thinking about him. And when I
am with him, I can't tear my eyes away from him.

Everything he does turns me on. The way his forearm flexes
when he's shifting gears. The way he runs his hand through his
hair. The wicked gleam in his eye when he looks at me. The way
he grabs me and yanks me into his arms the second we're alone
together.

And the sex...dear god, I can't even think about it without
flushing from my scalp all the way down to my toes.

It gets better and better every time.

He's a fucking magician with his hands. You can see it in the way
he touches any object—when he's tinkering with an engine or just
messing with something out of his pocket, like a lighter or a coin.

He can make a quarter dance across his knuckles and then disappear, moving the metal as fluidly as water.

And when he puts those hands on my body...I melt like butter on hot toast. He makes me come again and again, sometimes five or six times before he even starts fucking me.

It's the only thing keeping me sane. Because I now have to do all the work that comes into the shop myself, while taking care of my dad and keeping watch on Vic.

School has started back up. Vic did finish his AP summer course as promised, and he's been buckling down with his regular school-work. He works three shifts a week at the Stop & Shop, and he tells me he's got $600 saved for college, plus $240 for the mixing board he's been dreaming of buying. I don't even think he's been hanging out with that shithead Andrew, though I haven't asked him about it because I don't want to go full Gestapo on him.

A week ago, my dad went in for surgery to remove the lump in his lung. Now he's doing radiation treatments three times a week, to make sure there's nothing left behind. He's in rough shape—totally unable to get up and down the stairs without me. He doesn't want to eat, but I make shakes for him, and Patricia brought over her soup, too.

I completely broke down during the surgery. Bawled like a baby, alone in the waiting room.

Then an arm dropped around my shoulders.

It was Nero. I hadn't told him I'd be at the hospital—he must have heard from Patricia. He sat with me for hours, just holding me like that. The scent of his skin was so warm and comforting. I should have been embarrassed to cry in front of him, but I wasn't. Because I remembered that night on the beach when he told me about his mom, and his face was wet, too.

It's one thing to be comforted by somebody who's nice to every-one. It's an entirely different thing to get care from the last person in the world you'd expect to be nurturing. I knew this was as weird for

Nero as it was for me. That's what made it mean so much more to me. That he was doing something wildly out of character, just for me.

When I bring my dad back home, Nero's there again to help get him up the stairs and into his bed. He isn't just kind to me—he's kind to my father. Gentle with him. Respectful. Reminding him of a time a few years back when my dad found a bumper for an old Corvette that Nero couldn't get anywhere else.

"So I owe you a favor," Nero says. "'Cause I still have that Corvette. We should take a drive in it, when you're feeling better."

My dad can barely speak. He squeezes Nero's arm, before lying back in his bed, exhausted.

Before Nero leaves, he pulls me aside and says, "I called the hospital. I told them to send the bills to me instead."

"I don't want you to do that!" My face is burning. "In another week, I'll have enough to cover it myself."

Nero frowns. His face only looks more beautiful when he's angry, but also terrifying. Like an avenging angel.

"About that..." he says. "Schultz has been following me everywhere, like fucking gum on my shoes."

"I know. I've seen him, too. He even followed me to the hospital."

"That means he's seen us together."

"I know."

"A lot."

"*I know,*" I say.

Schultz hasn't been texting me. Which is probably an ominous sign. I know he hasn't given up—he expects me to turn on Nero, and Levi, too.

"The day of the job, I was thinking you should lead him off somewhere. As a diversion," Nero says. "You'll still get your cut."

"No way." I shake my head. "You're just trying to keep me out of it."

"I'm not!" Nero insists. "We need to get rid of him somehow. If he sees the whole thing go down—"

"Then we'll draw him off. But I'm still driving."

I'm the getaway driver. That's my job—and I'm doing it. I'm getting what Raymond Page owes my brother. And something else, too.

I don't want to say it, not to Nero. But I want to prove to him that I can be part of his world. I'm not the good little girl I was in high school. I'm Old Town to the core, just like him.

"Fine," Nero says, when he sees I'm not backing down. "That means we'll have to change the plan…"

"Then change it."

He lets out a rumble of annoyance. "It's not that easy!"

"You never do anything the easy way—why start now?"

"*God!* You're so stubborn." Nero flexes and clenches his fingers, like he'd enjoy strangling me right now.

"I can do this," I tell him.

"I know you can." Nero sighs. "That's not what I'm worried about."

"What, then?"

"I don't want you to get hurt!"

My heart does a little backflip inside my chest. Not at the idea of grievous bodily injury—at the look on Nero's face. His white-hot fury at the idea that anyone might lay a hand on me.

"Look," he says, reaching into his pocket and pulling out his knife. It's the one he keeps on him at all times, sometimes doing tricks with it when he's lost in thought or bored.

He tries to hand it to me.

I shake my head. "I'm not stabbing anybody."

"You might." He grabs my hand and forcibly closes my fingers around the handle. "You never know what might happen, Camille. Promise me you'll keep this with you, everywhere you go."

I hesitate, then slowly nod. "Fine," I say.

I don't have to actually use it. Just carry it around.

Nero shows me how to open the blade and close it again. He

shows me how to hold it, how to swing the knife upward or switch grips for a downward stroke.

I try not to get distracted by the scent of his skin and his warm fingers closed over mine.

"Remember, there's no fair fight," he tells me, his gray eyes as cold as steel. "You're always going to be the smaller opponent. You have to take any chance you can get. Go for the vulnerable spots—the eyes, nose, throat, groin, knee, instep. You've got to be ruthless and dirty. Or you don't have a hope of winning."

I swallow hard. "I don't think that will be necessary."

"Good, I hope not. We're still gonna practice," he says.

Nero folds the knife and slips it in my pocket, his hand lingering against my thigh.

Impulsively, I pull him into my room and shut the door behind us.

"I thought you had to go take care of your dad?" he teases me.

"I've got five minutes more." I push him down on my mattress, unbuttoning his jeans.

His cock springs out, already hard. I've never seen it in any other state—he seems to get aroused as soon as we're within five feet of each other.

I don't have much to compare it with, but Nero's cock is gorgeous, just like the rest of him: long, thick, with an upward curve. Just a little darker than the rest of his skin.

And here's the part I'd never admit: it tastes incredible.

I slide my tongue up the length of it, from base to tip. By the time I get to the head, a little droplet of clear precum is waiting for me. I close my mouth over the head of his cock, lapping it up with the flat of my tongue.

He tastes like salt and spice.

Nero groans, and I say, "Shhh! My dad will hear you."

I take as much of his cock as I can fit into my mouth. My mouth is watering from the taste of his skin, which makes his cock slide easily in and out.

I use my lips and tongue and both hands, sliding, squeezing, licking, and sucking all at once. Nero is rolling his hips, breathing deeply, and trying hard not to make any more sound. He can't help it, though. As I speed up my pace, he puts my pillow over his head and moans into that instead, pressing it into his face with both hands.

I love that I can do this to him. Nero is the most intimidating man I know, but for these five minutes, he's at my mercy. I can tease those groans out of him with my tongue, and I can make him explode whenever I want.

I draw it out just a little longer. Then I go to work on him, building the pace and intensity until I know he won't be able to hold back anymore.

Sure enough, his back arches, and he thrusts hard into the back of my throat. I feel his cock twitching before he lets loose a stream of boiling cum into the back of my throat.

He sounds like he's being tortured. The pillow can't cover it up.

I don't care—I love making him yell. He's done the same to me plenty of times.

I keep my lips wrapped around his cock until I'm sure he's done. Then I let go, wiping my mouth with the back of my hand.

"You're going to kill me," Nero says, from under the pillow.

I laugh, absurdly pleased with myself. "Now you can go," I tell him.

He throws the pillow aside, his eyes narrowed at me. "No fucking way. Not until we're even."

He pounces on me, throwing me on the mattress and climbing on top.

CHAPTER 22
NERO

PLANNING A JOB IS LIKE BUILDING A RUBE GOLDBERG MACHINE. One where you only get a single chance to move the ball from point A to point B. You set up all your pulleys and ramps, your levers and wheels. And then finally, when you're certain that every part of the machine is perfect, down to the tiniest angle, then you set your ball rolling. If it makes it all the way to the end, you get away with the money. If it falls short, you and all your friends are spending the rest of your lives in prison. As a best-case scenario.

I never really focused on the consequences before.

Having Camille involved changes that. I can't let her down. I just can't. She won't take money from me. But we can steal it together.

I've got Mason fabricating the equipment we need using his uncle's shop. Jonesy is back on his meds—or so he swears—and back to researching the alarm system of Alliance bank, instead of Canon conspiracy theories like he's been doing the past four months.

I'll be the one doing the actual safecracking. I built myself a scale model of the mag-lock door system and the electrical grid, which I've been practicing on blindfolded so I can do it by touch alone. And I'm figuring out exactly where Camille should be on the night of the heist, to lead our friend Schultz on a merry chase, with enough time left over so she can pick us all up afterward.

The only thing I don't have is muscle. Dante is still uninterested in the job, though at least he hasn't ratted me out to Papa about it. I could get someone else, but I don't trust anybody else outside my little circle. And it probably won't matter in the end. If all goes to plan, there won't be any blows or bullets exchanged.

If there is, I'll just have to handle it myself.

So there's one last thing to sort out. One little mystery I want to put to bed once and for all.

I have to take a road trip to do it. I was planning to go alone. At the last minute, I ask my little brother if he wants to come along.

Sebastian has always been on the periphery of the family business. He made it clear he had no interest in running poker rings or shaking down developers for cash. He wanted the straight life—college education, college athletics, maybe even a professional career.

Then he went from basketball star to barely walking in one night.

He doesn't hold a grudge against Callum or Aida; the feud between our families is water under the bridge. But it changed him. He went from gentle and dreamy to silent and unpredictable.

He's still attending classes at the U—in fact, he took them all summer long, staying on campus instead of coming home for a few months like he usually does. He barely ever comes home on the weekend anymore either. When he does, he looks hungover.

I know what it's like to have one night change your life. To have a demon crawl inside you and take up residence.

I call Seb up and ask him if he wants to drive out to Braidwood with me.

There's a long silence on the other end of the line. Then Seb says, "Yeah. Why not."

I take Dante's Escalade so Seb will have more room to stretch his legs. He's the youngest boy in the family, but the lanky bastard is near six-seven, taller even than Dante. And actually, he's not as lanky as he used to be either.

"You been lifting?" I ask him.

He nods. "I was doing it for physical therapy on my knee. Then I figured I might as well keep up with it. Since I'm not on the team anymore, I've got time on my hands."

He looks out the window, not smiling. His boyish face is filling out, his jaw widening. He used to have soft features and an even softer mop of hair. Now he's cut the curls tighter and stubble shadows his cheek.

"You haven't been coming home much," I say. "You seeing somebody?"

Seb shakes his head. "I don't have to ask you that question."

"Actually," I say, "I am."

"No shit?" Seb looks over at me, a bit of the old smile on his face. "What, did you meet Taylor Swift?"

"Nah." I grin. "You know Camille Rivera?"

Seb shakes his head.

"Her dad owns that auto shop on Wells."

"Oh…" Recognition dawns on his face. "You mean the Grease—"

"Don't call her that!" I bark.

"Sorry!" Seb holds up his hands. "That's just what some kids called her. I always thought she was cool. Kinda badass."

"She is."

My heart's racing, and I'm gripping the steering wheel too hard. I know Seb didn't mean anything by it—he doesn't have a mean bone in his body. Or at least he never did before. But the thought of somebody talking shit on Camille makes me want to track down every single kid we went to high school with and wring their fucking necks.

"Is it serious?" Seb asks.

I want to say yes. But I'm not sure I can answer for Camille. "To me it is."

Sebastian nods slowly. "I'm happy for you, man."

"She's helping me with a bank job in a week."

"Oh, yeah? What bank?"

"Alliance."

Sebastian lets out a low chuckle. "You're not fucking around, huh? Does Papa know?"

"No, so keep it quiet. Dante does, but he's not coming along."

"You want another hand?" Seb asks.

I look at him in surprise. "You serious?"

Seb shrugs. "Why not?"

"You know...I just thought you wanted the straight life."

Sebastian frowns. "Yeah, well, that was a fantasy, obviously. I'm not Michael Jordan. It was stupid to think that."

"Seb, you were really good. With some more therapy—"

"*Fuck* therapy!" he barks. "It doesn't fix it. Before the accident, I was playing nine hours a day, training constantly. I had to get better and better every game, always pushing. Now I can barely get back to where I used to be. And all the guys I was playing with have had months to keep moving forward. They passed me by. It's over."

I've never heard him admit that before. We all thought he'd keep trying, at least through graduation.

Before, I wouldn't have known what to say to him.

But if there's one thing I've learned from my time with Camille, it's that you can't say anything to fix a situation like this. And you don't have to try. You just have to be there for the other person.

So I say, "I'm really sorry, Seb. It's a shit situation, and you didn't deserve that happening to you."

Seb is quiet for a minute. Then he says, "Thanks, Brother."

"If you want to do this job with me...I'd be glad to have you."

"Yeah?"

"Definitely."

But first, our little late-night visit...

We pull into Braidwood about ten o'clock at night. It's a tiny town, maybe six thousand people. Most of them work at the nuclear plant. So does the man we've come to see. Eric Edwards is a security guard, preventing acts of industrial espionage for the princely sum of twelve dollars an hour.

It's a step down from the days when he was patrolling the city streets for the Chicago PD. He was discharged with no pension after he broke some kid's arm during a routine shoplifting arrest. Turns out that kid was the fourteen-year-old son of the fire commissioner, so that little act of aggression didn't get swept under the rug like the twenty-two complaints Edwards had received before.

But I'm not here about any kid.

I'm here because Edwards was one of the two officers who found Matthew Schultz outside Rosenblum Park on April 18, 2005.

Now he lives in a tiny saltbox house on the outskirts of town, between the Dollar General and Hicksgas and Propane.

I've seen photos from his policing days, when he had a thick black mustache and a muscular physique. I hardly recognize the sloppy fuck sitting by his firepit, dressed in a pair of gum boots, a moth-eaten robe, and a stained Ghostbusters T-shirt, his mustache now gray and so scraggly that it's overgrown half his face. He's roasting a hot dog on a stick, the first of many if the number of buns laid out on his plate is any indication.

He looks up as our car pulls into his drive. He doesn't move from the beat-up lawn chair that barely looks capable of supporting his bulk.

Seb and I get out of the car. We approach him from two sides, as Papa always taught us. Flanking like wolves.

"Whadda ya want?" Edwards demands, squinting up at us.

"Just a moment of your time," I say quietly. "I've got three questions for you. If you answer honestly, we can be on our way."

Edwards's piggy little eyes narrow even further as he looks between Seb and me. "Who are you? You work for Flores?"

I don't know who Flores is, and I don't care.

"That's not how the game works," I remind him. "I ask the questions. You answer."

"I don't have to play your fucking game, kid." Edwards nods toward his old service pistol slung over the arm of his chair in its holster.

I raise an eyebrow, pretending to be impressed. "You see that Seb? He's got a gun."

Sebastian and I lock eyes. Then, at the same instant, Seb uses his good leg to kick out the straining struts of the lawn chair, while I knock the gun and holster out of Edwards's reach.

The chair collapses beneath him, and he tumbles backward. He flails his arm, trying to grab his gun. I bring my boot down on his hand, pinning it in place.

Sebastian does the same with Edwards's other arm. Now he's lying on the grass, looking up at us, howling with fury.

"Quiet," I snap, "or I'll stuff one of those filthy socks in your mouth."

Edwards is wearing a pair of rancid wool socks under his sandals. He immediately quiets, knowing better than I do how disgusting that would taste.

"What do you want?" Edwards snarls.

"I told you," I say. "Three questions. First, who shot Matthew Schultz?"

"How the fuck should I know?"

"Wrong answer." I nod to Sebastian. He puts his other shoe on Edwards's throat and bears down.

Edwards chokes and gurgles, his face turning a congested red. Seb lets up just a little, and Edwards cries, "I don't know! Nobody knows!"

Seb starts to push down on his throat again, and Edwards sputters something I can't make out.

"Ease off," I say to Seb. Then to Edwards, I add, "Last chance. What were you saying?"

Edwards gasps and chokes, giving a phlegmy cough. "He had a lot of enemies."

"Who?"

"Everybody. People said he was working with Internal Affairs, turning in other cops."

"So who wanted him dead?"

"I don't *know!*" Edwards howls. Seb raises his foot again, and Edwards cries, "All I know is that we were supposed to be by the park that night. To answer the call."

"What call?"

"About the shooting. Only I didn't know it was gonna be a shooting till we got there."

"Who told you to be there?"

Edwards squirms, trying to wrench his wrists out from under our feet. He clamps his mouth shut and shakes his head side to side, like a toddler trying to refuse food.

"Who?" I demand, pressing down on his wrist until I hear the tendons pop.

"Owww!" Edwards howls. Then, as Seb starts to press down on his neck for the last time, Edwards gasps, "Brodie! It was Brodie!"

I nod at Seb to let him be.

Then I take my weight off Edwards's arm so he can sit up and rub his wrists with a sulky expression.

"Brodie told you to be there that night?" I say.

"Yes."

"Did you get the security footage that showed the shooting?"

"Yeah. But I never watched it. I gave it to my partner. Coop was supposed to log it. Instead, it disappeared."

"Convenient."

"What do you care?" Edwards mutters, glaring at Seb and me. "You're not cops. Who the fuck are you anyway?"

"I'm the guy who's not gonna kill you tonight," I tell him. "You're welcome."

After kicking his gun farther out of reach, I nod to Seb, and we head back to the SUV.

As we climb inside, Seb says, "Did you know who he was talking about? This Brodie guy?"

"Yeah. I know who that is."

I saw a picture of him pinning a medal on Logan Schultz.

CHAPTER 23
CAMILLE

I'm robbing a bank today.

It seems completely unreal. Standing in my tiny dingy kitchen, everything looks so prosaic and familiar that I can't imagine myself doing anything but the normal activities of cooking, cleaning, or working in the auto bay.

Yet tonight I move from (mostly) law-abiding citizen to full-out criminal.

Nero and I have our plan in place. I know what I'm supposed to do.

Yet I can't help focusing on the thousand ways it could all go wrong. If I forget a single part of it. If I make just one mistake...

No. That can't happen.

I try to picture my dad, the very first time he showed me how to take apart an engine and put it back together.

These are complicated machines. You've got to be like a machine yourself. There's no room for mistakes.

The plan is one big engine. I've got to be methodical and accurate like never before.

I'm painfully tense during the first part of the day. I remind Vic that he has a shift at the Stop & Shop after school. I make sure he remembers to grab his lunch bag out of the fridge. I bring my dad breakfast in bed. I swap out a pair of brake pads down in the shop.

Then I make lunch for my dad. This time, he's able to come sit at the table to eat with me.

"Are you all right, *mija*?" he says. "You look pale. Are you getting sick?"

"Of course not. You know I never get sick."

"Yes, you do," he says, smiling sadly. "You just never complain about it."

"I've got to go out tonight, Dad," I tell him. "Vic's at work—will you be okay here alone?"

"Absolutely. You don't have to baby me, sweetheart. I'm getting better all the time. I'll be back downstairs working soon enough."

Seeing as he can barely hobble around the apartment, I doubt that very much. But I'm glad he's feeling optimistic.

"You call me if you need anything," I tell him.

"I'll be fine. I'm gonna watch *Once Upon a Time in Hollywood* tonight—it's playing on Showtime. Now that's a movie with gorgeous cars. Tarantino loves a classic car. I read he used two thousand of them, just to fill the streets in the background. You remember what Brad Pitt drives in that movie?"

"I dunno." My dad and Vic and I all went to see the movie in a theater. We were mesmerized, all the way through. Not just by the cars—by the way it sucked us into 1969, like we were living every minute of it. "Oh, wait!" I say. "Was it a Cadillac?"

"You got it!" Dad grins. "A '66 DeVille. The same car Tarantino used in *Reservoir Dogs*."

"How do you know that?"

"I read *Entertainment Weekly* while I'm waiting in line at the grocery store. Not now, obviously. But when I used to get the groceries."

"Well, you better get back to that soon, Dad. 'Cause I keep forgetting the milk, and when I tell Vic to bring some home, he gets that awful pink stuff. Puts it in his cereal and everything. It's disgusting."

"Your brother is deeply disturbed," Dad agrees, nodding somberly.

It makes me so happy to see him joking around again. I reach across the table to hug him, ignoring the fact I'm covered in grease and he's still frail under his robe.

"Good luck on your date tonight." Dad winks at me.

I flush. "It's not a date."

"Sure, sure," he says. "I'm just glad to see you going out. You deserve it, Camille."

"Thanks, Dad."

It's stupid, but my father wishing me luck actually does calm me down a little. I head back down to the shop to finish my work for the day. Then I shower and change my clothes.

Only then am I ready to call Schultz.

The phone rings several times. I shift uneasily, worried he's not going to pick up.

Finally, I hear his drawling voice saying, "This better be good."

"It is. I found where Levi makes his product."

"Are you sure?" Schultz is unable to hide the eagerness in his voice.

"Pretty sure."

"Are you at the shop? I'm coming to pick you up."

"Yeah," I say. "See you in a minute."

Forty minutes later, I'm at the police station, having been brought in through the back door by Schultz.

I've got my shirt off so a female officer can tape a microphone between my breasts.

"Don't you have a better way of doing this?" I ask Schultz.

"This *is* the better way. This thing is a quarter the size it used to be. You got a transmitter, microphone, and battery pack, and it's all barely bigger than a Zippo."

"I just…I feel like someone will see it."

"Nah," Schultz says, letting his eyes roam over my breasts. "You've got a pretty big…crevice to hide it."

I see the female officer narrow her eyes, shooting a dirty look back at Schultz, but he doesn't even notice.

"So how do I know when you're all gonna bust in?" I ask Schultz.

"We can't just break down the door for no reason. You've got to get Levi to take you down to the lab. Then you gotta get him to incriminate himself on tape."

"What if he won't?"

Schultz smiles coldly. "Then you're on your own."

Bastard.

"You're all set," the female cop says.

I pull my T-shirt back over my head, turning and bending a little to make sure the microphone stays put.

"How does it feel?" she asks me.

"Weird."

"You'll get used to it," Schultz assures me.

I see a dozen other officers suiting up in bulletproof vests and tactical gear. They're planning to make a raid on Levi's lab.

But only if I can create probable cause for them to enter. If I fuck this up, Schultz says I'll be high and dry. All on my own in Levi's basement.

And that's not the worst part—the worst part would be Nero and Sebastian, stuck at the bank with no getaway driver.

That can't happen. I can't let them down.

As I'm about to leave the room, Schultz grabs my arm, pulling me back inside. It's just me and him—the other officers are getting ready.

"Where's your boyfriend tonight?"

"He's out of town," I say blandly.

"Does he know you're ratting out Levi Cargill tonight?"

"He doesn't give a fuck about Levi."

Schultz has his fingers wrapped around my wrist, holding me close so I can't take a step back from him. He's finally wearing his uniform again, like the first night I met him. The deep navy blue makes him look stern and formal. But his eyes are burning brighter than ever beneath the brim of his cap.

"I've seen you two together," he hisses. "I followed you out to the bluffs. Saw you in the back seat of his car…"

My skin crawls; I know what night he's talking about. Nero fucked me in the back seat of the Mustang until the windows were running with steam and both of us were drenched in sweat.

Schultz was watching us the whole time?

That fucking creep.

"That's an interesting use of police time," I mutter.

"I wasn't on duty that night."

I try to pull my wrist out of his grip, but he holds on tight, not letting me move an inch.

"I thought you were smarter than that," Schultz says. "A girl like you…with a body like that…you could have picked a better class of man. You still could."

"Are you talking about yourself?"

"Why not?"

I look up into his face, furious and disdainful. "Because say what you want about Nero…he never forced me to do a damn thing I didn't want to do." I twist my wrist, wrenching it out of Schultz's grip. "For a bad guy…he's a pretty good guy."

I push past Schultz, leaving him alone in the interrogation room. It's almost ten o'clock. I've got to get over to the lab.

———

I'm standing on the doorstep of 379 Mohawk Street. Nero and I found this place via the property records for Evan Cargill.

After Ali let slip her little comment about Levi and his brother,

Nero and I put two and two together. Levi sells drugs out of his house on Hudson Ave. But he makes them in his brother's basement.

While Evan has been squandering his inheritance in Ibiza, Levi's been using his house. Now that big brother is coming home, Levi's pissed because he's got to find a new location for his lab.

Nero and I confirmed all this by doing a little spying of our own. Taking a page out of Schultz's book, we tracked Levi to the Mohawk Street house, which he apparently visits every Thursday night to pick up the product for the week. Or I should say, his trusty bodyguard, Sione, picks it up, while Levi makes sure he never carries so much as a single pill on his person.

But he does come to the house. And that's where I've got to meet him. If I have any hope of Schultz getting rid of my unwanted "boss" once and for all.

I knock on the door, bouncing nervously on the balls of my feet while I wait for someone to answer. I can feel the microphone between my breasts. I'm sweating a little, and I'm afraid the tape might come loose. I try to hold still so I don't jostle it any more than necessary.

At last, the door cracks. I have to look up to meet Sione's stern, unsmiling gaze.

"I need to see Levi."

He stares at me like he's thinking about slamming the door in my face. Then he cracks it just wide enough for me to pass.

"What the fuck are you doing here?" Levi demands, the second I step inside. He's standing there with Pauly, Sione, and a guy I don't know. All four of them look tense and irritated. Nobody is lying around smoking weed here—the Hudson Street house may be for partying, but Mohawk is all business.

"Who the fuck told you about this place?" Levi shouts.

"Nero sent me," I say quickly.

"What?" Levi narrows his eyes.

"He wants to make a deal with you."

"What kind of *deal*?"

"He wants product. A lot of it."

Levi casts a swift glance at Sione. I think I see his huge shoulders lift and lower in a near-imperceptible shrug.

"Why'd he send you?" Levi says.

"I'm his girlfriend."

"His *girlfriend*?" Levi hoots.

Pauly mutters something to Levi, maybe confirming what I've said. Levi's face changes in an instant, becoming much more respectful.

"I didn't know that," he says.

"He wants me to check out the lab. If he likes what I tell him, his family will place an order."

"This ain't McDonald's." Levi frowns. "I don't usually manufacture for anybody else."

"Fine," I say coldly. "I'll tell the Gallos what you said."

"What, like…all of them?" Levi glances nervously between me to his men.

"Yeah, *all of them*. Enzo's been letting you run your little operation in his neighborhood. I'd think you'd want to stay on friendly terms with the Gallos. But don't let me tell you how to run your business."

Levi licks his lips, irritated by me but not quite bold enough to lip off about the Gallos. "Fine," he says shortly. "Let's go down."

I already told Schultz I was going to use the Gallos as a cover story. Still, I hope he doesn't get any bright ideas about using that part of the tape as evidence.

I follow Levi down the creaking wooden stairs to the basement.

It's about twenty degrees hotter down here. I was already flushed and overheated from the stress of lying to a bunch of tightly wound drug dealers. Now my skin starts to sweat worse than ever. I wipe my forehead with the back of my hand, not wanting Levi to notice.

"Don't you have AC?" I ask.

Levi shrugs. "It's hot in the kitchen."

The basement is large but low-ceilinged. Only tiny windows set high in the walls lead to the outside. The space is totally unfinished— bare concrete floors and exposed struts. Still, there really is an industrial "kitchen" of sorts, with vats, a distillery, and a hood that vents into the backyard.

The three "cooks" are dressed in boxer shorts, leather aprons, heavy-duty gloves, and rain boots. They're all wearing face masks. Sweat drips down their exposed skin.

I have no idea what they're doing. I can see various stages of drug making in process, but I don't know what any of it means.

"So where do you get your ingredients?" I ask Levi.

"The precursor ingredients come from China," he says. "You start with safrole. Then you make methylamine hydrochloride from formaldehyde and ammonium chloride."

I nod like I know what any of that means. Vic would understand. Hopefully, Schultz does, too, on the other end of the wire.

Levi continues his explanation, pointing out the various stages of drug making. I keep nodding and egging him on, hoping this is enough "incriminating evidence" for Schultz to bust down the door. In fact, I expect to hear the cops breaking in any second.

I sneak a quick glance at my watch. It's twenty to eleven. Not only do I need to get Schultz in here, I also need to get out myself. I'm supposed to pick up Nero and the others at 11:05 precisely.

"Then you crystallize the MDMA oil by combining it with hydrochloric acid and isopropyl alcohol," Levi finishes.

"Sounds like a lot of work," I say weakly.

"Yeah, it's a shit-ton of work. And don't touch anything 'cause there's mercury fucking everywhere."

Great. I'm probably taking a week off my life every minute I spend down here.

"Satisfied?" Levi sneers. "Gonna give me a good report to Nero?"

"Yeah," I say. "It all looks…great."

"What the fuck is that?" Pauly points to my stomach.

In slow motion, I look down. Without me even noticing, the tape peeled off my sweat-soaked skin, and the microphone fell out of my shirt. It's now dangling by my crotch, hanging at the end of its wire.

Quicker than I can blink, Levi pulls a knife and slashes the front of my shirt. He rips it open, revealing the loose tape, the microphone, and the battery pack. He rips it off me, throwing it to the ground and stomping on it until it's a mess of broken plastic.

"You're a fucking rat," he says, blue eyes alight with fury.

"Yeah, and the cops will be here any second, so don't even think about using that," I say, eyeing the switchblade in his hand.

To my shock and dismay, Levi just laughs.

"I don't think so. I have a signal jammer in every corner of this house. The cops didn't hear shit from that recording. Which means nobody's coming to save you." He jerks his head at Sione. "Get rid of her."

Sione seizes me by the arm and starts dragging me up the stairs.

"No!" I shriek. "You don't want to do this!"

"I absolutely do," Levi says carelessly.

Sione is dragging me like I'm a rag doll. It takes zero effort for him to pull me back up to the main floor and into the actual kitchen.

I struggle and flail with all my strength. I might as well be punching a wall. He doesn't seem to feel any of it.

"Don't!" I beg him. "If you kill me, Nero's gonna—"

"I don't work for Nero." Sione grunts. "I work for Levi."

With that, he closes his massive hands around my throat and starts to squeeze.

In the two seconds of blood flow I have left, I close my eyes and try to picture what Nero would do in this situation.

I remember what he told me: *You're always going to be the smaller opponent. So don't even try to play fair. Hit them in the vulnerable spots: eyes, nose, throat, kneecaps, groin, feet.*

With every bit of my remaining strength, I stomp down hard on Sione's instep. Then I boot him again, right in the kneecap. His trunk-like leg buckles under him, and his hands loosen slightly around my throat. That's when I kick him as hard as I can in the balls.

He lets go of me for an instant, doubling over. I grab the knife Nero gave me out of my pocket, and I whip it open just like he showed me. Then I stab it down into Sione's shoulder.

I could have tried to stab him in the neck. But even in my desperation, I don't want to kill him.

That turns out to be a huge mistake.

As I turn to flee, Sione grabs my ankle and jerks my legs out from under me. I crash down on my stomach, the air knocked out of my lungs. My chin hits the linoleum, cracking my teeth together and making me bite my tongue hard enough to fill my mouth with blood.

Sione is dragging me back toward him, his eyes rage filled and murderous. I flip over and kick upward at him, but it's useless. He's just too fucking strong.

He grabs me by the tattered remains of my shirt and jerks me toward him, swinging one massive fist at my face.

Wildly, I grab for the only thing at hand—a cast-iron fry pan on the stove. The pan connects with the side of his head a millisecond before his fist can cave in my face. The blow jolts him, and his fist grazes off my forehead instead, still hitting me hard enough to fill my vision with stars.

I manage to grab the handle of the knife and jerk it out of his shoulder.

We both stumble backward in opposite directions. I've got the knife, and he's got about a hundred and fifty pounds on me. We circle each other, Sione looking dazed but deadly.

Meanwhile, I hear somebody stomping up the steps.

Levi yells, "What the fuck is going on up there? Don't tell me you need help with one little—"

At that moment, the front door explodes inward under the force of a police battering ram. Somebody tosses a metal canister into the house, and it rolls into the hallway between the kitchen and living room.

Sione stares at it, his brain not quite back to normal speed.

I sprint toward the back door. I wrench it open just as the canister explodes. The light and noise are blinding.

The force flings me down the back steps onto the grass. Even though I only caught part of it, I'm crawling around blind, my ears ringing. I know I don't have a second to waste. I sprint for the back fence, only able to see a blurry outline of where I'm going. I vault over it, skinning both my arms but dropping safely on the other side.

I'm flooded with adrenaline, my body telling me to run, run, run away from Levi's house as fast as I can.

Instead, I army crawl through his neighbor's yard, circling back around.

I see the cops swarming into Levi's house, shouting, "GET DOWN! GET DOWN!" to everybody inside.

Looks like enough time passed that Schultz got worried. Or he managed to pick up some of the recording. I don't really give a shit anymore. Schultz is occupied, so I did my job. Or at least most of it. There's one more thing I need…

My vision is starting to come back, though everything still sounds muffled, with a constant high whine over it.

I'm creeping around to the back of the police cars, to the van at the edge of the roped-off street.

Taking deep breaths and staying low, I jog out from the neighbor's yard to the driver's side door. It's unlocked. There's no key in the ignition, but that's not a problem. Using Nero's knife, I turn the screws on the steering column, then strip the insulation off the battery and ignition wires. When I twist them together, the dashboard lights up. I take a quick peek out the front windshield, to make sure that hasn't attracted any attention. The cops are all facing the other direction, focused on the house.

I grab the starter wire and spark it against the other two.

The engine revs to life.

Fucking bingo.

Resisting the urge to burn rubber, I quietly pull away from the curb and drive off without anybody noticing.

CHAPTER 24
NERO

I DON'T PARTICULARLY LIKE SENDING CAMILLE BACK TO LEVI'S house. Especially with only that idiot Schultz to protect her. But I trust Camille to take care of herself. And Schultz to look out for his own best interests by keeping his informant alive.

Still, I'm more distracted than I've ever been, heading into this job. And that's not a good thing.

Because this shit is complicated. In fact, I'd almost say I'm nervous. If I were willing to admit to feeling an emotion like that.

Let's just call it…tense. A tightness that runs from my scalp all the way down my spine.

I look at my watch: 10:02. Camille should be going into Levi's house right now.

Fuck, fuck, fuck, I regret how we planned this. It seemed like the only way to make sure Schultz was occupied. But now it seems insane, pulling two jobs in one night…

We should have stayed together.

If we all get out of this alive, I'm not letting Camille out of my sight anymore. She can stay safe right by my side.

"You okay?" Seb says to me.

"Of course."

I shake my hair out of my eyes, determined to focus.

Sebastian, Mason, and Jonesy are all gearing up. We're at

Jonesy's house 'cause we're using his van. He's got this nice white windowless electrician's van from his time working for Brickhouse Security. That was four years ago, but Jonesy hasn't forgotten how to cut his way into most any electrical panel, including the one powering Alliance Bank.

I love Jonesy, but he's twitchy as fuck. When he's in a manic phase, he stays up all night hacking government websites, trying to prove his conspiracy theories. When he's in a depressive state, he holes up in his basement and won't let anybody come over unless they bring pizza and a six-pack and agree not to discuss anything but *Halo*.

You have to catch him right in the middle of those two states, when he can actually be productive.

Today he seems to be in good spirits. He's showered (always a good sign), and he's got a new pair of glasses that make him look a bit like John Lennon during his bearded Jesus phase.

Jonesy drives us to 600 North LaSalle, where we use a stolen key card to get into the underground parking garage.

This is a mixed-use building, with a bunch of law firms and private equity companies using the office space. It's not the perfect access point because lawyers and finance types like to work late at night, but it has one very special feature—a patio garden space that extends outward to within twelve feet of Alliance Bank.

We hop out of the van, taking a ladder and a couple of paint cans from the back.

"Let me know if you have any trouble," I say to Jonesy, tapping the earpiece nestled in my right ear.

He nods. "Don't cut the glass till I give you the okay."

Jonesy drives off, headed for the electrical grid that powers the Alliance building. It's about twelve minutes away, and he's got to stay there for the duration of the job, manually clamping off the signals for the perimeter sensors. He won't have time to drive back and pick us up again. That's got to be Camille.

Compulsively, I glance at my watch again. 10:16. She's definitely in Levi's house by now.

Mason, Seb, and I take the elevator up to the sixth floor. We're all kitted up in paint-spattered coveralls, but I'd rather not run into anybody who might wonder why a bunch of painters are headed into work at ten o'clock at night.

Luckily, the sixth floor is quiet. I see a light on down the hall— some junior lawyer slaving away over a huge stack of files, most likely. Our little painting crew quietly makes its way over to the garden patio.

It's a pretty space, full of outdoor lunch tables and open umbrellas to shade the lawyers from sun or rain.

I'm more interested in what lies on the other side of the railing.

We try to move in total silence. We're six floors up, with a street right below us. We don't want to attract any unwanted attention.

Carefully, we extend the ladder and stretch it over the gap between buildings. It's easy to secure the ladder on our side. On the opposite end, the legs rest only on a three-inch windowsill. The smallest jolt, and we could knock the whole thing down, with a whole lot of noise and a shattered spine for whoever was trying to climb across.

The person is me, to start with.

Sebastian and Mason hold the ladder steady while I start to crawl across. This is the worst part because there's nobody to secure it on the other side. I've just got to be slow and careful.

It's fine while I'm on the side being held by Seb and Mason. However, the farther I venture out to the middle, the more flexible and unstable the metal struts feel. I'm not afraid of heights. But it's not exactly pleasant to be ninety feet in the air over cement.

I feel like a mountaineer crossing over an icy crevice—only instead of the blessed cold of the alps, I'm sweating my ass off in coveralls and latex gloves and hundred-degree Chicago heat.

The ladder creaks and twists to the right, making my stomach lurch. The legs cling to the window ledge, just barely. I keep inching forward until I'm up to the glass.

Touching my earpiece, I say, "You all set, Jonesy?"

"Mm-hmm." He grunts. It sounds like he's holding something in his mouth. "Window sensors should be off."

"Should be?"

"Only one way to know for sure."

I start to cut through the glass, careful not to upset my precarious position on the ladder. I slice out a perfect circle, suction the glass, and push it through into the bank. Then I crawl through the hole.

I drop into an office. This isn't Raymond Page's office—that's two floors up. This is just the plain, boring space of a regular drone who has three mugs of half-drunk cold coffee on their desk and a depressing motivational poster on their wall—a picture of a kitten in the rain with the caption *It Will Get Better*.

I wait for Seb to follow me. He makes it across the ladder all right—getting through the hole is a bit harder. He's so damn tall and he's filled out enough that he almost gets stuck halfway, like Winnie the Pooh when he ate too much honey. His backpack isn't helping.

"Cut it a little smaller, why don't you." Seb grunts.

"I forgot I had Groot coming after me."

Mason won't be following us—he's got to pull the ladder back, and then he's going to hang out a while on the patio in case something goes wrong and we've got to come back that way. Plus, somebody's got to listen on the police scanner to give a heads-up if any unwanted company is headed our way.

"You nervous?" I say to Seb.

He thinks about it for a second. "Actually…no. I was before. Threw up twice this morning. But this is like playing in a big game— once you're on the court, you're not nervous anymore. You just do it."

"Good." I nod. "Let me know if that changes."

I check my watch again—10:32. With any luck, Camille will be out of Levi's house and on her way over in our getaway car. I wish I could text her. We have to stay incommunicado in case Schultz has her phone.

We strip off the painters clothes—nobody's gonna be fooled by the getup in here, and it's too hot with all the other gear underneath. Then we head to the closest elevator. I don't press the button to call the car to our floor. Instead, Seb and I force the doors open so we can climb down into the empty shaft.

The building has three elevators—two that serve the main floors and one that only runs from the ground floor down to the vault.

Disabling the cameras and sensors on that elevator would be difficult. But it could be done. The one thing we can't do is disable the alarm. If the elevator car moves, it triggers a remote alarm directly to remote security. There's no way around it—the elevator cars can't move outside of business hours.

However, I don't really need the cars to use the system. All three elevators share the same ventilation shafts. Ignoring the cars entirely, Seb and I can climb down the shaft, then across and down to the vault itself. Assuming my oversize brother can fit through several tight squeezes along the way.

We use clamps to slide down the elevator cables. It's like doing a rope climb in gym class but in reverse. Also, I fucking hated gym class.

Seb, of course, excels at this part. He's actually grinning, like he's having fun. "I feel like a spy."

"Oh, yeah? Just wait for the next bit. Then we're gonna look extremely cool."

Seb and I squirm through the horizontal air shaft between the elevators. It's slow, tight, and overwhelmingly hot. Sweat runs down my face. There's no way to hurry—all we can do is keep crawling forward, inch by inch.

Once we're inside the third elevator shaft, we climb down the last hundred feet to the vault.

"What now?" Seb says, his feet firmly planted on the ground.

"Now the moon suits."

Jonesy has temporarily disabled most of the external sensors. The seismic sensors are still running, which is why we can't tunnel over to the vault or blow the door open. Inside, the thermal motion sensors are still running, too.

Now, the good thing is that they won't go off unless they sense both motion *and* heat. But I need to get close enough to jam them up.

So Seb and I put on possibly the most embarrassing costumes ever, created by my friend Mason. They look like giant marshmallows made of shiny foil, covering us head to toe until we resemble two highly reflective mascots. I can barely see through the eyeholes, but the suits should block the heat from our sweating bodies just long enough for us to disable the sensors.

Seb and I open the elevator doors, and then I slip through. It's completely dark inside the space. I count my steps away from the elevator door, just like I did when I was down here with Bella. Remembering where each of the sensors is located, I spray them with foam concentrate. That should block their ability to see motion. And then, fingers crossed, it won't matter if they read a heat signature.

I spray the cameras, too. They're triggered by light, and I don't want to have to work blind the whole time we're here.

Once we've got all the sensors covered, Seb and I can pull down the hoods of our crinkly foil suits and turn on our headlamps.

Now we can see. At least a little bit.

I touch my earpiece, whispering, "So far so good?"

"Police radar is quiet," Mason says.

"Everything looks okay here," Jonesy adds.

Their voices are tinny and distant. It's shit reception down in the vault. We can't count on them being able to reach us, so we've got to work fast.

Seb and I approach the vault door, which looks like a massive porthole six feet in diameter and two feet thick, made of solid steel.

There's just one thing left in our way.

It's not the code to the vault—I already have that, thanks to the hidden camera I placed on my little field trip down here with Bella. I've seen Raymond Page and his bank manager punch in the code thirty times since then. They've only changed it twice, which isn't bank protocol, but I think Raymond is a little bit lazy.

No, the only thing left to deal with is the exterior magnetic lock.

The lock consists of two plates. When armed, they create a magnetic field. If you open the door outside of business hours, that field is broken. It triggers an alarm that even Jonesy can't intercept. There's no way around this—the field has to remain intact all night long.

I had to ponder the problem for a long time. How to move the plates without breaking the field?

Eventually, I realized I simply had to move them together, at the same time.

I had Mason make me an aluminum plate that looks like a rectangular serving platter with a handle on one side. He welded it together in his mom's basement, using her silicone oven mitts and his makeshift welding mask that's basically a bucket with a plexiglass window in the front. He looked like a proper idiot, but his work is always top-notch, down to the last millimeter.

Seb takes the plate out of his backpack. I cover the flat side with heavy-duty double-sided tape. Then I stick it onto the two bolts and unscrew them. Now I can lift out both bolts at once, while keeping them at precisely the same distance from each other, then move the whole thing out of the way. The field remains intact, even though it's no longer attached to the vault.

I set it carefully down against the wall, with the delicacy of a bomb-removal expert.

Seb watches, so quiet that he's not even breathing.

When I place it down successfully, he lets out a long sigh. "It worked!"

"Of course it did," I say, as if I never had any doubt at all.

"All right." Seb's practically rubbing his hands together in anticipation. "Punch in the code."

"I thought you had the code?" I say blankly.

Seb freezes by the vault door. "What?"

"I thought you were gonna memorize it?"

"You never told me that."

"Yeah, I did. Remember? It started with 779...something."

Seb stares at me with a horrified expression.

I laugh. "I've got the code, ya dummy."

"That's not funny."

"It was for me."

I punch in the code: 779374.

I hear four distinct clunking sounds as the bolts retract. Then I pull the vault door open.

I'm hit with the smell of stacked bills. Cash has a distinct odor: ink, cotton, leather, grease, dirt, and a hint of metal, from touching coins.

But Seb and I aren't here for bills. It's too heavy to haul out that much cash.

We want the diamond.

I take the drill out of Seb's bag so we can start drilling into the lockboxes. I drill out the locks, and then Seb checks the contents. Ingots and gemstones go in the bags. Everything else stays behind.

"Don't take anything sentimental," I tell him. "I don't want some gangster coming after us 'cause we stole his grannie's wedding ring."

There are two hundred and eleven lockboxes in the vault.

In the hundred and eighth, I find what I'm looking for.

It doesn't look like much: just a plain wooden box with a hinged lid.

Still, I feel the thrill of anticipation as soon as I see it. I grab the box and lift the lid.

The stone inside is unearthly in its beauty. It truly looks like it might have fallen to earth in the core of a meteor. It's about the size of a hen's egg, clear and sparkling, with just a hint of frosty blue. The Winter Diamond.

Seb sees my silence and stillness. He comes to stand beside me, gazing down on it.

"Fucking hell," he breathes.

"Yeah."

We stare at it for about ten seconds. Then I close the lid with a snap before slipping the box directly into my pocket.

"Should we keep going?" Seb says.

"No. We've got as much as we can carry."

Sebastian and I hoist our backpacks onto our backs. It's much more difficult this time because gold is heavy as hell. Not just gold—platinum bars, loose gemstones, and one original Babe Ruth baseball card in a Lucite case because fuck it, that's cool and I want it.

We can't go out the way we came in. It's too slow to climb up the cables. If the cops are called when we're halfway up, we'll be trapped like a couple of bugs in a bottle.

The only problem is that engaging the elevators will trigger the alarms. So once we press that button, we have about two minutes to get out the front doors. And pray Camille is waiting for us with the getaway car.

I touch my earpiece, saying to Jonesy, "We're about to head out. You can pack up." To Mason I add, "You, too, Mace."

Mason will leave the ladder, strip off the coveralls, and exit the perimeter on foot. He doesn't have anything incriminating on him.

Seb and I are a different story.

"You ready?" My finger hovers over the elevator button.

I'm holding a stopwatch in my other hand. From the time I hit the button, I calculate that we have exactly three minutes to get away from the two-block radius surrounding the bank before the cops block it all off.

Seb looks tense but resolute. "Ready."

I hit the stopwatch and the elevator button simultaneously.

The elevator starts to descend.

I don't hear anything besides the jolt and hum of the elevator car coming down, but I know the moment that car started moving, it triggered a silent alarm to the firm that handles the bank's security and to the Chicago PD.

The elevator seems to take forever to come down. If I weren't watching the stopwatch, I would never believe it was only twelve seconds. As the doors part with aching slowness, Seb and I hustle inside. I press the button for the lobby.

The doors close again, and we lurch upward. My heart is beating three or four times every second that passes.

As soon as the elevator stops, Seb and I push through the doors, hustling across the dark, empty space. Our footsteps echo on the polished marble. It's still deathly silent, but I know our presence isn't a secret anymore.

When we get to the glass doors, I pick up the closest brass stanchion, and I launch it through the window like a javelin. The glass shatters, splintering like so many jagged icicles. It doesn't matter how much noise we make anymore. The point is to get outside as quickly as possible.

Seb and I step through the glass, hurrying out onto the steps leading to the street.

I look down to the curb, where Camille should be waiting for us.

There's nobody there. No car, no truck, nothing but an empty street.

"Where is she?" Seb says, a note of panic in his voice.

"She'll be here."

The seconds tick by. The road remains empty.

"Should we just run?" Seb says.

We're halfway down the stairs. We could sprint off down the street.

But I told Camille to meet us right here.

Someone barks, "*Don't move!*"

Slowly, I turn and look over my shoulder.

A security guard is standing behind us, his gun pointed at Seb and me.

Not just any security guard—my good buddy Michael, who let us down into the vault a couple of weeks back.

Michael is not supposed to be working tonight. No security guards are supposed to be working tonight.

The question of why Michael is here at 11:00 p.m. is a mystery. If I had to guess, I'd assume he was doing something less than legal for Raymond on one of the upper floors. That's not what I care about, however. I'm concerned solely with the gun pointed at my face.

Seb and I are wearing Kevlar vests. I really don't want to test their functionality or Michael's aim.

"Take it easy," I say, keeping my voice low and calm.

"Don't fucking talk, and don't fucking move, or I'll put a bullet between your eyes," Michael barks.

"What do you want to do?" Seb murmurs to me, so quietly that even I can barely hear it.

I see his body coiled like a spring. He wants to try to get the jump on Michael, thinking he's just some rent-a-cop. That's a bad idea—I doubt Raymond Page picked a schmuck as the head of his security team. This guy is probably some ex-SEAL or worse.

Carefully, keeping my body turned to hide what I'm doing, I slip my hand in my pocket. I intend to close my fingers around the handle of my switchblade. If Seb can distract this dude, I might have a chance…

My hand grasps at nothing. I don't have my knife anymore—I gave it to Camille.

Well, shit.

At that moment, I hear sirens—distant, but getting closer by the second.

Michael chuckles. "You're fucked now."

Then I see something so odd that it looks like an optical illusion. The shadow behind one of the bank's marble pillars peels away from the wall, looming up behind Michael. In one swift motion, it grabs the guard's wrist, wrenching his gun upward, and wraps one massive forearm around Michael's throat.

The security guard squeezes his trigger three times in a row, but the bullets shoot harmlessly into the air. Meanwhile, my big brother, Dante, puts Michael in the most painful-looking headlock I've ever witnessed. Dante chokes him out in about eight seconds, until Michael slumps over unconscious.

Dante drops him on the top of the steps.

"Hey!" Sebastian greets him cheerfully.

"What are you doing here?" I demand.

Dante shrugs his heavy shoulders. "Thought you might need help."

"We had it covered," I tell him.

"Clearly." He snorts, stepping over the security guard's slumbering frame.

The sirens are getting closer. Now's the time to leave.

Dante must have a car somewhere around.

But I don't want to leave without Camille...

"Let's go." Dante grunts.

"One more second..." I say.

A white police van screeches up in front of the bank.

Seb and Dante are about to take cover behind the pillars.

"Wait!" I say.

Camille pokes her head out the driver's side window. "Come on!" she shouts.

We book it down the stairs.

Dante and Seb climb into the van. I grab the last of Mason's inventions from my bag and fling one of the grenades up the north end of the street and one south. Then I jump in the passenger seat, shouting to Camille, "Go west on Monroe!"

Cop cars are zooming up LaSalle from both directions. I can see them closing in on us from two sides.

Then the grenades explode.

Not in the normal way—there's no charge inside. Instead, the grenades release two smoke bombs of massive proportions. They create dual pillars of dense black smoke, twelve feet in diameter and a hundred feet tall. This blocks the view in either direction with apocalyptic panache.

Camille floors the gas pedal, shooting the gap between the pillars of smoke. She zooms down Monroe Street, taking us out of the financial district, out toward the river.

She's driving fast and aggressive, handling the van like it's a sports car. I can't help grinning, watching her. The only thing I don't like are the ugly marks around her neck and the gash on her chin. Not to mention the fact her shirt looks like it was cut off her body.

"Are you okay?" I ask her.

Camille gives me a quick smile before turning her eyes back to the road. "Never better."

I feel myself grinning, too, a bubble of elation building inside me. *We're doing it. We're fucking doing it.*

I hear sirens everywhere. Probably twenty cop cars, headed toward the bank from all directions. It'll take a miracle to get through them all without being spotted.

Camille is headed toward the bridge, to cross over the river.

Instead, I say, "Turn right here. Then turn right again."

"But that'll take us back—"

"Trust me," I say.

Camille wrenches the wheel to the right, then takes the next right again.

Now we're headed back toward LaSalle on Washington Street. Sure enough, two cop cars are racing down the road after us, sirens blaring. Camille's hands are stiff on the wheel, and her face is pale.

"What do I do?" she says.

"Just keep going."

The cop cars shoot past us on either side, zooming down Washington.

Camille lets out a startled laugh.

"They think we're with them," I tell her. "It's way more suspicious to drive in the opposite direction."

We keep driving back toward the bank, letting another squad car pass us by. Once we're sure the bulk of the cops have passed, we take a left to head north instead.

The sound of sirens fades away. Seb and Dante start laughing. Camille joins in, her voice higher than usual and a little skittish.

"We did it," she says, like she still can't believe it.

"Did you get what you were looking for?" Dante asks me.

"Of course I did."

Now Dante and Seb are looking curiously at Camille.

"Thanks for the lift," Dante says in his rumbling voice.

I can see Camille's cheeks turning pink. She hasn't officially met any of my family yet, but she knows who my brothers are, like everybody does in Old Town. "Sorry I was late."

"How'd it go?" I ask her.

"There were a couple of...bumps along the way."

"But you're okay? Really okay?"

"Yes," she says, her dark eyes flitting over to me again.

I can feel my brothers watching us. I don't give a shit.

I grab her hand and bring it up to my lips, kissing it. "You're incredible," I tell her.

CHAPTER 25
CAMILLE

"Turn here," Nero tells me.

We're weaving through Roscoe Village. It's funny being in such a sleepy little neighborhood, just minutes after pulling off a bank robbery. We're passing by Whole Foods and Trader Joe's. Hipster lofts and coffee shops seem like the antithesis of criminal activity.

I know we need to get rid of the police van, but Nero seems to have his own destination in mind.

"Right here," he says, pointing to a parking garage.

I turn into the first stall, mildly confused. "Are we leaving the van here?" I ask.

"Nope," Nero says. "Come on."

I get out of the van. Dante climbs into the driver's seat instead.

"Nice to meet you, Camille," he says in his deep voice.

"See you again soon, I'm sure," Sebastian says, giving me a little salute.

They drive away, leaving Nero and me alone in the garage.

I turn to face him, utterly bemused. "Where are they going?"

"To burn the van," Nero says.

"How are we getting home?"

"I dunno." He grins. "I was hoping you'd drive me."

I have no idea what he's talking about. All I know is he's definitely excited about something. Not just the insane amount of money we just stole. This is something else.

"What are you up to?" I say suspiciously.

"I'm talking about your new car."

He pulls the dust cover off the car parked in the nearest stall.

I gasp, putting my hands over my mouth.

I see a long sleek body with outrageous curves, painted a deep oxblood red. The chrome grille and round headlights gleam in the dim parking garage. The wheels are pristine. I can smell the fresh leather even from here.

"You're joking…"

"I'd never joke about a car," Nero says. "Especially not this one."

I turn to look at him. His eyes look darker than usual, intently focused on me. His expression is serious.

"Nero, I can't take this… You may never find another one."

"Camille…" He touches my cheek with his hand. "I've always felt things intensely. Or I thought I did. But every emotion I ever had my whole life through is nothing compared to what I feel when I look at you. I don't care about the car or the money we just took. Next to you, everything else just fades away."

"This is crazy," I whisper.

The Grand Sport is beautiful, utterly beautiful. Priceless, in that there's not another one like it in the world, and you could never buy the countless hours of time that Nero put into it when he thought it would be his.

But it's not the car itself that's making my heart race like mad and hot tears spring into my eyes.

It's what it means for Nero to give it to me.

Nero is the most gorgeous man I've ever laid eyes on. He has a fire inside him that burns hotter than the surface of the sun. I know how strongly he hates—I can only imagine the kind of love he feels. It terrifies me.

I don't know how or why he's given it to me.

I feel like a mortal chosen by a god.

And yet…

It feels right.

The way our hands fit together. The way our bodies fit together, too. The way I understand him, when no one else seems to. And the way he sees me, when no one bothered to before.

The way we find peace in each other, when we're two restless souls.

For a long time now, I've known he was the one for me.

I just never thought I could be the one for him.

Then Nero says something even more insane. "Do you think you could ever love me, Camille?"

I'm so startled that I almost laugh.

He mistakes the look on my face.

"I know I've got an awful history, and honestly, I'm not much better now. My temper's shit. I want to kill any man who looks at you. I'm not…good with words or feelings." He takes a deep breath, and I realize Nero is nervous—almost as nervous as I am. "But I love you, Camille. I'll never hurt you. You can trust me for that, if nothing else."

I'm speechless. Desperate to answer him, yet totally unable to make a sound.

All I can do is grab him and kiss him. I kiss him like the very first time, hungry and aching. Then I kiss him like we kissed in my tiny glassed-in room—as if the whole universe has passed away, and he and I are the only two things in existence.

When our lips part, I can finally speak. "I'm scared to tell you, scared to even let myself feel it. But I love you, and I have for a while."

"Good," he says, with infinite relief.

He kisses me again, crushing me against his body.

When he lets me go, he grins and says, "Now take me for a drive."

He hands me the keys. Even the fob is original to the car, made of old silver polished bright again.

I slide into the driver's seat, inhaling the fresh leather and paint. The dash is all round dials, with the huge steering wheel in the center.

I turn the key, listening to the engine turn over with a roar before subsiding into a patient purr.

"When did you know you were going to give this to me?" I ask Nero.

Nero smiles. "The moment you touched it and I saw the look on your face."

I pull out of the parking garage, my heart soaring with every turn of the wheel. The car operates flawlessly. Nero truly is a magician.

He looks perfect in the passenger seat—stylish, haughty, and outrageously handsome.

He says, "It suits you. It was made for you."

I take us east to Lake Shore Drive so we can drive along the water. A cool breeze is blowing. The maples are turning red. It's finally fall.

We stop at Montrose Point, parking the car so it faces the city. Chicago is lit up, the skyscrapers reflecting on the water.

I climb over onto Nero's lap, straddling him. He reclines his seat so he can look up at me.

The moonlight illuminates one side of his face; the other is deeply shadowed.

He's always going to have two sides of him: the side that's dark and vengeful, but also a side unearthly in its beauty.

I can feel Nero's cock, already raging hard, pressing against me with too many layers of clothes between us.

I see myself reflected in his eyes. I see the longing radiating from his face.

And finally, for the first time, I accept that Nero wants me as badly as I want him. He loves me like I love him.

I never realized how deeply certain insults had buried under my skin. I told myself I didn't care what people said. But it was the compliments I deflected, while I clung to the belief that I was ugly, undesirable, and pathetic.

Now the most beautiful man in the world is looking at me with love and desire. And I realize it's impossible that he could feel those things for me if I were truly undeserving.

If Nero and I are a perfect match—and I feel certain we are—then I'm his equal. His analogue.

It's a strange realization to have, after all this time, but I finally believe it. I'm beautiful. I'm intelligent. I'm worthy of love.

"What is it?" Nero asks me.

I take a deep breath, pressing my forehead against his. I'm breathing in the scent of his skin and his lips, just an inch away from mine. Taking in his breath—then giving it back to him again.

"I'm really, completely happy."

"So am I," he says. "It's weird, isn't it?"

I laugh. "Do you think this is how other people feel all the time?"

"No." He wraps his arms around me and pulls me close. "I don't think anyone has felt exactly like this."

He kisses me again, with those full lips that spark a thousand sensations everywhere they land.

He pulls off the remains of my shirt, already cut to tatters and filthy with sweat and blood. He takes off my bra, too, letting my breasts spill into his hands. He traces their curves with his palms, brushing his fingertips over my nipples until they stiffen and throb under his touch.

He puts the palm of his hand in the center of my back and pulls me closer to him so he can take my breast in his mouth. He sucks on my nipple, gently at first, then harder, so that my whole breast is aching with pleasure.

With his spare hand, he massages my other breast, running his thumb down the muscle of my chest, then pinching and tugging on the nipple with just the right amount of pressure.

He always finds that perfect balance point between pleasure and pain—taking the sensation to its fullest intensity, without destroying the enjoyment beneath.

When it comes to sex, Nero has infinite patience. He spends ages just on my breasts, kneading and sucking and teasing them, until they reach their fullest erogenous potential. They become more sensitive than I ever would have thought possible. I get so aroused that I'm about to come before he's even touched anything else.

In fact, the moment he slides his hands down the front of my jeans, I start to climax. He still has my breast in his mouth. All he has to do is apply a little pressure to my clit, a few strokes with the flat of his fingers, and I tip over the edge. He sucks on my nipple and lets me grind against his hand. I feel the rush that flushes through my body—joy and satisfaction and release all at once.

Nero raises his hand to his mouth and licks the taste of me off his fingers. Like an aperitif, it seems to ignite his hunger. He throws me down in the back seat and rips my jeans off, flinging them who knows where. He yanks my panties to the side and licks the length of my slit, flicking his tongue up under my still-throbbing clit.

I gasp and try to wriggle away, but he pins me down, thrusting his tongue all the way inside me, then licking all over my pussy lips and clit. He's ravenous for my taste. He drinks it down, coming back again and again for more.

My pussy is already swollen, thudding with each pulse of my heart. When he takes two fingers and slides them inside me, I yell, barely able to stand it.

He eases the intensity by lapping at my clit with his tongue. Then he slowly slides his fingers in and out, finding that sensitive spot on my inner wall, teasing it with his middle finger.

I feel like I'm possessed. My back is arching, and I'm making all kinds of embarrassing sounds, but it's impossible to care. He's building up another climax, this one much stronger than the one that came before.

I'm squeezing around his fingers and grinding my pussy against his tongue, barely able to handle what I'm getting but still wanting more and more.

He switches to gently sucking on my clit. I explode. I almost black out for a minute, from the insane euphoria that bursts through my brain.

Nero is grinning with that wicked, devilish smile. Nothing pleases him more than playing my body like an instrument.

He climbs on top of me, thrusting his cock inside me while my pussy is still burning from before.

"Oh my god," he groans. He can feel how molten hot I am, soaking wet all the way down my thighs.

Nero's cock is much bigger than his fingers. It fills every bit of space inside me. In fact, with every thrust, it demands more room than exists. Like Nero himself, it straddles the edge of serious discomfort. And yet it's intensely satisfying on a whole other level.

He kisses me tenderly. He fucks me roughly. He doesn't give one good goddamn what he's doing to the brand-new leather seats.

He slams into me harder and harder, as if he wants to take possession of me all over again, as if this is the only way he can exorcise that demon in him.

His breath quickens, and I know he wants to let go.

But he won't let himself do it, not until he's wrung one more climax out of me.

He presses my body tightly against his so my clit grinds against his abdomen as he thrusts into me. And sure enough, I feel one last orgasm building, even though I'm already weak from the ones that came before.

Nero is full of strength. He does all the work, fucking me with relentless intensity. Until I turn my face into his neck and scream as a final wave crashes over me.

Only then does he let himself come, thrusting as deep as he can inside me and unleashing the load he's been holding back.

He comes so much that I can feel it running out of me before he's even pulled out. I would never say it out loud, but I'm wildly aroused by the volume he produces—the evidence of his virility and his desire for me.

He collapses on top of me, our limbs tangled.

I realize how cramped it is in the back seat. But I don't care—in fact, I love it. I love how tightly we're pressed together. I love the smell of the car and the scent of our skin, mixed. I love the stars through the windows and the silver glow on Nero's skin.

He's right—there's never been another moment exactly like this one.

CHAPTER 26
NERO

OFFICER SCHULTZ IS ON TOP OF THE WORLD. HE'S GETTING another commendation for his bust of the MDMA lab on Mohawk Street. Levi Cargill is sitting in a holding cell in the Metropolitan Correctional Center, along with four of his dealers.

Schultz is out celebrating with about twenty other cops in a little pub called Frosty's.

Nobody parties quite like an off-duty cop. You can hear them hollering and singing from two blocks away. Not that drunken singing is anything unusual in Cabrini-Green.

Even the top brass stops by, including Commissioner McKay and Chief Brodie. They buy a round for all the officers, then leave the pub together, climbing into the back of a limo headed for the Celestial Ball at the Adler Planetarium.

Papa will be there, along with the Griffins. Drumming up support for our South Shore project, which we now have ample funding to get rolling.

Not me, though. I got the money—they can get the permits.

I hate tuxedos, and I hate bullshit schmoozing.

I've got my own deal to make tonight. No tuxedo required.

I drive over to Schultz's apartment on Kingsbury Street.

It's not very high-security, as far as a cop's house goes. It only takes me about eight minutes to break in, scaling the fire escape and forcing the lock on his window.

Then I poke around the place for a bit. Honestly, it's pretty depressing. Schultz lives alone—not even a cat or dog or budgie to keep him company. No roommate or girlfriend.

He's got a pretty clean apartment, if you're only considering tidiness and not the fact he probably only vacuums about once a quarter. His dishes look selected at random, and there are basically no decorations anywhere.

He's not a total psychopath, though—I see a few sparks of personality.

First, there's a bunch of battered baseball gear in the closet. So he's probably on some kind of rec league. And he really is a Cubs fan—about half the shirts in his closet have some kind of Cubbies logo on them. The one and only photograph in the apartment is a picture of blond boyish Schultz at Wrigley Field with his dad.

I recognize Matthew Schultz immediately. He looks exactly like his son, only a bit slimmer. Same square jaw and same Captain America set to the shoulders.

It's Logan Schultz who looks different in the photograph—he's grinning so hard that he can hardly see, holding up an autographed baseball in triumph. He looks absolutely joyful, without any of the bitterness of the adult cop I've come to know.

That's the only sentimental item in the whole apartment. That and his father's old badge, stuffed in the top drawer of his nightstand, right next to the bed.

I take a beer out of Schultz's fridge, pop the cap, then sit down to wait.

It's another hour and a half before he stumbles home. I hear his keys scratching in the lock, muttered swearing, and then Schultz himself shuffling into the apartment. I wait for him to take off his service pistol and lay it on the table before I make my presence known.

"Congratulations," I say, snapping on the light.

Schultz jumps like a startled cat, grabbing for his gun.

"Relax," I tell him. "This is just a friendly visit."

"You know I could shoot you right now." Schultz scowls. "Or just arrest you for breaking and entering."

"That wouldn't be very hospitable, considering I've brought you a gift."

Schultz has his hand curled around the stock of his gun. He pauses, then stuffs the pistol into his waistband instead. He crosses his arms over his chest, fixing me with a bleary stare. "What is it?"

"Well…maybe 'gift' is an exaggeration. More like an item in trade."

"Trade for what?"

"Camille Rivera."

Schultz gives an irritated snort. "You gonna try to pretend you give a shit about her?"

"Oh, I give a lot more than that," I say quietly. "Camille is mine now. You're not going to come near her again."

"Or what?" Schultz sneers.

"Or the next time I break in here, you'll wake up to a blade severing your vocal cords."

He doesn't like that. His right hand drifts down toward his gun again.

I don't give a fuck. I'm deadly serious. This is Schultz's one and only chance to leave Camille alone. I'll do whatever it takes to protect her. I'd take down the whole Chicago PD if I had to. I'd murder every man in this city, one by one.

Deliberately and slowly, so he can't misunderstand, I tell him, "You don't look at her. You don't talk to her. You don't come within a hundred feet of her. She's done being your CI."

"Oh, yeah?" Schultz scoffs. "Then you better have brought me something pretty fucking fancy. Like maybe whatever you pulled out of Raymond Page's vault. Oh, yeah, I know that was you. Page knows it, too. He saw you on camera, taking your little field trip down to his vault with his daughter."

"Let me worry about Raymond Page."

I hold up the present I've brought for Officer Schultz. It's a VHS tape with a handwritten label. He stares at it blankly, like he forgot about that piece of technological history.

"What the fuck is that?"

"It's the tape from the security cameras on Jeffrey Boulevard. Taken the night of April 18."

Schultz goes pale beneath the ruddy hue of his tan. It makes him look almost yellow in color. All intoxication fades from his eyes, and they burn brighter than ever.

"That's impossible," he says.

"Not impossible. Just difficult to get."

Schultz looks at my hand holding the tape. He sees my knuckles, swollen to almost twice their normal size, scabbed over and bruised.

He licks his lips convulsively. "Give it to me."

"I will," I tell him. "But first, your promise. You leave Camille alone."

"Yes," he snaps.

"Permanently."

"YES!"

I hold out the tape. He snatches it out of my hand, clutching it as if it really were one of the gold bars from the bank.

He narrows his eyes at me, saying, "This changes nothing between me and you."

"Obviously."

His knuckles are white, and he's almost shaking with anticipation. He can't help himself from asking me, "What does it show?"

"The shot came from inside the car, not out. Your father wasn't alone."

His jaw tightens like he already suspected that. "Who?"

"Daniel Brodie."

Schultz is perfectly still, his eyes wide and unbelieving.

"You know they were partners," I say.

Now Brodie is the head of the Organized Crime Division—Schultz's boss. He was toasting Schultz just a couple of hours ago at Frosty's.

Schultz has been sitting just a couple of desks away from his father's murderer all this time.

"What you do with that information is up to you," I tell him. "But I'd be very careful. Internal Affairs is not your friend. Your father trusted them—and look what happened to him."

I shrug, standing from Schultz's chair. "That's your business, though. All I care is that you stick to our deal."

Schultz is still rooted in place, paralyzed by the bomb I've dropped on his head.

He doesn't move at all while I brush past him, heading out through his front door.

CHAPTER 27
CAMILLE

I wait for Vic to wake up, then stumble out to the kitchen where I've left his present on the table. I know he's seen it when I hear his whoop of surprise.

I poke my head out of my room, already grinning. "You like it?"

I bought him the best damn mixing board money can buy. I promised Nero I wouldn't use the bank heist money for anything flashy—just my dad's medical bills and Vic's college. But I figured we could get one little luxury without anybody noticing.

"Are you kidding me?" Vic's face is incandescent with joy. "It's fucking fantastic!"

"Hey, put a quarter in the swear jar." Dad shuffles out of his room. He's looking not terrible today, which is an improvement.

"If you enforced that rule with Camille, we'd have a million dollars," Vic says.

"What? My baby girl?" Dad pretends to be shocked.

"I don't know what he's talking about," I say innocently.

Vic rolls his eyes at me, turning his attention back to the mixing board. He looks like he wants to kiss it.

"Uh-oh," Dad says. "I think Vic's finally fallen in love."

Vic gives me a mischievous grin. "I hear I'm not the only one."

"Wait, what? What did I miss? Don't tell me we're talking about Nero Gallo…"

"Uh…" I blush. "Yeah. I mean, yes. We're together."

"Nice work." Dad gives me an approving nod.

"You don't mind about…you know." I don't have to mention the Gallos' colorful reputation.

"I never expected you to fall for anyone normal," Dad says.

Vic snorts, and I can't help laughing, too.

"Me neither, I guess," I say.

As Vic tries to sneak his gift back to his room, I add, "Don't think this means you're dropping out of school! You still need to get a degree. Even if you are making sick beats on the side."

Vic groans. "Please don't say 'sick beats.'"

"Why?" I tease him. "Is that not 'fire' anymore?"

"What's 'fire'?" Dad says, mystified.

"You two are killing me." Vic pulls his hat down over his eyes in embarrassment.

"I'm starting to think he doesn't think we're cool," I say to my dad.

"Impossible." He shakes his head.

I grab the last piece of toast and head down to the auto bay.

Even though my cut of the money was an utterly insane sum, it's business as usual for the foreseeable future. For one thing, Nero drilled it into my head again and again that we can't behave any differently. Cops, gangsters, and Raymond Page will all be sniffing around, looking for the slightest sign of bank robbers flush with cash. Even the gorgeous Grand Sport is currently hidden under a dustcover in the garage so I don't draw attention to myself.

Funnily enough, I don't mind buckling down to work now that it's a choice instead of a necessity. I guess it helps that if some dickhole comes into the shop, hollering about the quote we gave him, I can tell him to bugger off. It's nice to have a cushion so you don't have to cling to every job that comes your way.

I work straight through lunch so I can leave early tonight. I've got a date with Nero—one I'm a little nervous about.

Once I'm finished, I head upstairs with plenty of time to shower and scrub my hands clean.

I wish I had Patricia to doll me up, but I'm on my own tonight. She's got her own date with Mason.

She called me up to tell me all about the reconciliation.

"He flew Nana out to visit—it was a total surprise! *And* he remembered to pick her up at the airport, right on time. He had this whole thing planned for us where we did the architecture river cruise, and the Skydeck, and ate at Smoque...Nana was so happy, she said it was the best trip of her life. I swear, Camille, it's like he got this fire lit under him. He says he found an apartment, and he wants to start a business renting portable movie screens... I don't know what happened to him!"

"That's amazing," I said, trying not to laugh. "I'm really happy for you, Patricia."

I feel a little guilty having to play dumb with Patricia, but I'm sure Mason will tell her in time.

I've got a different secret weighing even heavier on my conscience.

It's the secret of Vic's birth father.

I know he's told me a hundred times that he doesn't want to know. And he might be better off—Raymond Page is an absolute ass. But I keep thinking of Bella. That burst of empathy I had the night on the beach hasn't entirely left me. I think Bella is the way she is because of her parents. I wonder if she'd be different if she had a family member who wasn't coldhearted. Someone funny and kind. Someone like Vic.

Once I've showered and put on my robe, I knock on Vic's door.

"Hey," I say, poking my head inside. "Can I talk to you for a second?"

"Sure."

I'm pleased to see he's got his homework spread out in front of him, even with the temptation of the new mixing board right next to him.

"Vic, I know we've talked about this a bunch of times. But sometimes when something's theoretical, it's different than reality…"

"What are you talking about?" Vic chews the end of his pencil.

I take a deep breath. "I found your father. And a sister, too."

For once, Vic doesn't dismiss the subject immediately. He sits very still, looking up at me with those big dark eyes.

"A sister?" he says.

"Yeah."

"How old?"

"Uh…my age, actually."

Vic puts the pencil down. "I guess…that is different."

"Yeah. I know where she is. If you want to meet her."

Vic runs both hands through his hair, thinking hard. I give him time, not interrupting.

Finally, he says, "Ask me again in a year. When I graduate."

I let out the breath I was holding. "Yeah? You sure?"

"Yup." Vic gives me a quick hug. "I've got enough sisters for now."

I ruffle his hair, hugging him back with my free hand. Then I leave him alone so he can get back to work.

I feel relief as I walk back to my room. If Vic wants to meet Bella in a year…I'm okay with that. It gives me enough time to get used to the idea.

Plus time to figure out how to do it without seriously pissing off Raymond Page.

I get dressed much more carefully than usual. I put on a new red dress Patricia helped me pick out. It's got sort of a Latin vibe to it, bright and playful, which isn't exactly how I'd describe myself, but Patricia assured me that it was the perfect "meet the family" outfit.

I put my hair in a braid while it's still damp, and then I carefully dab on a little lip gloss, the same color as the dress. I slip my feet into a pair of sandals, then head back down to the auto bay for Nero to pick me up.

The black Mustang pulls into the drive, right on time.

Nero jumps out and kisses me before he opens the door for me. "You look stunning."

"I feel like I might throw up," I admit.

"Don't worry. They're going to love you."

We drive west through Old Town. As we cross over Sedgwick, I hear bagpipes. A police procession marches down the road. The end of the street is blocked off, with a wall of uniformed officers lined up.

"What's all that about?" I ask Nero.

He raises an eyebrow at me. "You didn't read about it?"

"No."

"Papa gets the paper every morning. This was front-page stuff."

"Are you going to tell me?"

"Chief Brodie got shot in the back of the head in Rosenblum Park."

"What? By who?"

"That's the mystery. It happened in the middle of the night. He was all alone in the park." Nero has a strange look on his face, like he's trying not to smile.

"What's going on?" I demand. "You look like you know something."

"Maybe I do."

"What is it?"

"I'll tell you…" he growls. "If you convince me."

"I don't have time to convince you! We're almost at your house!"

"Later, then," he says, in his most infuriating tone.

We pull up to the Gallos' mansion, which intimidates me much more than last time because I know the whole family is waiting inside.

Nero takes my hand. He leads me up a dark, rickety staircase, all the way to the rooftop deck.

There I see the loveliest dinner imaginable. The place settings are laid out on a massive old table, big enough to seat twenty people or more. The dishes look heavy and handmade, like they might have come from Italy a hundred years ago. Fairy lights twinkle from the bare grapevines that arch overhead, growing all across the pergola.

Nero's family is already seated, waiting for us. I see Enzo at the head, looking older than the last time I saw him but still intelligent and distinguished in his dinner jacket. On his right side is Dante, imposing in his bulk and his humorless scowl, until he gives me a nod of recognition. Sebastian sits next to Dante, much more cheerful than his eldest brother. He waves to me.

On the other side of the table is the baby of the family, and the only girl—Aida Gallo. I've never actually met her because she's so much younger—not even a freshman by the time I graduated. I heard stories about her, though. How she was wild like Nero but kind like Sebastian. So I was always disposed to like her.

She's quite beautiful—the same gray eyes as Nero, paired with a grin so impish that I don't know whether to smile back or be terrified of her.

Her husband, by contrast, is almost as serious as Dante. He's starkly dressed in a dark suit, with carefully combed hair and pale blue eyes that are a little unsettling when they land on me.

However, he nods politely. I can tell from how close he sits to Aida, and the way he lays his hand on her thigh, that they're a tightly bonded couple, no matter how mismatched they might appear.

The seat next to Aida is empty. I take it, with Nero sitting on my other side.

"Welcome," Enzo says to me. "We're very glad to meet you, Camille. I know your father, of course. I'm sorry to hear he's been ill."

"Thank you," I squeak. "He's getting better now."

My heart is fluttering. The beauty of the table and this outdoor space, and all the handsome, well-dressed people sitting around it, are exactly the kind of things that remind me that Nero has always been wealthy and well-connected, while I've always been a nobody.

Nero is squeezing my hand tight. When I look at him, his expression is fierce and proud. He's not embarrassed of me.

Greta starts bringing the food up from the kitchen. Sebastian jumps up to help her. I can see him limping just a little. Otherwise, he looks healthy and strong. He easily carries several platters at once before setting them in the center of the table.

I'm not Italian, but you can't grow up in Old Town without learning about proper Italian cuisine.

I can see Greta knows what she's doing. The platters are heaped with roasted vegetables, eggplant Parmesan, radicchio panzanella, Italian wedding soup, giant meatballs, and freshly made pasta with clams and hot Italian sausage.

Once all the food is brought up, Greta sits down to eat with everyone else. It's clear that she's family, too. That makes me feel just a little more comfortable, as evidence that the Gallos aren't snobs.

"Take a meatball!" Aida encourages me. "They're the best you've ever had, I guarantee it."

"Don't hype it up too much," Greta says. "I'm sure Camille has had plenty of meatballs in her life."

I take a bite, chewing carefully so I don't burn my tongue. "Not like this," I say, seriously impressed. "This is amazing."

"You should open a restaurant," Sebastian says to Greta.

"Don't tell her that!" Aida cries. "She'll never come back here if she knows she has other options."

Greta snorts, pouring herself a generous glass of wine.

Seeing that she can't get a rise out of Greta, Aida turns her attention on me instead. "Don't take this the wrong way," Aida says, with a concerned expression. "But have you suffered a head injury lately? Because it appears you actually like Nero..."

Nero scowls at her. "You promised to behave yourself tonight."

Aida lets out an infectious peal of laughter. "Is that by your standards, big brother? Because if that's the case…I think anything short of burning the house down is acceptable."

"You're the only one at the table who's set a house on fire," Aida's husband reminds her.

That's Callum Griffin—probably the richest and most influential person at this whole table. He looks stern. But there's no malice in his tone—he's only teasing Aida.

"One library," she says airily. "Not a whole house."

"That was *my* library," he growls.

"Well, now you have a whole new apartment! And a wife!" Aida grins. "What a good trade."

I feel Nero sitting tensely next to me. I glance over at him, afraid he is embarrassed of me after all.

Then I see that he's looking at Aida, not at me—nervous at how I'll take her jokes.

I realize he's worried what I'll think of his family now that I've seen them all in their natural state.

I squeeze his hand, smiling up at him. "These really are the *best* meatballs," I whisper to him.

He relaxes a little, smiling back at me. "I know," he says. "You can't oversell them."

In the end, the dinner is just as lovely as the setting. Nero's family is warm, charming—and most of all, just a family. People who love and drive one another crazy, in equal measure.

I feel like I could fit here.

I know that's what Nero wants.

He put me right in the center of the table. He looks at me with an expression that plainly shows he wants me to feel at home. A part of this group.

I'm not a fool—I know this is the Gallos at rest. In their den, so to speak. When they're out hunting, they become a different sort of beast entirely. Violent. Calculated. Vengeful.

But that doesn't concern me. There's a core of darkness inside me, the same as Nero. We recognized it in each other.

The Gallos see it, too.

I do belong here.

———————

After the meal, Nero takes me for a drive, like almost every night.

Sometimes he's behind the wheel; sometimes it's me. Either way, we never tire of the wind in our faces and the road unspooling beneath the wheels of the car.

Tonight, he takes us out to Peoria Heights. Teddy Roosevelt once said this was the most beautiful drive in the world. Admittedly, Nero and I might be more fascinated by the car Teddy Roosevelt drove than the view itself, but either way, he wasn't wrong. On a clear night like this, you can see thirty miles across the Illinois River Valley.

It's always easiest for Nero and me to talk while we're driving. It puts us in our calmest state. The car is like a bubble, containing only the two of us, where anything can be said.

"What did you think of my family?" Nero asks me.

"I loved them."

"All of them?" he asks in disbelief.

"Yes, all of them." I laugh. "You're lucky to have so many people who have your back."

"Well, tonight they were there to see you," Nero says, looking over at me. "They know how much you mean to me. But it was nice—having everyone together again."

"Do you remember the first time I came to your house?"

"Of course."

"You said you weren't anybody's favorite."

He shrugs. "No, probably not."

"You're *my* favorite," I tell him. "You're my favorite person in the world."

He looks over at me, a slow smile spreading across his face.

Nero looks fierce or moody almost all the time—even when he's relaxed. But his smile is truly stunning. It's slow, it's sexy, and it makes him look more wicked than ever.

It makes my chest burn and my whole body go weak.

"Is that right?" he says.

"Most definitely."

He puts his warm palm on my bare thigh and slides it up a little under my skirt. "You're driving me insane in this red dress," he growls. "You should do something about that…"

He finds a place to park, with the valley spread out below us.

I don't think there's ever been a couple who spent so much time taking each other's clothes off in cars.

I love being inside Nero's car. It smells like him. It feels like him. The gearshift and steering wheel have been worn by constant contact with his hands. His shape is indented into the driver's seat.

I love the way he lays my seat back and climbs on top of me, pinning me down in the confined space. I love how close his face is to mine, as he slides his cock inside me.

He's fucking me slow tonight, more gently than usual. His arms are wrapped around me, his hands thrust into my hair.

Our lips lock together in one long kiss that goes on and on.

I run my hands down his back, beneath his shirt. I've never met a man with skin so phenomenally smooth. The softness of the skin and the hardness of the muscle beneath is a dichotomy I never tire of exploring.

Every time he thrusts into me, I feel his back flexing, as well as his ass. I run my palm down the hard curve of his ass cheek, thinking what an underappreciated part of a man this is. The Greeks and Romans knew how to take an ass like this and immortalize it in marble.

Nero should be a statue.

If he were, I would worship it.

I press my face against the side of his neck, inhaling his scent. That's all it takes—that's the catalyst that pushes me over. I start to come, and he's coming, too. It almost always happens at the same time now. Whether he starts first or I do, the clenching and squeezing of our flesh puts the other one over the edge.

Every time we do this, I fall more and more into my obsession with this man. I realize I could never feel this way about anyone else. If I lost Nero, I would spend the rest of my life remembering what it was like to experience desire on this level. Pleasure on this level. Connection, admiration, love on an all-encompassing scale.

That's the harrowing thing about falling in love.

I'm Eve in the garden. Once I eat the fruit, I can never go back. I can never forget what I tasted.

And I don't care. I would give a thousand gray and lonely years for one hour of this.

I would give anything to have Nero.

We lie together in the cramped passenger seat, wrapped tight in each other's arms.

After a while, Nero says, "I have to tell you something."

"What is it?"

"I found something out about your mother."

The silence in the car seems enormous. Even in the warmth of Nero's arms, I feel cold. I already know what he's trying to tell me. I can read him so well by now. I feel the stiffness of his shoulders and the tension in his voice.

"She's dead, isn't she?"

Nero nods. "I'm sorry."

The finality of that is like a door slamming in my face. All the things I wanted to say to her, all the things I hoped she might say to me one day…it all waited on the other side of that door. Now it's closed, and it can't ever open again.

"I think I knew it. When she hadn't called in so long…not even once. I guess I knew what it meant."

"Still," he says. "Knowing for certain is different."

I bury my face in his chest, clinging to his arms around me. He's the only thing holding me steady right now.

"What happened?" I ask him.

"From what I could find, it was an overdose."

I sigh.

I had a fantasy in my head that she might have gotten clean. Moved to another city. Changed her whole life. I thought she might come back one day, looking as beautiful as she used to. She'd knock on the door, just like the night she brought Vic. But this time she wouldn't run away. She'd come into the kitchen and sit with us and tell us where she'd been.

I almost believed I could make that happen for her, just by holding that picture in my head. A possible future she could step into, as long as I kept it ready for her.

"I shouldn't have told you." Nero wipes the tears off my face with his hand.

"I'm glad you did. So I'm not wondering anymore."

"I won't ever leave you," Nero says. "Never, Camille. You'll never have to wonder where I went. I'll be right by your side."

I look up into his face.

I've spent a long time with a hole in my heart.

Nero fills all the empty space inside me. He heals every wound. I know how dangerous he is. How intelligent. How ruthless. He makes me feel invincible because with Nero next to me, nothing can hurt me.

I'm sorry about my mother.

But it's time for me to finally start the next chapter of my life.

I'm moving forward—Nero and I, together.

BONUS SCENE
BLOCK PARTY

AUTHOR'S NOTE

The first time I heard the song "Tamagotchi," I saw an image in my mind of Nero and Camille dancing together at a neighborhood block party. I ended up writing a bonus scene for *Savage Lover*, which is what you're about to read.

One of the things I love about Nero and Camille's story is that in many ways, Camille is the "girl next door" to Nero—they grew up around each other and went to school together without ever really being friends. I loved the idea of their families socializing before the two of them really figured out what they are to each other.

I like to think of this as a "deleted scene," or an alternate version of how Camille could have been formally introduced to Nero's family, instead of the way it actually happens at the end of *Savage Lover*.

You'll notice I made one other small change, which is to decrease the age gap between Nero and Aida. I wanted Aida to be in school at the same time as Nero and Camille because I thought her interaction with Camille would be more fun if they had also observed each other from a distance back in high school.

———

CAMILLE

WHEN I SHUFFLE DOWN THE STAIRS SUNDAY MORNING, MY DAD'S already in the kitchen impaling bits of pork on steel kebabs. He's got a pot large enough to bathe a toddler bubbling away on the stove behind him, full of gallons of simmering *pollo guisado*.

"What on earth are you doing?"

He stares at me like I'm the crazy one.

"It's *las fiestas de Santiago Apostol*."

"You can't be serious."

"Check the calendar."

"I know the date, Dad—I'm wondering why you're making food for an army in your boxer shorts when you're supposed to be resting. Your surgery's two weeks away!"

He gives me a wounded look. This is his move, and Vic learned it from him, too—the puppy-dog eyes to get me to agree to whatever insane plot they're devising.

"I know it's two weeks away. That's why I'm cooking—this could be our last block party."

"*Block party?* DAD!"

Vic ambles into the kitchen, hair sticking up in all directions, hand down the front of his pants.

"Camille's already yelling? What time is it?" He checks the digital display on the microwave. "6:20—new record."

He opens the fridge and reaches for the orange juice.

"First," I say, "stay out of it. Second, wash that crotchy hand before you touch the communal orange juice."

Vic grins, popping the lid off the juice and chugging down half the carton, mouth-to-spout. I guarantee he hasn't even brushed his teeth yet. "You haven't heard the best part."

Vic is gleeful, while my father squirms like a kid who got caught raiding the popsicles.

"Spill it," I say.

"Dad invited the Gallos. And they're coming, too."

It's like he's actively trying to ruin my life. Like he sits up at night dreaming of ways to do it.

"Which Gallos?"

"All of them."

I wheel on my father. He gives me a sheepish grin, hands outstretched.

"They're part of the neighborhood."

"DAD! They go to parties with the mayor. Parties with waiters and tuxedos and nine hundred-dollar bottles of champagne. They don't want to eat one pot chicken stew and play dominoes with us!"

"Now you're just being silly," my dad says, placidly. "Everybody likes dominoes."

"Oh my god." I put my hands over my face and breathe into them. "Why did you do this? You never invited them before."

"Actually, I always send an invitation to Enzo. This time he accepted."

My head snaps up.

"He did?"

Vic smirks.

"Said yes right away. Probably wants to see who his son's been ba—"

I shoot my brother a look about as subtle as a full-bore blast from a flamethrower.

"—dating," Vic finishes.

"That must be the reason," my dad nods approvingly. "It's a compliment to you that they're coming."

I haven't met Nero's family yet, not a single one of them. I've seen Enzo Gallo from a distance, when he used to visit my father's shop. Once he patted me on the head and gave me a crisp twenty-dollar bill to buy candy. Because I was six, and the daughter of his mechanic.

I highly doubt I'm as acceptable to him now as the person dating his son.

If we're even dating. I think what Vic was about to say is more accurate.

"This is not how you're supposed to be introduced to someone's family," I inform my father.

"You're not being introduced. You've lived in the same neighborhood your whole life. Enzo Gallo has seen you running around in a diaper."

"That's not helpful, Dad. Actually, it's worse."

I've spent my entire life embarrassed by my poverty, my lack of class. High school was a living hell because I showed up grease-stained and reeking of diesel every day, while the popular girls drove cars fancier than anything I'd even worked on.

Our "neighborhood" encompasses Victorian mansions passed down through generations, of which the Gallo's is the largest and most venerable, right next to the tiny saltbox houses and tightly-packed apartment buildings that house the Polish and Puerto Rican immigrants who settled the less desirable parts of Old Town—not to mention the army of sex workers from Wells Street, and the old-timers from Chicago's original "gay ghetto" that preferred not to move to Lake View or Lincoln Park.

Old Town contains two highly incompatible demographics: people who swipe their credit cards like they're swatting flies, and people who scrounge the couch cushions for gas money.

Our block parties are supposed to be for the latter group.

We're talking flip-flops, belly out, bad beer, worse jokes, potluck, hard-luck kinda parties.

It's trashy as hell and I fit in just fine, because this is where I grew up, and who I am at my core.

My dad is putting us on display to the people I want to impress most.

"Tell them it's canceled," I say, desperately.

"Uninviting them would be worse."

I don't think that's true.

My phone pings in my pocket.

I pull it out, feeling the intense pressure that blooms in my chest whenever I see the name *Nero Gallo* on the display. That feeling doesn't go away. In fact, it's only getting worse.

What should I bring tonight?

I hold the phone angled away from Vic so he can't see who I'm texting. That would work if I had other friends.

"Is that Nero? What's he saying? Is he offering to make *papas rellenas?*"

Vic is laughing so hard his nose is running.

I type back madly:

No need to bring anything or to come at all. Party's canceled.

I've barely hit Send when Nero fires back:

Nice try. See you at eight.

Oh my god. I need to date someone stupider. And less rich. And less good-looking. This is way too stressful.

"He didn't buy it," Vic says, reading over my shoulder.

"Knock it off!"

I stuff my phone in my pocket.

"Think his sister's coming?"

"She's married. And too old for you."

"What about cousins—"

I escape to the garage so I don't have to answer.

Elbow-deep in engines, I try to forget that in a few short hours I'll have to form coherent sentences while facing the Don of Old Town and his son, who happens to have my heart twisted up in a pretzel. Plus several other highly-intimidating Gallos.

I should have asked Nero who was coming so I could mentally prepare.

No, that would just make it worse. Better to live in denial.

I tell myself the Gallos will make an appearance to be polite, then leave before anybody pulls out the karaoke machine or tries to start an illegal cock fight.

"This will be fine," I mutter, about eight hundred times.

The day flies by—the one time I wish it wouldn't.

Before I know it, I'm scrubbing my nails with steel wool, trying to remove every trace of grease and grime.

I hunt through the clothes in the hall closet, which takes about two seconds. No outfit magically materializes. Usually, I wear jean shorts and one of Vic's old T's—which would be too casual to meet Nero's dog, let alone his dad.

Feeling a kind of wild recklessness, I raid the old coffee can in the kitchen, stealing $60 from the stash of folded bills we keep socked away for emergencies.

We need every penny we can get for my dad's medical bills, but I'm not delusional enough to think that sixty bucks is gonna make much difference to the thousands of dollars of debt we're about to incur.

Sometimes you need one little ray of sunshine in the middle of a storm. Even if it's frivolous. Even if you can't really afford it.

I take my money to the shop three doors down from Axel Auto, Minnie's Boutique.

Minnie's shop is smaller than most people's closets, so stuffed with racks of dresses that I have to wedge myself sideways to access the wares in the back.

Minnie was my mom's best friend when they were kids. I don't think she sees her much these days, but from the nuggets Minnie has let slip over the years, I get the impression my mom calls her friend a hell of a lot more than she ever called me.

Minnie must know that too, 'cause she never asks how my mom's doing.

Instead, she says "How's Axel?" when the chime over the door brings her running.

"Apparently, he's made a miraculous recovery. 'Cause he's throwing a block party tonight."

Minnie laughs.

"I know, I'm closing the shop early—you barely caught me. You want something to wear?"

"Yes, please. I'm sort of…bringing a date."

My cheeks burn.

Minnie has more tact than Vic. She doesn't ask questions, though I can tell she desperately wants to as she briskly flicks through the racks.

"A date, you say…" Her smile knows too much already. "So you'll want something pretty…something flattering to the figure…"

"Not too revealing," I add.

Minnie's own stunning figure is perpetually displayed to its advantage by the best her boutique has to offer. She likes to call herself the Puerto-Rican Dolly Parton, and she's got both the sequins and the cleavage to do Dolly proud. However, I do not fancy introducing myself to Enzo Gallo in a dress cut to the navel, dripping in feathers and fringe.

Minnie winks at me. "Don't worry sweetie-pie, I'm only gonna take you two steps out of your comfort zone."

"So…coveralls with a skirt?" I tease her.

"You wish." She pulls something yellow and ruffled off the rack. "This is the one."

I touch the material, soft and flowing like it could float on a breath of warm air. It feels expensive.

"I only have sixty bucks. I should have told you that."

Minnie yanks off the tag, tucking it in her pocket before I can get a look at it.

"This is forty," she lies.

"Minnie—"

"Don't argue with me. And get outta here—I need at least an hour to do my hair."

Since Minnie's mountain of curls are already arranged in an elaborate beehive, I have no idea what another hour will do.

"Shouldn't I try it on?"

She waves me off. "Trust me—this is the one."

I take the dress back upstairs to our apartment over the auto shop. There's no mirror in my room, so I stand on the toilet to get a view of myself above the bathroom sink.

Minnie was right. The dress clings to every curve. If you can call it a dress—really, it's a top and a skirt, with a strip of bare navel in between. The hint of skin remains innocent, the flounce of the skirt too playful and the marigold color too cheerful to read as anything but adorable. I look like I live in a musical—like the whole world should burst into song around me.

Vic whistles when he sees me.

"I always forget that you're pretty."

I mess up his hair.

"You're *too* pretty—let me help you."

He shoves me off, furiously finger-combing.

"I've got better lashes *and* better legs—if I put that skirt on, it'd be game over for you."

"I had you both beat before I got bald and fat," my dad says, strolling into the kitchen in his own version of party-wear, which means a Hawaiian shirt older than he is and a pair of sandals patched with duct tape.

If Minnie is Dolly, then my dad was James Dean. He had a gorgeous head of hair and a vintage Harley that drew the girls of Old Town like an ice cream truck swarmed by kids.

He's bald as an egg now, but not fat. The weight fell off him when he got sick, so fast that I should have known something was wrong. His Hawaiian shirt hangs off his shoulders, and even his sandals flop loose on his feet.

"You're still handsome, Dad."

"Yeah—for an old geezer," Vic says, playfully cuffing Dad on the shoulder. He picks up the huge pot of *pollo guisado* before our dad can try to carry it.

I scoop up the hefty roasting pan of pork skewers just as quick. They've been soaking all day in my dad's citrus marinade, for which he's never revealed the recipe, not even to me and Vic. The fresh orange rind reminds me of Nero's scent, which carries something mouthwatering and exotic on its edge.

I want to see him. Desperately. Even when I'm dreading it.

We carry the food four blocks over to the long alleyway between two brownstone apartment buildings. The alley has been cleared of trash bins and filled up instead with mismatched tables and chairs, including the plastic folding kind, spindly wooden dining chairs carried down from people's kitchens, and an assortment of benches, stools, and even stepladders.

Five or six grills are going strong, pouring smoke and the delicious scent of roasting meat.

My dad's friend Marley is heating his ancient kettle grill for the pork kebabs. He helps my dad lay the metal skewers crosswise, then closes the clamshell lid.

The party forms around us like a magnet drawing in metal filings from all sides.

The apartment-dwellers hang colored lights down the fire escapes on both sides of the alley, flinging rolls of lights across the gap.

A band of musicians assembles—neighbors who play together often without ever holding anything as formal as a "practice session."

The mismatched tables are soon heaped with an even odder assortment of dishes: spicy bulgogi, pierogis heaped with onion, tacos and tamales, a huge platter of hot dogs, baked pig's feet, fried green tomatoes, a dozen kinds of rice, Jell-O salad, Cajun shrimp, funeral potatoes, deviled eggs, sweet plantains, and that's before you even get to the desserts…

It's chaotic and marvelous, it makes your eyes water, and your mouth too. I can't help but be swept up in the mood of celebration as the people I've known all my life shout and laugh together, eating and teasing, flirting and dancing, all mixed up like ice in a shaker.

I almost forget to be nervous—until a cream-colored Chrysler as long as a boat pulls up at the end of the alleyway. The doors crack open and five dark-haired Italians emerge.

Everyone tries not to stare, but it's impossible for the Gallos to avoid attention.

Though he's spent the last decade in increasing isolation, Enzo Gallo is still the most infamous man in Old Town. Anybody who owns a business around here has kissed his ring—figuratively or literally.

Dante Gallo is a hulking giant, making even the Chrysler land yacht creak beneath his weight. Nero's dark beauty would jump-start the heart of a corpse. Aida bounces like there's a little extra rubber in the soles of her shoes. And Sebastian Gallo ambles along behind them, smiling at everyone, but sad behind his eyes.

They tried to dress casually. For Enzo Gallo, this means a light linen summer suit that still probably cost as much as his car. I've only seen Nero in something other than a black T-shirt once—today is no exception, though it's a slightly newer black T-shirt than usual. Aida is dressed like a farmer's daughter in denim shorts and a gingham top, a red scarf wrapped round her ponytail.

I take several deep breaths, then stride forward to meet them.

As soon as our eyes lock, Nero breaks away from his family. He plants his arm firmly around my waist, presenting me to his father.

"Papa, this is Camille Rivera. Her father is Axel Rivera."

"Of course, of course." Enzo takes my hand between both of his. His palms are warm and dry, his knuckles swollen. His large hands easily close around mine. "I know your father well. And I remember you."

"You gave me money for candy once." I want to thank him, but I'm horrified by a sudden thickness in my throat. It's too much, remembering that I had never held a twenty-dollar bill in my life at that point.

"I hope you spent it all." Enzo smiles.

Actually, I hid the money away inside a book under my mattress.

It stayed there for years, untouched, cherished, until I got my first job delivering fliers.

"You were very kind," I say, when I can speak.

"Our families have long been connected. Your grandmother sewed my wife's wedding dress by hand. Designed it, too. Did you know that?"

I shake my head.

"She was an artist and a craftsman—I've never seen a finer stitch. A famous beauty, too—all the Vega women are. I remember when your mother was crowned Queen of Old Town."

I've seen the picture—my mother on a float of orange carnations, sash across her chest and tiara on her hair, waving with a cupped hand like a trained beauty queen. Really, she'd signed up for the pageant just that morning. She was so lovely that she won, even though her talent was reciting the periodic table to the tune of a song from *Pirates of Penzance*. So joyful that her smile could still blind you from a faded photograph tucked in a drawer.

I wonder if Enzo knows she works at the strip club three blocks from here.

If he does, he's kind enough not to mention it. Or to point out that I look nothing like my mother, much more like my dad.

Enzo pats my hand and lets go.

"You'll forgive an old man for reminiscing."

"I'd love to see a picture of the gown. My grandmother died before I was born. I've never seen anything she made."

"You can see the actual dress," Aida offers. "It's still hanging in her closet."

I want this so badly I can't possibly refuse. "That would be incredible."

Aida grins. "I always liked you since you dumped spaghetti on that cunt Bella Page."

"*Aida...*" Nero gives a warning look that his sister blithely ignores.

"She deserved it! And she definitely didn't see it coming..." Aida laughs heartily at the memory.

I don't love that Enzo is hearing the gory details of the one and only time I snapped on my high school bully.

"I wish the principal shared your opinion—I almost got expelled."

Plus, Raymond Page's lawyer sent me a nastygram, threatening everything short of the electric chair if I laid a finger on his baby girl again. Completely ignoring that said baby girl had just drenched my end-of-term art project in chocolate milk. It was a self-portrait. Bella said it needed a few grease stains.

"I got expelled twice," Aida says, cheerfully. "It's not as permanent as they pretend."

Though Aida was only a freshman when I was a senior, I heard her outrageous laughter ringing in the halls and witnessed her unrepentant figure parked in the principal's office on multiple occasions. I always felt a funny kinship for her, and I'm pleased to hear she might have felt the same.

"Well…" I grin. "Would you guys like a drink? There's a slushie machine."

Marley owns the bodega on the corner. Every time there's a party, he hauls out the Coke slushie-maker and dumps in enough rum to knock a horse off its hooves. Remembering this, I try to think how to revise my endorsement.

"We brought drinks, too!" Aida says. "And food."

She whistles for Dante and Sebastian, who had already wandered off toward the buffet tables after the initial introductions.

She needs the help of all three brothers: the Gallo boys unload boxes and trays from the Chrysler's capacious trunk, bringing out a second feast of the best Old Town's delis and bakeries have to offer, as well as a dozen bottles of wine so dusty, I can only assume they're from Enzo's private store.

My father joins us as they lay out the spread.

"Pistachio croissants from Hendrickx!" Dad nods approvingly. "You always had an eye for the best, Enzo."

"That's why I only trusted you to work on the Rolls."

"What a machine," my father sighs. "I miss it."

"A casualty of Nero's mechanical education," Enzo chuckles. "He cannibalized two of my favorite cars to make a Frankenstein's monster."

I stare at Nero in horror. "You didn't."

The silver Rolls-Royce was a treasure. I drooled over it every time Enzo visited the shop.

Nero shrugs. "I've done worse."

He grabs my arm. "You promised slushies."

We're barely away from the tables when he pulls me close against his side and growls, "You're driving me crazy in this dress..."

I turn my head, letting my lips brush the rim of his ear.

"When were you ever sane?"

His dark eyes look into mine. "Not since the moment I saw you bent over a car..."

He seizes my hand and presses it once, hard, against his cock. The shaft lays like a steel bar down his leg.

"I don't think I've been fully soft ever since..."

He pours us two massive rum-and-Coke slushies, then gulps his down without using the straw.

"Don't you get brain freeze?"

He winks. "I'm too hot-blooded to freeze."

Over the next hour, I realize that my father understands the Gallos better than I do. I watch Sebastian playing dominoes with Marley and Dante shoveling down pork kebabs as fast as my dad can grill them. I see Aida learning to bomba from a pack of little boys who can't stop giggling at her mistakes. Enzo Gallo makes his rounds slowly and methodically, greeting more people than I could name.

The Gallos really did grow up here the same as I did.

I put the barrier between us—the barrier of money and power. I thought it meant everything.

I thought I'd be embarrassed by the pig's feet, by the half-naked children who've taken off their clothes to play under the mister that spritzes the tomatoes outside the grocery store. I didn't think the Gallos would dance to music where the drums are upside-down plastic buckets.

But it's Nero who pulls me out on the cracked cement, under the confetti-colored lights of a hundred strings of mismatched Christmas bulbs.

♫ *"Tamagotchi"—Omar Apollo*

I slip into his arms like I belong there. Like he belongs here with me.

We sway back and forth, connected down the whole length of our bodies. I turn so my back is against his chest. He puts his hands on my hips, his fingertips resting on the twin wings of bone. I lean my head back against his shoulder, warm and relaxed.

He runs one hand up my side, all the way up my arm to my fingertips, taking my hand, bringing it to his mouth, pressing it to his lips. I turn and trail my fingers down the side of his face, looking in his eyes.

The yellow ruffled top slips off my shoulder. My bare skin glows with colored light. Nero presses his lips against that spot and a shiver runs all the way to my toes.

I'm full of delicious food. The most beautiful man I've ever beheld is dancing with me and me only, his eyes locked on mine.

"I was surprised your dad accepted the invitation," I murmur. "I know he doesn't get out much."

"I asked him to come."

Nero twirls me around so the marigold skirt flares out like the petals of a flower around the stem of my legs. Then he drops his arm around my waist, pulling me in tight. His face is an inch from mine. He's sweating a little in the humid summer night. His back is damp beneath my palm, his scent far more intoxicating than the rum.

I look up into his eyes.

"Why?"

"So he could see you like this, in my arms."

The moon is rising. It hangs directly over the alleyway, silvering the edges of the rusted fire escapes.

The dancing is slower now, lazier. Couples sway with their arms around each other's necks.

A stern-looking man in a smoke-gray suit has joined the party. He's wildly overdressed, as if he just came from the office even though it's a Sunday. He pulls Aida away from a game of horseshoes and spins her with surprising grace.

My dad has abandoned his grill at last. He shuffles his sandaled feet through a gentle merengue with a plump redheaded woman Nero knows very well.

"Greta's here!" I say.

"She just got back from visiting her sister. We made her go 'cause she hasn't taken a day off in a year, but my father gets lonely, even when the rest of us try to pick up the slack."

I think of my own dad, of the nights Vic and I go out, and I return home to find him asleep on the couch in his bathrobe, the TV still going, a single bottle of beer half-drunk on the coffee table and one used plate and fork in the sink.

"I wonder if it's worth it to fall in love, if you just end up alone in the end."

Nero's fingers tighten in my hair. His words are hot against my neck.

"If you were mine, I'd never let you go."

I turn my lips to his.

"Then never let me go."

He pulls me away through the warren of alleyways, through short passages of brick and stone, until we're in a tiny back garden, weedy and overgrown, with a stone statue of an angel weeping into a mossy fountain.

Nero presses me against the soot-stained wall, biting and sucking at the side of my neck. His hand slips inside my top, cupping my breast in his warm palm.

I seize his face and kiss those full lips, tasting his mouth. He's as tender as a rosebud and sharp as a blade. His fingers are savage as they pluck at my breasts, yet I feel nothing but pleasure everywhere he touches.

He drops to his knees, lifting my skirt. I put my legs over his shoulders, back up against the wall. He noses my underwear to the side, licking along my slit, delving his tongue between my pussy lips, finding my clit with the tip of his tongue. He licks till I'm flushed and panting, then lightly latches on my clit, fluttering his tongue until I'm whimpering like a puppy, until I'm squirming and grinding, locked in place with his hands gripping my ass.

The orgasm comes in waves over pulses, like melody over the beat of a song. The waves are each roll of my hips, the pulses the flick of his tongue.

He drops me down from his shoulders, my pussy sliding from his chest down onto his cock. He slots himself inside me, the marigold skirt rucked up around my waist, my legs locked around his hips.

He fucks me slow and deep, each thrust pressing all the way to my back wall. There's magic in the way we fit together; it's not like normal sex. Each stroke drags a moan out of me, so pleasurable that I could never keep quiet, not if I were being hunted by wolves.

Nero has to clamp a hand over my mouth. Still, I groan against his palm, biting down hard with my teeth.

He puts his hand on my throat instead, squeezing till my head spins.

"If you're gonna moan, you better moan my name."

I love his name. Every time I groan it out, my body flushes and my head spins.

"Nero…oh, Nero…"

He runs his tongue up the side of my neck, hot and wet and electric.

I start to come, my pussy clenching around his cock.

Then I don't just moan his name—I scream it.

The effect is galvanic—Nero's legs shake like an earthquake as he erupts inside of me. His fingers dig into my flesh, and his arms tremble around me. His cock twitches, flooding me with cum.

When he pulls out, the cum runs down my leg, dripping down my inner thigh. He scoops it up with his fingers, pushing it back inside me, slippery as oil. I'm spongy and warm, helpless in his hands.

"That pussy belongs to me," he growls in my ear. "Every time I touch it, I want to feel my cum already inside you."

I'm dizzy with lust. I seize him by the wrist, pushing his fingers deeper inside me. I hold his wrist, riding his hand, fucking myself on his fingers.

"Feel it now."

My eyes roll back. I cum on his fingers like I'm riding a cock, top pulled down from my bare breasts, Nero's teeth nipping at my tits.

When I'm finished, Nero lifts his gleaming fingers to his mouth. Then he kisses me softly.

"See how good you taste."

I lick my tongue across his lips, tasting us both.

The moon is the only light in the weed-choked garden. The thick green moss mottles the stone skin of the angel, smelling of caves and damp. All the city is alive around us, but we stand still in its silent heart.

"To think you tried to uninvite me," Nero says.

"I thought it might not be fancy enough for you."

He snorts. "What the fuck made you think I was fancy?"

I laugh. "Definitely not your manners."

He pulls back slightly so he can look in my face. So I can see his expression, so I know he's serious.

"I like you, Camille. Not some version of you. Not a Camille without a dad or a brother or grease under her nails. I like the girl who grew up here, right in this place."

I lift his hand and hold it pressed against my cheek.

"You have grease under your nails too, you know."

He smiles.

"That's how I knew we were meant for each other."

PATREON

Want to see uncensored NSFW art and stories too hot for the printed page? Check out my Patreon:

BRUTAL BIRTHRIGHT

Callum & Aida

Miko & Nessa

Nero & Camille

Dante & Simone

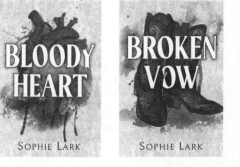

Raylan & Riona

Sebastian & Yelena

ABOUT THE AUTHOR

Sophie Lark writes intelligent and powerful characters who are allowed to be flawed. Her stories are dark, twisty, and full of surprises. She lives in the mountain west with her husband and two kids.

The Love Lark Letter: geni.us/lark-letter

The Love Lark Reader Group: geni.us/love-larks

Website: sophielark.com

Instagram: @Sophie_Lark_Author

TikTok: @sophielarkauthor

Exclusive Content: patreon.com/sophielark

Complete Works: geni.us/lark-amazon

Book Playlists: geni.us/lark-spotify